A SIMPLE
request

COOPER TOWN BOYS
BOOK ONE

USA TODAY BESTSELLING AUTHOR
LACEY BLACK

A Simple Request
Cooper Town Boys Series, book 1

Copyright © 2026 Lacey Black
Cover Design by Kristie Leigh, Vanilla Lily Designs
Photographer Eric McKinney, 6:12 Photography
Model Bryan B

Editing by Kara Hildebrand
Proofreading by Sandra Shipman, Joanne Thompson, and Karen Hrdlicka
Formatting by Champagne Book Design

Published in the United States of America.
All rights reserved.

ISBN-13: 978-1-951829-71-1

A SIMPLE
request

CHAPTER ONE

Collin

I PULL OPEN THE OLD WOODEN DOOR AND SMILE. CLASSIC GEORGE Jones pours through the speakers, not too loud, but loud enough all patrons can enjoy the good music. The regulars at the bar turn and wave when I enter, earning me a round of welcomes and hellos from the people I'll be serving drinks to for the next several hours.

"Hey, Collin," Guy hollers, throwing me a wave and a grin.

"Evening," I reply, walking behind the bar and dropping my duffel bag into the cubby hole where we keep personal possessions. "How's it going?"

"Oh, not too bad. The game's on," he informs me, nodding to the TVs lined up on the wall above the bar. The St. Louis Cardinals are taking on the Chicago Cubs in a much-anticipated rivalry game. Our red birds are up by one in the series but look to be down already in game two. "How are we doing?" I ask, even though the score is pretty telling.

"Bats are cold," Guy states, moving to the tip jar and cleaning it out. "Hey, so I heard something today," he adds, stepping closer and lowering his voice. "Chuck sold it."

The hairs on the back of my neck stand up and my mouth drops open. "You're shittin' me. He really did it?"

Guy gives me a sad smile and a nod. "'Fraid so."

My heart sinks with the news. Chuck has been talking about selling this place for years, but no one ever thought he'd actually do it. He's worked here his entire life, buying the bar in his late twenties. Now, he's pushing seventy, and I thought for sure he'd be here until the day he died.

This place won't be the same without him.

"I guess he's signing the papers Friday."

I turn my attention to the older man standing beside me. "What?"

He gives me a knowing look. "Yeah. He told me earlier when he stopped by. This Friday, we'll have a new owner."

"Who?" I ask, my mind spinning.

"I don't know, but it sounds like he's from out of town."

I exhale loudly and catch one of the regulars sliding his empty beer bottle toward the inside of the bar top, a sign for a refill. "Well, maybe this is my time to get out too. I've only really stayed because of Chuck and you. I don't need the money," I confirm.

"I know, kid. I just thought you should know. As of Friday, looks like some changes coming our way."

I nod and head toward the customer who's ready for another drink, grabbing his brand from the cooler on my way by. "Here ya go, Tom," I state, twisting off the top and placing the beer on the old, faded coaster.

"Thanks, Collin," he replies, taking a sip from the fresh brew. "Did you hear the news?"

"Guy just told me. I can't believe it," I reply, reaching for a cloth to wipe down the bar top.

"Me either. Do you think there's gonna be any changes?" he asks, his eyes bouncing between me and the Cardinals' game on the TV.

"I hope not. We've gotta pretty good thing going here," I state.

"Damn right, we do," he says just as the sound of a bat cracking a baseball fills the bar. Everyone cheers as our batter hits a double, sending a runner home.

After Guy takes off, I check on the rest of the patrons and refill a few drinks. Everyone seems to be engrossed in the game, so I take the opportunity to do a little cleaning behind the bar, all while my mind is spinning.

I can't believe Chuck is selling. This place has been part of my life since I was twenty-one and could finally—legally—enter. It's a small bar with lots of character. The bar is original but has been refinished a few times, keeping that old charm intact. I'm not sure the stools have ever been replaced except when they break, leaving them mismatched and well-loved. Hell, a few of them are leaning and don't even spin anymore. The walls are covered with neon beer signs and paraphernalia and maybe a thick layer of cigarette smoke. No, you can't smoke in here now, but back in the day you could, and I'm pretty certain Chuck didn't do any sort of deep cleaning after the updated smoking laws were passed.

This place is old, but it's one of my homes away from home.

The other place I call home is the Sycamore Fire Station West. Ever since I was a little boy, I knew what I wanted to do with my life. Fighting fires is a calling, and I answered. I went through basic training at Lackland Air Force Base, and then specialized technical training at Goodfellow Air Force Base, both in Texas. I spent my four years fighting fires around the United States and learned an invaluable skill set doing it.

Now, I work as a full-time firefighter in Sycamore, a large city of thirty-two thousand people about an hour north of us. I love it there, but not enough to move, if that makes sense. I actually prefer the small-town lifestyle, which is why I returned to Cooper Town after my discharge from the Air Force.

Cooper Town, Ohio.

Home of four-thousand busybodies.

And the stories of me and my brothers and our friends growing up?

Legendary.

There are three Miller boys and one daughter, but don't let that fool you. My sister caused just as many sleepless nights, and as much mischief, for my parents to ensure their sainthood status for putting up with us all. I'm the oldest, by five minutes, before my twin brother, Cade. We may look identical, but we're as different as night and day. I'm the serious, broody twin, as many people have referred to me as, while my brother is the life of the party. He's witty, charismatic, and quick with a smile and can charm the panties off anyone.

Up next is our sister, Charli, short for Charlotte. Growing up with twin older brothers and a younger brother would cause a young girl to shy away from the mischief her rambunctious brothers caused. But not Charli. That girl was the instigator, and often times, the ringleader of Miller family trouble. And don't get me started on her now, as an adult. Charli is just as much of a troublemaker as she was in our youth.

Finally, there's Camden bringing up the rear. He's the baby of the group, nine years younger than my thirty-two years of age. I swear that kid got away with anything and everything growing up, because at that point, our parents were just tired. He's almost as charismatic as Cade, always having a lady friend to keep him company, much to our mother's dismay.

So there you have it. The Miller kids, along with their mischievous friends, wreaked havoc on this town. The things we'd done in our youth teeters the line between legendary and outrageous. Want to hear about some of the tales? Just ask any of the guys sitting at the bar right now. Every one of them will have a story about the Cooper Town kids.

I'm quite certain most of this town is surprised any of us turned out to be productive members of society upon adulthood.

Not that I blame them.

I hear a throat clear behind me, causing me to spin around and take in the regulars at the bar. Jarrod waves his empty can, letting me know he's ready for another. I grab the brew and pop the top before placing it in front of him. "Kind of a slow night," he says, taking a swig of the beer.

"I prefer it that way, Jarrod," I state with a chuckle. A slow night usually means no trouble.

He lifts his eyebrows and just grins. "I recall, not that long ago, a certain group of boys who'd come in and always get a little rowdy when they were here."

I feel my face heat up a bit, knowing he's talking about me, my brothers, and our friends. "I don't know what you're talking about, Jarrod."

He barks out a laugh. "Sure you don't."

"I'm ready to cash out, Collin."

I turn my attention to Tom, who's sitting with Larry. I go to the register and key in the quantity of beers Guy and I had marked on the piece of paper. "Fifteen bucks," I tell the man, who pulls cash from his wallet.

Handing over a twenty, he says, "Keep the change."

I nod and cross off his name on the paper, indicating he's paid his tab, and slip the five bucks into the tip jar.

Now, our system may not be the most up-to-date way of doing things, but Chuck has always had a level of trust for his regular customers. We tally their drinks throughout their time here, and then they pay up before leaving. He only lets a select group of patrons do that. Everyone else pays as they order.

"See ya later, guys! I gotta take the missus out to dinner," he states, earning a round of goodbyes from the others at the bar.

I shake my head, knowing Tom's wife, Betty, probably isn't going to be too happy with him for sitting in the bar up to the moment he's supposed to take her out to dinner, but that's none of my business. Grabbing the rag, I start to wipe down the bar where he sat, tossing the empty bottle into the trash can to be recycled. Another crack of the bat has the bar erupting into cheers. I glance up at the TV and find the Cardinals within one run now of their rivals.

I take the opportunity to restock the coolers with a few of our most popular brands. My mind returns to the shocking news of Chuck selling. I still can't believe it. I thought for sure he'd own this place forever. Now he's selling? And to an outsider? Should be illegal, if you ask me. The last thing we need is someone coming into our little town and changing up a good thing. This place isn't filled to the brim with patrons seven days a week like the other bar across town, but to me, this is better. It's familiar and relaxed, and I'd take that over crowded and noisy in a heartbeat.

I hear the door open and close with a thud and movement catches out of the corner of my eye. I glance up and…wow. The most beautiful woman I think I've ever seen is walking toward the bar. Her curly blond hair is pulled back in a ponytail and her clothes scream casually comfortable. She's wearing a pair of blue jeans and an oversized crewneck sweatshirt with a logo on the front. I recognize it right away as a business from a nearby town that sells amazing burgers.

When she takes a seat at the far end of the bar, away from the regulars watching the game, I head in her direction. I toss a coaster in front of her and ask, "What can I getcha?"

She looks at the wall of liquor, her light green eyes shining like emeralds under brilliant sunlight. I'm not sure I've ever seen eyes so stunning in my entire life. "Do you have any local beers on tap?"

My eyebrows shoot upward. "Sorry, we don't."

She's disappointed. "Oh, well, you should look into it. There's a regional brand that originated not too far from here."

I nod, knowing which one she's referring to. I've actually mentioned it to Chuck a few times in the past, but he never seemed too interested in adding to his lineup. Chuck sticks with what works, and that is usually the tried-and-true staple brands, like Anheuser-Busch, Miller, and Coors. "I'll mention it again, but the owner is kinda stuck in his ways."

The blond beauty smiles and says, "Then I'll have a Coors Light, please."

"Draft?" I ask, earning a nod.

I move to fill the glass and can feel her eyes on me the entire way. Call it a boost to the male ego, but I can't help and smile a little. Once I pour a perfect beer, I return to where she sits. The woman is looking around the bar, taking in the old décor.

"Kinda slow in here, isn't it?" she asks, setting a five on the bar and reaching for her drink.

I take the money, go to the register, and return with her change. "Not too bad. This is mostly normal for a weeknight."

She looks around some more and leans in so no one else can hear her. "You don't get a lot of women in here?"

I shrug and prop my hands on the bar. "On the weekends, sure. Not as many throughout the weeknights. A few every now and again, small groups having a quick drink after work or whatnot, but really, this is our norm."

"Huh," she replies, seemingly surprised by my statement. She reaches for her glass and takes a hearty drink. "Kinda sad, really. This isn't a bad place. Could definitely use an update, but it has great bones and probably some interesting history," she adds, looking up at the ceiling, which is covered with a variety of beer décor and customer-signed dollar bills. She points up and laughs.

"I have no idea," I confess. "I believe it started well before I was born. Chuck, the owner, bought this place about forty years ago, and I guess the story goes, on opening night, patrons were asked to sign their tips and then at the end of the night, Chuck stapled them to the ceiling. Over the years, more have been added, but a lot of those bills go back four decades."

The beautiful blonde smiles. "I love that story."

"Yeah, well, hopefully the new owner loves it too," I mutter before I can stop myself.

"New owner?"

"Apparently, Chuck's Place will officially have a new owner this Friday. In just four short days, all this history will probably be gone."

She looks around the bar once more, including up at the ceiling. "You don't think the new owner would find a way to mix the history with a new style?"

"Probably not," I confess, turning and propping one elbow on the counter so I can check on the guys down the bar. "Heard it's an out-of-towner. I can't see them appreciating what's here. They'll end up changing the entire place, from top to bottom, like they did over at The Tall One. About four or five years ago, someone came into town and bought the bar, gave it a complete makeover that caters to the younger crowd, and changed the entire vibe of the place."

"Enticing more customers isn't exactly changing the vibe," she states, focused on our conversation.

"It is when your old clientele doesn't really go there anymore. They don't want to deal with the uppity college kids who come to down the twenty-four kinds of draft beers."

"Twenty-four?" she asks with a surprised chuckle.

"Yep. Can you imagine?"

She looks over at our five-tap system and shakes her head. "I can't. I mean, maybe a couple more, so you can work in some popular imports or maybe that regional brand I mentioned, but twenty-four is too many."

I give her my complete attention once more. "You seem to know an awful lot about bars."

She smiles and glances down. "I grew up in one, but that's not a bad thing. My dad runs an amazing establishment." The pride reflecting in her eyes and in her words is evident. "I look up to him a lot."

"Yeah? That's cool," I say, as someone hollers my name behind me. "Be right back."

I move down the bar and refill Bud's draft beer and add a hash mark beside his name on the log. I know I should hang down around the guys or at the very least, watch some of the game, but that's not what happens. My legs carry me right back down to the end of the bar where the beautiful woman sits.

"So, what brings you to town?" I find myself asking.

"Is it that obvious I'm not from here?" she asks with a grin.

"Well, I did grow up here and know just about everyone, so it was a safe assumption."

"I'm here for business," she replies after another sip.

"And to watch the Cardinals and have a cold beer?" I ask with a grin.

"Absolutely," she says, turning her attention to the bar top and running her fingers over the marred wood.

The sound of her voice is like a good country song I can't help but listen to over and over again—only without the country twang. This woman's from the Midwest, that's for sure. "So, what kind of business?" I find myself asking, doing anything I can to keep her talking.

A light blush creeps up her fair skin. "Oh, well, I'm buying a business."

The hairs on the back of my neck stand up. "You are?" I ask, my throat suddenly very dry.

Green eyes lock with mine as she extends her hand. Her nails are painted, but kept short and clean, and the moment my hand touches her fingers, I feel the sizzle of electricity.

"Lizzie Meyer," she states before going in for the kill. "As of Friday, I'll be the new owner."

Fuck.

CHAPTER TWO

Lizzie

A WHOLE PLETHORA OF EMOTIONS CROSSES THE HANDSOME bartender's face as I tell him who I am. Shock, caution, a bit of anger, and then shock once more. Now that I've rendered him completely speechless, I take a moment to appreciate the view. He's tall, probably just a bit over six feet, has the darker side of sandy-blond hair, and the bluest eyes I've ever seen. And his body?

Bangin'.

Please don't tell my younger brothers I said that.

They'd be completely mortified.

No, his body is something to write home about. He's muscular, yet doesn't scream one of those guys who spends hours in a gym. He appears to be the type to get them organically, most likely from manual labor. I'm not sure what that is, but I don't think it's from working at a bar.

"Miss Meyer," he finally says, running his hand through his hair.

"Lizzie, please," I reply, smiling over the rim of my glass as I take a sip.

He exhales and turns a much chillier shade of blue eyes my way.

"Lizzie," he starts, swallowing hard, "I apologize for complaining. It was unprofessional of me."

I snort and shake my head. "You didn't say anything wrong," I reassure him. "Besides, I want to hear the unfiltered version. If you knew who I was, then you were less likely to be forthcoming about everything."

He pins me with an icy-blue gaze. "I don't lie."

"I'm not saying that," I insist, taking another sip of my beer. "I just mean that sometimes, people don't want to hurt someone's feelings, so they gloss over the ugly or beat around the bush."

He leans on the counter once more, the corded muscles in his forearms flexing in all the right ways. "I don't do that. What you see is what you get." His tone is firm, and his demeanor is somewhat gruff.

I nod, fighting a smile. He reminds me of someone I'm very close to. "What?"

"What what?" I ask.

"You were trying not to grin."

This time, I let the smile fly. "You just remind me of one of my uncles."

He slowly lifts his chin, as if absorbing the info. Before he can say anything, a man at the opposite end of the bar hollers his name. He moves with ease, his jeans hugging his hips and molding to his ass.

Well, he's definitely pretty to look at.

Too bad for me, that'll be all it ever is.

I'm not buying this bar, uprooting my life, and devoting everything I have to creating the future I want, just to jump into bed with the first hot bartender I cross. Hell, good-looking guys behind the bar are a dime a dozen. It's not like I haven't seen them a thousand times before. It's how my dad made a name for himself back in the day, if I'm being honest.

It's the same with women.

Employees with the right personality and the drive to do the job quickly earn the tips. It's a fact.

He doesn't return to my end of the bar right away, and I'm certain it's because he's now dubbed me the enemy. I'm the one buying the place he loves from the man who has built it into what it is today. From the moment I heard about Chuck's Place from a friend of a friend—the second friend being my uncle, Jameson—I saw the potential. This place has great bones, and even though it's a bit rundown and dated, I can totally work with that. It's what I've been saving for since I got out of high school. I knew I wanted my own place, my own bar.

My own legacy.

I learned everything I could from the best in the business. I knew in high school my heart was calling me to the industry, but I wasn't going to take what could easily be handed to me. I've spent the last decade working the business, learning everything I could from four of the best men I know, and saving every penny I could, so one day, I'd have a nest egg ready when the time was right.

That time is now.

Am I scared to shell out all the money I've been saving, signing papers for a business loan for the rest, and praying my business plan is right? Hell yes, I'm scared. But you live or die by the sword, and I refuse to die. I will do what it takes to turn my dreams into reality.

I am Walker Meyer's daughter, after all.

The man is the definition of determined.

And I didn't just learn from my dad. I spent countless hours with my uncle, Numbers, as well as Uncle Tank. I didn't shadow my uncle, Jasper, as much as the others, because food wasn't my passion, but that didn't mean I didn't learn a lot from him too. All four of them are honorable, hardworking men who have put so much into their business, building it from the ground up.

That's what I want.

But I want my dream, not an extension of theirs.

When my beer is almost gone, the bartender returns to my end of the deserted bar. "Another?"

"No, thank you," I reply, knowing I won't be staying too much longer. One beer is my limit so I'm able to drive back to Stewart Grove. My plan is to grab food at the diner down the block and then be on my way. Friday will be here before I know it, and I'll have a ton to do between now and then.

He nods.

"Can I ask you something?"

He opens his mouth but flashes hesitation. "Sure," he finally agrees.

"What's your name?" I ask, sliding my empty glass toward him.

"Collin. Collin Miller." He swallows hard but keeps his crystal-blue eyes locked on me.

"Well, it's nice to meet you, Collin, despite the circumstances," I say, pulling another five from my wallet and setting it on the bar. "I don't want us to be enemies. I think what is here has a solid foundation, and all I'm looking to do is build on it and grow. I hope you will one day see that."

He continues to stare at me before giving me a nod. I can sense his ire with me, even though he basically shut down after learning who I am. He clearly isn't a fan of Chuck selling the bar, which is something I understand and respect. He doesn't know me from Adam, and the last thing he wants is someone coming in and changing everything. That's not my intention, even though I do plan to make some updates to attract more clientele.

With that, I slip off my stool, noting the wobble to the chair and making sure I add matching stools to the list of purchases I'll need to make soon, and head toward the door. My eyes scan the front of the room and I can already see the changes I want to make. The windows are high and covered in neon beer signs, and while those are important, I'd love to see a little more natural light filtering inside.

I sense Collin's eyes on me as I reach the door, and even though I'd love to glance back and confirm my suspicions, I don't. I keep my focus forward as I pull open the heavy door and exit the bar. When I'm outside, the cool late-April air hits me in the face. It wasn't a particularly brutal winter, but the roller-coaster temperatures sure seem to be hanging around longer than normal in the Midwest. I'm ready for the warmer temps to be here to stay.

I turn and face the building. In just a few short days, I'll call this place my own. I've even settled on a name. Hell, it's been the name I've had in mind since I started dreaming of owning my own bar. Not only is this one the perfect size—not too big and not too small—it has an old living quarters in the upstairs. Chuck says it hasn't been used in years for anything other than a little storage, and with a little TLC, it'll be perfect for me. I'll live close to where I work and won't have the added expense of either renting a place locally or traveling the hour between Stewart Grove and Cooper Town.

Closing my eyes, I let the moment wash over me.

I did it.

This place will be mine on Friday.

I can't wait.

"Hello."

I smile as the familiar voice calls from the front of my apartment. I don't get up from my perch on the floor. I know my mom will come looking for me.

"How did I know this is how I'd find you?" she asks, laughing when she spots me sitting on my bedroom floor, surrounded by everything from my closet.

"Because you know it's crunch time, and my plan is to move this weekend."

She hands over an iced coffee drink and a white paper bag. Immediately I notice the logo for my aunt Lyndee's bakery. Taking both items, I sip the sweet, caramelly coffee drink before peeking inside the bag. I gasp. "Is that a raspberry strudel?"

"You know Lyndee. She made a batch just for you," Mom confirms before moving a pile of clothes on my bed and dropping onto the mattress. "How's it going?"

I take a quick bite, savoring the sweet raspberry taste mixed with pastry and frosting. "It's going. Besides my bathroom, this is the last room to pack up."

She glances around. "You're doing well."

"I'm about to just pitch it all," I confess, earning a chuckle.

"Don't do that. You never know when you'll need this…thing." She looks up at me, picking up the bright orange object and giving it a once-over. "What is this?"

A giggle slips from my lips. "It's a puppy life preserver with a shark fin."

"But…why do you have it?"

I shrug. "It was an impulse buy."

Mom tosses it aside and shakes her head. "All right then. What can I help with?"

"I thought Em had a game," I state, referring to my little sister, Emberlyn. She's a senior in high school and plays on the softball team. These extended colder temps, mixed with a bit of a rainy spring, has made it difficult to get all her games in before the end of the season.

"The field is too wet," Mom confirms. "They're doing a practice in the gym, and then she's gonna stop by here to help."

I don't necessarily need my sister's help, but I'm excited she's stopping by. Em and I are best friends, despite the ten-year age difference. I have two younger brothers, who are just as rowdy and wild as you'd expect them to be, so when I was ten and my mom had my sister, she was like a little gift from heaven. Don't get me wrong, I love my brothers, but growing up, they were a lot to handle. Especially when we'd all get together with the cousins.

"She's going to miss you," Mom states quietly, causing my throat to tighten.

"It'll be completely mutual," I tell her. "I'll only be an hour away. I was farther when I went to Ohio State."

"I know," Mom confirms, standing up and taking the box I just filled and taping the lid closed. "But you came home as often as you could back then, and after four years, moved back home for good. Now you're leaving once more and staying." Her green eyes fill with unshed tears.

Climbing to my feet, I pull her into a hug. I feel wetness hit my shirt as a few tears slide down my cheek too.

When she pulls away, she gives me a sad, watery smile. "I'm so proud of you, Lizzie."

"Thanks."

She wipes the tears from my face, much like she did when I was growing up. "We're all very proud of you."

I nod, unable to get words past the lump stationed in my throat. "Dad has been…quiet."

"Because he's sad, Lizzie, not because he's not happy or proud of you. You following your dreams is a parent's ultimate goal in life, even if that goal takes you away from us."

"I'm not going far," I remind her.

"I know, and that's why he's as calm as he is. If you were moving farther, he'd struggle. He'd still be proud of you, but he'd really have a hard time letting go. You remember what it was like that first time we dropped you off at college, right?"

I bark out a laugh as one of my favorite memories replays in my mind. We had everything in my dorm set up, but he kept finding little things to do or fix to draw out their departure. He even went as far as to go to the big box home improvement store and replace the bathroom faucet because it dripped and strengthened the closet clothing rod because it felt a touch loose.

"Oh, I remember. My roommate thought he was a Stage Five Clinger," I say, referring to one of my favorite movies, *Wedding Crashers*.

Mom laughs. "He was. But he got over it, and he'll get over this too."

I sigh and rest my head on my mom's shoulder.

Not a lot of people know this, but my dad isn't my birth dad. He adopted me when I was four, after my birth dad went to prison. He signed over his rights, thankfully, allowing the only man I've known as a father to raise me and give me his last name.

"You'll come see me, right?" I whisper.

She snorts. "Try to keep me away."

I hug my mom and commit her familiar scent to memory. I don't know why it feels like I'm leaving forever, because I'm not. I'm not even going that far. An hour is an easy day trip, and if I know my family, there will be plenty of visits. Especially in the beginning. My dad and his partners—my pseudo uncles—have already promised to be just a phone call away, ready to help. But they also understand my need to do this on my own.

That's why I love them all so dang much.

"Hello? I'm raiding your kitchen!"

Mom and I both laugh. "Your sister is here," she says, pulling away and giving me a small smile filled with both happiness and sorrow.

"She's probably already found those brownies I bought from the diner in Cooper Town."

"Oh, you know she has," Mom confirms, throwing her arm around my shoulder. "Let's go make sure she doesn't eat them all."

We walk side by side to the kitchen, where my suspicions are confirmed. My sister already found the brownies and has poured herself a big glass of milk. "Where did you get these?" she asks, her mouth full of chocolatey goodness.

"From the little diner in Cooper Town," I confirm, handing the container with one remaining brownie to Mom.

My sister narrows her eyes at me. "I suppose that's a good reason for me to visit often. Brownies."

I can't help but giggle. "They actually had several different options. Not anything as elaborate as Aunt Lyndee has, but a small selection of pastries for dessert."

Em takes a huge bite of her brownie and follows it up with a big gulp of milk. Her gaze remains locked on mine. While I resemble our mom in many ways, she has several of Dad's features. "So, you're still going, huh?"

"Yeah, I'm still going."

She sighs dramatically in a way only teenagers can do. "Does that apartment have two bedrooms?"

I flash her a grin. "It does."

"Good. Make sure the spare room is always made up. We'll just call it Emberlyn's room."

"Done," I confirm, even though I don't have a spare bedroom set to put in it yet.

"I mean it. It's my room. Don't let the smelly boys sleep there."

I fight back a smile and reply, "I wouldn't dream of it."

Our two brothers, Duncan and Waylon, are twenty-four and twenty-one, respectively, and both work at the family's bar and restaurant, Burgers and Brew. They're at that age where they have the whole world in front of them, and life is one big ball of fun. I highly doubt they're going to come to Cooper Town and hang with me at my little hole-in-the-wall bar. Besides, Duncan lives with our cousin, Rorik, at Uncle Jameson's old house, and between Waylon and any one of the other cousins or friends, there's always someone crashing on the couch.

Em steps forward, swallowing her snack and leveling me with a look. "I know I'm just your little sister, and I'm technically eighteen and going off to college in a few months, but this feels really big to me. Bigger than when you went to college. This is like…life. Forever."

Her eyes fill with unshed tears as I pull her into a tight embrace. "It's not forever, Em. You're always welcome at my place."

"I better be. I'm coming to visit all the time. Like every weekend. Promise me it's okay."

I don't think she will, but I don't argue with her either. Once she gets settled at school, she's going to have the best time ever. She probably won't even spare a thought for her older sister, working her ass off in Small Town, USA to make her dreams come true. "That bedroom is always open for you. Promise."

She sniffles and wipes her nose on the shoulder of my shirt.

I bark out a laugh and jump back. "Oh my God, Em. So gross."

She giggles and wipes her eyes.

"You used to do that to her when you were little," Mom says to Em as she pulls her in for a hug. "It was nasty then, and it's nasty now."

Em just laughs. "I only did it to rile her up."

"Keep it up and your bedroom will become a Duncan and Waylon room," I grumble, even though I'd never do that to her.

She gasps, her eyes wide. "You wouldn't!"

"If you wipe your nose on me again, I will."

Mom throws her other arm around my shoulders, pulling us into a three-way hug. "I love you both. I don't know what I'm going to do with both of my girls gone."

"Way still lives at home," Emberlyn confirms.

"Only on paper. Between the bar and your brother's house, he only comes home to raid the refrigerator and pick up clean clothes."

She's not wrong.

"All right, ladies, no more tears. We have packing to do," Mom announces, stepping back and quickly wiping away moisture from her own face.

I'm going to miss this. I'm incredibly close to my family, and the thought of not working with them, seeing them all the time, or even just living in the same town as them has my insides in knots.

But I know this is the right step.

I feel it in my heart.

This is me, chasing my dreams.

"Let's do it."

CHAPTER THREE

Collin

I LOOK AT THE CLOCK AND SIGH.

It's done.

As of noon, Chuck's Place officially changed hands, and the bar I've known and loved since I was old enough to drink is officially gone. No, the bar itself is still there, but it won't be the same. It can't be. Not with some out-of-towner buying it.

Lizzie.

Beautiful, spirited Lizzie Meyer.

Her emerald eyes still haunt my dreams. Four nights of tossing and turning, closing my eyes and not being able to get any real sleep. I tell myself it's because of the job—my full-time one—and not because of the woman I picture when trying to get some shut-eye. But that would be a lie. Every time I close my eyes, I see her face, which only elevates my annoyance all over again.

"Hey, dumbass, you okay?" The question is followed up by a swift slap to the side of my head.

"What the fuck?" I ask Gio, instantly bringing my hand up to shield any additional blows.

"I've been talking to you for a solid two minutes, and you haven't heard a word I've said."

"That's because you always talk. I'm so used to it, sometimes I have to tune you out just to get a second of peace," I counter, teasing one of my closest friends and coworkers.

"Fucker," he grumbles, reaching over to slap me a second time, but this time, I'm prepared and block the swing.

"Anyway, what were you saying?" I ask, giving him my full attention. Right now we're the only two in the day room, and while the TV is on, I have no clue what we're even watching.

"I was saying I heard from Clara. She's gonna come by this weekend so we can talk," he states, making me feel like an even worse friend than before when I wasn't listening to him. Gio and Clara have been on again, off again for as long as I can remember, and last I knew it was off once more.

"Yeah? Is that…wise?"

Gio sighs and closes his eyes. "I don't know, man. Honestly, I don't know what to do. I love her, but she has a hard time handling this life I lead."

I nod, knowing exactly what he's talking about. Gio and I are full-time firefighters, and our job, while incredibly important, comes with a lot of risks. It's similar to that of a military individual or police officer. It's dangerous and, sometimes, that's hard for some people to accept. Clara is one of those people. Every time she hears of a situation involving a firefighter on the news, she freaks out and says she can't handle his job. It weighs on him, heavily.

"I can't really tell you what to do, my friend, but you can't keep riding this seesaw all the damn time. The constant up and down, on and off, is hard on you." Every time they break up, he's a mess for about a week afterward. Then, they'll start talking, and she'll start coming around again. I don't judge, but as a friend looking in from the outside, their time together has run its course, and it isn't healthy for either of them.

After a few seconds, he says, "I know." Then, as if flipping a switch, he asks, "So, what's going on with you and that bar you work at when you're home? Today was the sale date, right?"

"Yep," I mutter, wishing I hadn't confessed my irritation with him back on Tuesday, because now he'll keep needling me to talk about it. "I think I'm just gonna quit. It's not like I need the money."

"True," he states, checking his watch. "Almost time to start chow."

I nod but don't get up.

"Why would you quit? Just because it's a new owner?"

"It's someone from out of town."

"So?"

I exhale deeply, my brain instantly drawing her image when I close my eyes. "She won't get the nostalgia and comradery that comes with the place. She'll make changes."

"Change isn't always a bad thing."

"Says the man who's about to meet up with Clara to possibly reconcile for the hundredth time in the last three years." As soon as the words are out of my mouth, I wish I could take them back.

Gio makes a face, but states, "Don't do that. Don't pull punches, man. That's why I come to you about this shit. You tell it like it is."

"Yeah, but it's not my life, it's yours."

"I know, but still. We're friends, and I value your opinion. Like when you came to work on Tuesday like someone with a thorn in his paw and told me all about the hot chick buying the bar where you work part time."

My eyes narrow as I level him with a look. "I did *not* tell you she was hot."

He shrugs. "Well, she has to be to get you this worked up."

"Maybe it's the fact she's going to wreck my favorite bar, huh? Maybe it's because I hate change, and she's about to change everything about one of my favorite places."

"Or *maybe* it's because you think she's hot and don't know what to do about it."

"Fuck off," I grumble, refusing to confirm or deny my attraction.

"You're proving my point, friend."

"How was that proving anything?" I ask, getting irritated with him all over again.

He snorts and smiles widely. "Because if you didn't like her, you'd be aloof, not getting your panties in a twist every time the bar is mentioned."

I just stare at him, wanting to call him on his bullshit, but unable to do so.

"Listen, if you really don't want to work with her, then quit. Like you said, you don't need the money. You just enjoy hanging out there with the old men so you're not stuck at your house all the damn time because you have no life."

"I do too have a life," I argue.

He just laughs. "Sure you do. I'm not judging, my friend, really, but the only thing you do is work at that bar or hang out with your family. When was the last time you got laid?"

I refuse to answer that question, because the answer is too fucking embarrassing.

"Exactly," he says, pointing a meaty finger my way. "You're sexually frustrated."

"Am not."

That's a lie.

"Oh, you definitely are. You're even more surly than normal. That screams blockage, if you know what I mean."

I snort. "Everyone this side of the Mississippi knows what you mean."

Ignoring my comment, he continues, "All I'm saying is, either give her a chance and see what kind of changes she makes or quit."

"That's not at all what you said."

"Sure it is. If you stay and like working with her, maybe she'll play with your dick. If you quit, you're just a patron who wants angry sex, and she'll play with your dick. It's a win-win."

I shake my head. "I don't even know why we're friends."

"Because I give solid advice," he states, kicking his feet back onto the coffee table.

"That's the biggest pile of bullshit I've ever heard," I reply with a chuckle, feeling surprisingly lighter after talking to him.

He's not completely right, obviously. There will be no dick-play, despite how quickly my cock stood up and paid attention to her when she was at the bar. But he is right on the rest of it. I can either give her a chance and see what kind of changes she makes, or I can quit. Hell, I can quit even after she makes her changes. I'm not married to the place, that's for sure. I just enjoy it.

Perhaps she won't even be involved in the bar much. She could hire someone—Guy, for example—to run the day-to-day for the place. She'll make random appearances to collect her money and then be on her way.

I could get on board with that.

A smile spreads across my lips. I bet Lizzie won't even be at the bar when I'm around, and that'd be fine by me.

That thought is silenced by the wailing of the alarm. Instantly, Gio and I both jump up and run toward the apparatus bay. Any thoughts of Lizzie and the bar are pushed out of my head. Right now, I have a job to do, and all my focus turns to my training. I'm geared up quickly and heading for the awaiting truck.

It's time to roll.

"Hello." I say, answering my phone when I spot the name on the screen.

"Good morning," Mom greets, her chirpy, happy voice filtering through the speakers in my truck. "On your way home?"

"I am," I reply, trying not to yawn. The fire we battled last night took several hours to get under control, and fortunately, we kept it from spreading to a neighboring building. By the time shift change happened this morning, our heads had barely hit the pillow. The next shift will most likely deal with a few hot spots today, but at least the building isn't still burning.

"I just wanted to call and remind you we're having Charlotte's birthday dinner tonight at six."

I want to groan, but I hold it back. The last thing I want is for Mom to think I don't want to attend my sister's birthday celebration. I was just hoping, the moment I get home, I could sleep for about twenty-four hours straight. Looks like that won't be happening, but I can still grab about seven hours before I need to get up and go to my parents' house.

"Your brothers are coming, and I'm sure that means Quinn will be there too."

I'm sure she's right. Quinn has practically lived at their house since the first time he was invited over for dinner and realized my mom could cook about anything. Even as a kindergartener, Q ate about anything and everything, never wanting to be at his own place. I'm sure that had something to do with his parents and the fact his house was slightly dysfunctional. At our home, he found stability, warm food, and love.

He's been part of the family ever since.

"Do you want me to bring anything?" I ask, unable to control my yawn this time.

"No," she replies with a chuckle. "Just yourself. Dad's got some ribs on the smoker. I'll make baked beans and mac and cheese, and your sister requested red velvet cake."

My stomach growls, reminding me we didn't get dinner last night because of the fire. "Sounds good. I'm starving."

"Well, you might find some biscuits and gravy in your refrigerator, waiting."

My mom is the fucking best. Even now, at the age of thirty-two, she's still taking care of me, and I'm not just talking about the food that randomly appears in my fridge after a long, forty-eight-hour shift. I know that's why she called me on my ride home when she could have easily texted to remind me of the gathering. She calls to keep me company while I drive so I don't fall asleep.

"Damn, Mom. If I get a ticket for speeding, it's your fault."

She chuckles. "Don't blame your lead foot on me. We both know you got that from your father."

A gravelly laugh fills my truck cab. "No one would believe it if I tried to tell them otherwise. You're a saint for putting up with that man and then having four kids just like him," I tease. My dad had a wild streak a mile wide growing up, and everyone said my mom was crazy getting together with him. The truth is—and he'd be the first person to admit this—it took the love of a good woman to help him grow up and settle down. Now, he's a damn good father and husband.

"Well, if the crown fits…"

I bark out another laugh.

The drive back to Cooper Town goes quickly, thanks to chatting with Mom. We catch up on what's happening with my siblings, my parents, and even their neighbors. By the time I reach the welcome sign at the edge of town, I feel pretty relaxed, yet alert, thanks to her. I mean, I haven't once thought about the woman who shall not be named in the last hour. That might actually be a record.

"I'm getting ready to pull into my driveway," I tell Mom, turning my truck onto Oak Street.

"Good. Go inside and heat up some breakfast, take a shower, and go to bed. Don't forget to set an alarm for five."

Smiling, I reply, "Yes, Mom."

"Don't sass me, Collin Andrew Miller."

"I wouldn't dare," I respond, earning another bark of laughter through the speaker.

"Right," she sasses, not believing it for a second. "Anyway, get some rest, and we'll see you later."

I pull into my driveway and park in front of the garage. No reason to put it away when I'll be leaving again later. "Sounds good."

"Love you," she states, which I repeat before we disconnect.

Grabbing my duffel bag off the seat behind me, I head for my back door and step inside. Familiarity wraps around me, like it always does when I get home after a two-day shift. I drop my bag in front of the washer to deal with later and go straight to the fridge. The container inside has a Post-it on top with a heart, and like always, it makes me grin.

I rip off the note and set it on the counter before placing the plastic container in the microwave and pressing the button for one minute. I don't even wait for the beep. The food is still cold after about thirty seconds, but I don't care. I'm starved. I grab a fork and dive in, closing my eyes and savoring the first bite of homemade biscuits and gravy.

Thank God for Mom.

It's loud before I even have one foot inside the door.

"'Bout time you got here," my youngest brother, Camden, hollers when I enter the kitchen.

I glance at my watch. "Dinner's at six," I remind him, noting I'm fifteen minutes early.

"Yeah, but the food's ready now and we've been waiting on you," he argues, reaching his hand inside the chip bag and pulling out a fistful.

Ignoring his obnoxious chewing, I head for my sister and press a kiss to her cheek. "Happy birthday, brat."

Charli rolls her eyes. "I'm twenty-nine."

"And still a brat," I argue, setting a card in front of her.

She immediately rips into it, not even bothering to wait until later, where there usually is a designated time to open gifts around the consumption of cake. "Oh, thanks," she says, shaking the gift cards out of the card without even reading the message.

"You're not even gonna read it?" I ask. "I spent all that time picking out the perfect card."

Lies. I literally just grabbed one.

My sister just rolls her eyes a second time. "I call bullshit. You just grabbed a card. Wanna know how I know?"

I take a seat and wave my hand. "Enlighten me."

She holds it up and points to the big gold letters on the front of the card that read "Happy Birthday, Granddaughter."

I bark out a laugh and reach for some chips. "You may have a point."

"But seriously, thank you. These are my two favorite places," she states, confirming what I already know. She loves fancy coffee drinks from the little corner shack near the bar and shops the bookstore often.

"Finally!" my twin brother, Cade, announces dramatically as he enters the kitchen.

"Shut up," I grumble before shoveling chips into my mouth.

He falls into the chair beside me and takes the bag of chips. "So, we thought we'd head up to Chuck's Place after this," he says with a mouthful.

I don't say a word, not really wanting to go up there.

"Heard there's a hot new owner, so we all thought we'd go check her out."

I can feel his eyes on me, but I refuse to look his way.

"I can't believe you didn't tell us," Cade says, filling the silence with his words, like always. "No worries though. It's all anyone is talking about."

"When do you work next?" Camden asks, smiling at me from across the table.

I shrug. "Don't know. Chuck usually texts me, but as you mentioned, he doesn't own it anymore."

"So, are you not working there?" Cade asks, his blue eyes penetrating past my defenses.

Again, I lift my shoulders casually. "I don't know. Haven't talked to her."

"But she is hot, right?" I narrow my eyes at my twin, who just laughs. "She is!"

"I didn't say that," I retort way too quickly and with too much venom.

He just grins that cocky little smirk of his. "You didn't have to."

Charli leans over and smacks my arm. "We're all going. It's for my birthday."

I exhale and close my eyes, knowing there's no point in arguing it now. If Charli wants to go, then we're all going. "Fine."

"Yes!" Cade hollers, throwing both arms up in the air victoriously. "I can't wait to meet the new hottie. She'll fall hopelessly in love with the twin who actually got all the charm and good looks."

I just stare at my brother. My *identical* twin brother. "You're an idiot."

He shrugs and grabs more chips. "Maybe so, but I bet by the end of the night, I'll have her number."

I don't take that bet.

Why?

Because the thought of him getting Lizzie's number and calling her sits in my gut like a lead balloon. It's a picture I don't want to see, a thought I don't even want to enter my brain.

But maybe that's just what I need to get her out of my mind. My brother and I have never fought over girls. Well, not since fourth grade and we both fell hopelessly in love with Missy Johnson. I shared my grapes with her and Cade his Cheez-Its. It caused a huge issue at home between brothers, considering we lived in the same bedroom.

It was at that moment we vowed to never let a woman come between us. If one brother saw a girl first, they got first dibs, and that was that.

Except…

I saw Lizzie first.

CHAPTER FOUR

Lizzie

"READY FOR ANOTHER?" I ASK BURT, ONE OF THE REGULARS I'VE come to get to know a little tonight, my second official day as owner of the bar.

Or Lizzie's Place as I'm calling it. Temporarily, until I unveil the new name.

"You betcha, Lizzie," he replies with a nod and a toothy grin.

Burt is one of the several regulars I've come to know since signing the papers yesterday. The moment I opened the doors on Friday with the keys I was just handed, I've met Tom, Larry, Gus, and Jarrod. Of course, there have been plenty of others who I've met, especially tonight, which is definitely a little busier than it was both Monday and last night. But from what I've heard, word has gotten around that Chuck's Place is under new ownership, and it appears everyone is curious.

I pour another draft beer and set it on the counter. He nods and reaches for his drink. From what I learned the day before, the regulars are used to paying at the end of the night. The previous owner let them keep a tab on a slip of paper and then settle up when they were ready to leave. I'm not against that, and I told them that fact. But I do believe we need a better system in place. I agreed to continue to do it that way for a short time, until I could get a new pay system installed and could count drinks electronically there. Sure, there were a few grumbles, but the regulars agreed we'd revisit the discussion at a future date.

"It's a lot busier than normal. That's because of you," Jani states with a laugh.

Jani is the only other female bartender, working two or three nights a week. She's twenty-six and a single mom of two-year-old Evan. She's already shown me a dozen photos of the cute little guy, with his black hair and dark chocolate eyes. Considering she has lighter hair and hazel eyes; I'm going to assume he favors Dad in his features.

"Because everyone is being nosy," I state with a chuckle.

"Exactly! But that's good. At least they're buying drinks while they're here," she replies, pouring a Jack and Coke for a guy wearing too much cologne.

I can't argue with her there. Last night, we had a handful of patrons stop by to see the new owner, but tonight is on another level. Every stool is full at the bar, and the tables too. Plus, there's a handful of small groups around the room, including four guys playing pool.

I'm ecstatic the employees Chuck had have agreed to stay on under my leadership. Well, everyone but Collin. I haven't had a chance to talk to him yet. I found out he's a full-time firefighter and works here a day or two a week, as his schedule allows. He's supposed to work tomorrow, and even though I have big plans to really dive into the apartment upstairs and get it a little more livable, I can work if needed. I had every intention of texting him today to see if we could meet, but the entire day just got away from me. Poor communications skills on my part, and hopefully he'll accept my apology.

My phone vibrates in my pocket, and I quickly pull it out to check the screen. I smile instantly when I see the name.

Dad: We're coming tomorrow. No arguments.

Dad: Love you, Lou. So fucking proud.

I shake my head and fight back the tears as my fingers fly across the screen.

> **Me: See you tomorrow. Love you more.**

> **Dad: Impossible.**

I slip the device back into my pocket and grab a Bud Light for someone at the bar. How I've managed to hold off my family this long is beyond me. Mom came over with me to sign the papers and take possession of the bar, leaving my dad chomping at the bit to help. I brought over just enough personal items to stay in the apartment upstairs for a few nights, knowing the big move would be happening first of the week. But weekends are the busiest time at my family's bar and restaurant, so I couldn't pull them all away from their own place to help with mine, even though they would have done it in a heartbeat.

Plus, I just wanted a couple of days to feel the ground settle beneath my feet.

No one argued, at least not to me. I'm sure Mom got an earful from Dad, but he hasn't said too much to me, other than reminding me they're all here for me when I need it. He understands my desire and drive to do this on my own, and he does support that decision, even if it's killing him.

Apparently, their sitting back and waiting is over. Honestly, I'm surprised they lasted forty-eight hours. It wouldn't have surprised me if they would've shown up Friday at noon when I turned the key and opened the door.

"What's so funny?"

"Huh?" I ask, turning my attention to Jani.

"You had this look on your face and a little smile on your lips," she says, pulling a couple of beers from the cooler.

"Oh, nothing much. My family. They're coming tomorrow."

Her eyes widen. "All of them?" Jani knows of my large, extended family, something we chatted about when I met with her earlier today.

"Well, I can assume so, yes. They don't do anything small," I state, moving to the end of the bar to grab a couple of drink orders.

"I'm kinda sad I'm not working tomorrow," Jani replies with a laugh when she's close enough to speak over the noise. "Collin will get first look at the Meyer clan."

"Eight bucks," I tell the guy buying the beer I just grabbed.

He hands over a ten, flashes a mega-watt smile, and says, "Keep the change, pretty lady."

Jani snorts and shakes her head. "Stay away from that one. He flirts with everything and everyone, and his dick falls into any vagina it gets near."

My eyes widen at her comment before a burst of laughter slips from my lips. "That sounds…yeah."

She rolls her eyes. "Town manwhore. Charming as all get out, which is probably why it's so easy for him. He's cheated on every girl he's ever dated longer than a month."

"Good to know," I reply, even though he's not really my type. Not that good-looking, a great smile, and fit body aren't my type, but I can tell he's a player. It oozes from his pores, and after finding myself dating one exactly like him back in my early twenties, I've vowed to stay the hell away from guys like him.

The only thing they're good for is breaking your heart, because even the orgasms they swear they can provide are somewhat lackluster.

"…he's pretty good. Just usually a little on the quiet side."

I shake my head, snapping out of my own thoughts and try to focus on what she's saying. I quickly realize she's talking about Collin still. "Oh, uh, I actually haven't talked to him. I meant to text him, but the day got away from me, so I don't really know if he's coming in tomorrow or not. He might just assume he doesn't have a job, thanks to the new owner," I state with an awkward chuckle.

She scoops ice into two glasses and starts mixing drinks. "I'm sure he'll be here. He's incredibly loyal."

"Yeah, but he was loyal to Chuck, not me," I reason, grabbing six different beers out of the cooler and setting them on the bar before twisting off the tops.

The front door opens and slams with a thud. Most people would hate the sound, but for me, I love it. The old door adds to the charm of the building.

"Well, here's your chance to find out."

I look up and find the man in question, as well as a handful of others, headed my way. My heartbeat quickens, and I feel my cheeks start to heat.

I'm blushing?

Seriously!

Frustrated, I clear my throat and finish my order, ignoring every set of eyes I feel on me. They're nothing new. I've had eyes on me for the last two days, everyone wanting to see the new girl in town.

When I finish filling the order and take the customer's cash, I finally turn my attention to the end of the bar where Collin stands. His intense blue eyes are all-consuming and all-knowing as he watches me work. "Hi," I greet, offering a brief smile.

"Hey."

I glance around the bar, noticing the brief lull in customers waiting for a drink, so I quickly add, "Do you have a second to talk?"

If he's surprised by my request, he doesn't let on. "Sure."

I point toward the back room, where Chuck had a small office set up. Over my shoulder, I hold up two fingers to Jani. "Give me two minutes."

She nods, waving me to go ahead, before jumping in and washing dirty glasses.

We step inside the small room, and I swear, with his presence, it feels so much tinier than before. I'm not claustrophobic, but the walls are definitely closing in around us. Not to mention the little space seems to amplify his woodsy, fresh scent, sending zings of pleasure to my core.

"I won't take but a minute of your time, but I needed to apologize."

That seems to catch him off guard, because his eyebrows shoot upward. "Why?"

"I've been meaning to call or text you. I was told you were working your other job yesterday, so I was holding off, and then today just got away from me. Chuck had you on the schedule for tomorrow, and I'm hoping you're still planning to work here."

He swallows, considering me with those intoxicating eyes. "I'll be honest, I assumed you were starting fresh with employees."

I shake my head, feeling even worse about not clearing things up with him before now. "No, and again, I'm sorry for that. I've talked to everyone who worked here prior to me purchasing this place, and they're all staying on. I hope you'll consider it too."

"Uhh, I'm not sure. This might be the perfect time for me to step away. My full-time job keeps me pretty busy, and I was just doing this to help Chuck out a day or two a week."

I take a step forward. If I were to reach out, I would touch him. I don't, of course, because that would be completely unprofessional of me. "I understand that, but honestly, it would help me out too. You know this place, and even if you still work one or two nights a week, you'd give me a chance to take a break or work on some of the changes I've been hoping to make."

At the last part, I see the corner of his jaw tick as it tightens. Clearly, he doesn't like the idea of me making changes. I can understand his reluctancy, but he's annoyed without even hearing what I have planned for this place, and that *annoys* me.

"Listen, you and I got off on the wrong foot. I'd like to start over. I'm not a bad guy—or woman, actually. Yes, I do plan to make some improvements and changes here, but I'm not about to destroy what Chuck has already built." An idea quickly forming in my mind, I add, "Give me thirty days. It's a simple request."

He holds my gaze, not saying a word for several seconds. Finally, he asks, "A simple request?"

I nod. "Yes. Thirty days, and at the end, if you don't like what I'm doing or simply don't like working here anymore, just say the word and I'll take you off the schedule. No questions asked."

"Just like that?"

"Just like that," I confirm.

He exhales, running his hand across the back of his neck. "Thirty days."

"Yep."

After a few seconds he finally agrees. "All right, thirty days."

Relief washes over me at his agreement, mostly because I don't want to worry about hiring someone right now. I have a long list of projects to work on, and training a new employee isn't near the top of that list. "Great. Thank you."

He nods, glancing toward the door. "You should probably get back out there. It was pretty busy."

"Yeah," I reply, moving to the closed door. "The entire town seems to be here tonight," I add with a big grin.

"The entire town is curious…about you."

"I'm nothing special," I state with an awkward chuckle.

I swear I hear him murmur, "I beg to differ," but when he doesn't elaborate or say anything else, I assume I just made it up. My mind wants Collin to be different for some reason, to prove good guys really do still exist.

Just as I pull open the door and step forward, I smack square into the chest of…Collin?

"There you are," he states, a big, wolfish grin on his face.

My mouth drops open and my neck practically gives me whiplash as I look behind me. "What the hell?"

The man in front of me barks out a laugh. "Well, hello to you too, darlin.'"

Collin exhales loudly before saying, "Lizzie, meet my brother, Cade."

"Brother," I whisper, looking forward once more.

"*Twin* brother," Cade announces, reaching his hand forward and giving mine a gentle shake before bringing it to his lips. "I'm the better looking one."

I bark out a laugh, because from where I'm standing, there's not much difference between the two. Actually, I take that back. There are a few subtle differences, like a small scar under Collin's right eye, and the slight lump on the top of Cade's nose that indicates it's been broken at one point. Not to mention Collin's eyes appear a bit more vivid and a lot more hypnotic, while Cade's blue eyes just scream mischief.

Collin sighs once more and steps between us, practically pushing his brother out of the way. "She's gotta get back to work."

Cade just smiles. "What were you two doing in here…behind a closed door…alone?"

"Talking," Collin insists, his tone leaving no room for nonsense.

Cade barks out a laugh. "Is that what you kids are callin' it these days?"

"Actually, we were just talking, and now I really do need to get back up to the bar," I insist, finding myself smiling. While I don't feel the same attraction to Cade as I do Collin, I can appreciate his lighthearted, fun nature.

"You do. The natives are starting to get restless," Cade confirms, glancing toward the bar.

I pass by him and quickly make my way to help Jani. "Sorry," I mutter before jumping right in and filling orders.

She doesn't seem fazed by my absence, nor does she appear frazzled to be busy. She just goes with the flow and fills drink orders as quickly as possible. I like her and hope she sticks around. She's a hard worker with a good head on her shoulders.

Recognizing we're getting low on a few different beers in the cooler, I start making a mental list of what needs brought up the first chance we get. Movement catches out of the corner of my eye, and I stop what I'm doing as Collin appears behind the bar, carrying cases of beer. Without being asked—and without being on the clock—he gets to work on stocking the coolers with beer from the back cooler.

When he looks my way, I offer a grin full of appreciation, and all I can hope is this is us crossing the bridge of understanding. I think if he sticks with me for the next thirty days, he'll like what I have planned. Of course, if he doesn't and he leaves, there's no skin off my back. I'm not doing this for anyone but myself, and the only person who needs to be happy with what I do at the end of the day is me.

By the time it slows down enough for Jani and me to catch a breath, I head out and start clearing tables. The crowd has thinned as we approach eleven, but there's still some groups of patrons enjoying their evening. I pull a large trash can on wheels toward the pool table where Collin, Cade, and their friends play.

"So, you must be Lizzie, huh?"

I turn and find a woman with ocean-blue eyes and lighter blond hair sipping a mixed drink and watching me. "I am."

"I'm Charli," she states with a friendly smile.

"It's her birthday," Cade announces, coming over and giving her a hug.

"Well, happy birthday," I tell her.

"Thanks," she says, glancing over at the table, where Collin is lining up his shot. My eyes follow hers, and I'm treated to a nice view of him bending over. When he makes the shot, Cade hollers in victory, while two others show their displeasure. "Sorry, my family can be a little loud."

I can't help but laugh. "No worries. This isn't exactly a quiet place."

"You know Collin and Cade, right?" When I nod, she continues, "The other two idiots are Camden, my youngest pain in the ass brother, and his bothersome friend, Quinn."

Grinning widely, I reply, "I have two younger brothers and a sister, and a whole slew of cousins, so I understand."

Charli raises her glass in salute. "Lizzie, you and I are gonna be good friends, I can tell."

I don't know why, but I believe her, and the thought of having friends here in Cooper Town makes my anxiety over my big move lessen even more. Not that I didn't think I'd make new friends eventually, but I'm already getting along with everyone I've met.

Except Collin.

The jury's still out on him.

CHAPTER FIVE

Collin

"I LIKE HER," MY SISTER SAYS WHEN I DROP INTO THE SEAT BESIDE her.

I just stare at her in question, waiting for her to elaborate.

"Lizzie."

My annoyance shoots heavenward at the mention of her name. "You don't know her."

"No, but I know people, and she seems like a good egg," my sister reasons.

I watch as Camden and Quinn rack the balls, since they lost the previous game. Of course, my silence is all my sister needs to continue to talk.

"She comes from a big family too. Sounds like she's the oldest with a couple of younger brothers and a sister," Charli announces, taking a final sip of her drink.

"Another?" I offer, but she waves me off.

"Nope, that was my last one. Back to Lizzie," she starts, earning a groan from me.

"Let's not."

"Let's," she pushes, her blue eyes twinkling with mischief.

"Nope," I reply, standing up and stretching.

"She was totally checking out your butt when you were shooting pool."

That makes me pause, but I school my features so nothing registers. I'm a pro at making sure my siblings can't get a read on me, something I perfected when I was younger.

"I think she likes you."

I sigh and face my sister. "Butt out, Char. There's nothing there."

She shrugs and flashes a sweet little grin. "If you say so."

"I do," I reply, suddenly unable to ignore the fact she was staring at my ass. Not that it means anything, like Charli is stating, but it's nice to hear. "You're up," I state, bending down and placing a kiss on her cheek. "I'm out."

"You sure?"

"Yep. I'm exhausted and ready to crash. You okay to get home?"

My sister rolls her eyes. "Of course I'm good. Cade told me he'd get me home."

I glance over at my twin, who stopped drinking a while ago. "Make sure he gets the idiots home too," I state, referring to our younger brother and his sidekick friend.

Charli sighs dramatically. "They're on their own."

I narrow my eyes at her, knowing she'd never actually make them figure out their own ride home after they've been drinking. "Anyway, be safe. Love you."

"Love you too, Col. See you soon."

I nod and wave at my brothers. "Charli's got my spot."

I don't miss the way Quinn's face lights up, but my attention is quickly pulled to my twin. "Can't hang, huh?"

"It was a long shift last night, into this morning."

He flashes a cocky smile. "So, that means Lizzie's all mine tonight," he states, slapping his hands and rubbing them together.

"Whatever," I reply, even though I suddenly feel like I just swallowed gravel. The thought of my brother hitting on her, taking her home, has my gut in knots and my brain ready to explode.

He barks out a laugh, throwing his head back for dramatics. "You should have seen the look on your face."

"Fuck off, Cade." With that, I turn around, the sound of his laughter echoing through the bar as I head for the door.

Just as I reach the old wooden door, I pause and glance over my shoulder. Lizzie and Jani are behind the counter, but only one pair of eyes are on me. If she's embarrassed about being busted watching me, she doesn't let on. Just lifts her hand to wave and gets back to work. I know I should probably go check to see if they need anything before I go, but Jani is good, and if Lizzie is correct, and she's practically grown up in a bar, I'm sure they'll be fine.

The thought of my brother offering to help causes my feet to falter as I push through the door, but I don't stop. I forge on and refuse to look back any more than I already have.

Something tells me that woman is nothing but trouble.

Best keep my eyes straight ahead and remember exactly who she is. My boss.

I open the door to…chaos.

There are people everywhere, and I'm not talking about customers. The bar isn't open yet. On Sundays, we're here one to nine, which covers most major league sporting events throughout the year, and Chuck usually covered it.

A mixture of people, mostly men, turn to face me when the heavy door slams. "Uhh, hey?"

"Collin," Lizzie hollers from one of the tables farthest from the door. She gets up from the chair and moves in my direction. "Hi, sorry about all of this."

"What's going on?" I ask, noticing everyone is still standing where they are, watching me.

"Oh," she replies, glancing down to try to hide her blush. "This is my family. They showed up to...help."

"Help?" I inquire, but before Lizzie can reply, a man with dark hair and blue eyes appears at her side.

"Everything all right, Lou?"

She smiles lovingly up at the man beside her. "Yes, Dad. Dad, this is Collin, one of the employees. He's agreed to stay on through the transition for thirty days."

I extend my hand, and I see a touch of hesitation in the man's eyes. "Nice to meet you, sir."

"Walker Meyer," he replies, giving my hand a little bit of a squeeze. "The other guys are my friends and business partners, Jasper, Jameson, and Isaac."

Why do those names ring a bell?

I politely wave toward the other men, some behind the bar and another sitting at the table Lizzie just vacated. There are a few women floating around too. One is painting a sign over near the pool table, while the other three are doing what appears to be some spring cleaning. Not to mention a couple of teenage kids, who look like they'd rather be doing anything else than wash windows.

"I know this is a little...yeah," she finally says when her dad walks away.

I take another look around the room. "It's good to have such a big support system," I tell her. Actually, it reminds me of my own big, rambunctious family. "So, what do you want me to do?"

"Well, my dad and Uncle Tank are setting up the bar a little differently. They're not allowed to do anything without my approval though. Do you want to help? I know we're getting ready to open the doors, but they'll stay out of the way so you can take care of the customers."

I lift my chin, showing my agreement, and head back to where two big guys are cleaning and reorganizing liquor bottles. I grab for the clipboard hanging beneath the counter to "clock in" but notice it's not there. Looking toward the table Lizzie returned to, she holds up the clipboard and says, "Got you."

I glance around, not really sure what to do. To the big guy who's not-so-subtly watching me, I say, "Hey, I'm Collin. Where do you need me?"

His whiskey-colored eyes bore into me like an inquisition. I'm a man who's comfortable under pressure, but the way this giant is staring at me makes me want to squirm. If I were a lesser man, I'd be very intimidated by him.

Slowly, he extends his hand. "Jameson. Lizard asked us to organize the bar to make it a little more accessible for faster service."

The question is out of my mouth before I can stop it. "Lizard?"

I swear if I weren't staring directly at him, I'd miss the way the man's lip ticks in the briefest, faintest smile. "Lizzie. We've always called her Lizard."

"That's where she came up with the name for the bar," a woman says. She extends her hand and adds, "I'm Mallory, Lizzie's mom. You met my husband, Walker, and this guy, Jameson. The one over there is Jasper, and the guy at the table is Numbers. Also, Madelyn and Lyndee are the ones cleaning, and BJ is painting a sign for over the door."

My head's spinning a little bit as I follow along with her finger as she points.

"We're not making any big changes," Lizzie's dad states. "Lou put her foot down."

"Lou?"

Mallory laughs. "Lizzie. Her dad's always called her Lizzie Lou."

I slowly nod in understanding.

"If I had it my way, we would have ordered the same setup as Burgers and Brew," Walker mutters.

"Yeah, but you don't get your way in *my* bar!" Lizzie hollers, a hint of humor in her voice.

"Has she always been this sassy?" Walker asks Mallory, who just grins.

And that's when it hits me.

Hard.

Like a two-by-four to the chest.

"You guys own Burgers and Brew." It's not a question.

Holy shit, how did I not realize this?

Everyone in this part of Ohio knows about Burgers and Brew. Hell, I've been there, traveling the hour distance just to have one of their famous burgers. It's probably the biggest, most well-known non-chain restaurant in the area, and I can't believe these are the owners.

Which means the bar Lizzie grew up in was that one.

"I take it she didn't tell you that?" Walker asks, clearly witnessing my confusion and realization.

"Uh, no. She said she grew up in a bar and restaurant, but never said which one."

Walker snorts and shakes his head. "She's worked there since she was old enough to legally be on the payroll, but her love for the place goes way back. She practically cut her teeth there."

"Wow," I reply, not really sure what else to say. Knowing that she was always referring to Burgers and Brew and never so much as mentioned the name of it is actually pretty telling. She learned from the best, but didn't use their name or notoriety to get ahead or what she wanted.

My admiration of her just increased tremendously.

"Finished!"

All eyes turn toward the tattooed woman with black-and-pink hair. Lizzie jumps up and practically runs over to where she's been working and looks down. "Oh my gosh," Lizzie states, her hands moving to her mouth as her green eyes fill with tears. "I love it so much."

Everyone else slowly makes their way toward the sign, all anxious to see the finished product. I watch as they ooh and ahh over it, giving the woman who painted it kudos for a great piece of art.

"It's positively amazing, Aunt BJ," Lizzie says, beaming at the woman with a wide smile and love in her eyes.

"You made it easy. It's a great name for a bar," she informs her niece, giving her a warm hug.

Walking around the bar and toward where everyone is standing, staring down at the sign, I can't help but ask, "And what name is that?"

Lizzie just smiles, her excitement rolling off her in huge waves. "The Tipsy Lizard."

Lizzie's family spends pretty much the entire day at the bar or in the apartment upstairs. I've always known about the living quarters, having gone up there once or twice to get some things Chuck stored up there, but as far back as I can remember, it's been empty. I learned quickly that the new owner of this place has been staying up there since she was given the key, but it's in desperate need of some TLC. Once everyone got the bar area cleaned up a bit, the small changes they were making complete, and the new sign hung above the door outside, they all turned their attention above us, where they've been the last few hours.

"This place already looks better."

I turn my attention to Larry, one of the regulars, and nod. "It does."

"And I don't hate the name," Burt adds, studying the freshly painted logo on the mirror behind the bar. Once BJ finished the sign, she turned her attention to the mirror and duplicated the business name and logo from the sign. It still makes me smile. The lizard holds a beer in each hand, looking like he's had a few too many. It's a testament to BJ's talent as an artist, to be able to bring the character to life and actually make him look a little tipsy. I learned BJ's an accomplished tattoo artist, married to Isaac— or Numbers as everyone calls him—and is Jameson's sister.

I grunt in response, because to be honest, I don't either. I thought I'd disapprove of anything she came up with, but that's not the case. And knowing the connection beneath the lizard nickname and her pseudo-uncles is kinda sweet. It's like an ode to her extended family yet still keeping true to herself.

Don't tell her, but it's all sort of growing on me.

"And it's brighter in here, right?" Gus asks, glancing around the room. "Don't tell me that's just from cleaning."

I snort. "I think they took two inches of smoke and dirt off the windows," I tell them, wiping off the counter near where they sit.

"Maybe that's it," Tom replies with a hearty laugh.

"She said she's gonna paint too but promised to take care of saving what she can from what's on the walls and ceiling. My very first dollar bill tip to Chuck is hanging right there," Jarrod announces, pointing to the spot above the bar where he signed and stapled his contribution to the then-new owner.

In less than twenty-four hours, since she asked me to give her thirty days, she's already making good on her promise. Of course, the little things she's done so far are small, cosmetic updates. I know some of the bigger, more costly ones are yet to come, so I suppose we'll see if she holds true to keeping the same feel this place has always had.

I hear movement at the back of the bar and watch as Walker makes his way toward me. "Hungry?" he asks, putting the pizza box on the counter.

My stomach growls the moment it smells the Italian goodness in the box, causing Walker to chuckle.

"Have at it," he says, taking a step back and leaning against the bar. He looks around the room and greets the regulars while I take a bite of sausage pizza. It's from the diner down the block, and even though they're not an authentic Italian restaurant, their pizza is pretty damn good.

"Thanks," I tell him when his attention is returned to me.

He lifts his chin in acknowledgement, and even though he doesn't say a word, I have a feeling there's something on his mind. So, I wait him out.

It's not until I've finished my first slice when he finally speaks. "It wasn't easy for me to step back and watch as my oldest daughter picked up and moved away from the only home she's ever known. She's embedded in the walls of Burgers and Brew the same way my best friends and I are."

He glances at the mirror behind the bar where the new name is proudly declared and smiles. "I thought she'd always be there, with her blond hair, green eyes, and big smile, but that's not where her heart lies. It's here."

He pins me with a look so intense, so forceful, I almost take a step back from the pressure. "I'm not asking you to watch out for her. She doesn't need a babysitter. My Lou is the strongest fucking girl I know, second only to her mother. Both of them are total badasses," he says, a faint smile on his lips.

"What I *am* asking is that you respect her, as your boss and as a woman. This industry, like many, can be harsher on the fairer sex, but I'm not worried about her. She knows what she's doing, and she'll lead by example. She'll follow her gut and her heart. She'll earn the love and respect of everyone around her, I'm certain. I'm asking you to give her a chance and to treat her right."

My throat is a little thick as I gaze at a man—a loving father—who is asking me to be good to his daughter. Not in a romantic way, of course, but as a woman and a superior.

He's not wrong. This industry can be harder on women. Men who come to a bar and think they can say or do whatever they want to the woman behind the counter. Not that it doesn't happen the other way around too, but it seems even more troublesome for women. The respect I have for Walker Meyer is endless, and I just fucking met him.

Extending my hand, I vow, "I promise. She's in good hands here."

He seems to relax a little more, having said what he felt needed to be said about his daughter. "Thank you," he replies, taking my offered hand and shaking it. "Also, don't tell her I gave you this, because she'll hand me my ass on a platter," he adds, reaching into his pocket and pulling out a business card.

I take the card and glance down. It's a Burgers and Brew card with a list of names and numbers on the back.

"That's my cell, as well as the three guys you met today. The last number is for Garreth Taylor, our manager. If for some reason you can't get ahold of the four names above it, call him. Every name on that list I trust with my life...and my daughter's."

I nod and slip it into my own pocket. "I hope I never have to use it."

He cracks a little smile. "Me too. Might not be pretty for anyone involved." After a beat he adds, "I'll let you get back to work. I need to get back upstairs before they come looking for me."

With that, he turns and walks away, leaving me with a rapidly beating heart and a list of phone numbers in my pocket.

One thing's for certain.

I hope I never have to reach out to Walker Meyer and his friends.

CHAPTER SIX

Lizzie

"S O, WHAT DOES HE DO?"

The question from my aunt, BJ, makes me pause. "Who?"

"The hottie behind the bar downstairs," she whispers so no one else hears her.

My eyes widen at her bluntness.

"What? He's hot, right? I can't be the only one who sees it," she states, shrugging her delicate shoulders before sliding the paintbrush carefully along the top of the wall.

I clear my throat, trying to figure out what to say. She doesn't push me as I rewet my roller with paint and place it against the wall. "No, you're not the only one who sees it," I finally confirm without taking my eyes off what I'm doing.

"I knew it. So, what does he do?"

"He's a full-time firefighter. I haven't really had much of a chance to talk to him, but that's what I've been told. He worked for Chuck a night or two a week when he is off."

"Oh! A firefighter? That just raised his level of hotness by like a thousand!" my aunt bellows, making me giggle.

"Says the woman married to the accountant," I reply.

Aunt BJ stops and turns to face me. "Don't let that fool you, sweetheart. Sometimes, the structured ones are the most…wild."

I make a face of disgust, which causes her to giggle. "Don't ever say that again!" I insist, wishing I could bleach my brain and remove the statement I'll probably never forget now.

"I'm just saying," she replies before returning to her painting. "Honestly, it doesn't matter what their job is. Passion doesn't care about professions, honey. Sometimes, complete opposites work out best of all. Look at me and Numbers, Jameson and Madelyn. Hell, even Jasper and Lyndee."

I nod, understanding what she's saying. The problem is, she's thinking Collin and I are headed toward some sort of relationship, which we're not. "We just work together, Aunt Beej."

She smirks, and without breaking stride of the line she's painting, says, "That's what your parents thought."

I don't reply, because, honestly, there's nothing I can say. I can't deny that isn't exactly how my parents' relationship began all those years ago, when I was three. Dad had some rule about not dating where he worked, and it had worked for a while…until my mom came along.

I don't remember a time when Dad wasn't in my life, or my uncles for that matter. I've heard all the stories, seen the photographs. Four bachelor friends, all working and running a business together, and while most of them dated, it all changed the day Mom started working at Burgers and Brew. Dad fell hard for her, and with that, fell hard for me too. And my uncles? Well, let's just say I was incredibly spoiled by a group of big teddy bear men who doted on me. They did everything and anything they could to help me and my mom out of a tough situation and made us all a family.

And look at us now.

They're still right here, helping me.

"All I'm saying is keep your eyes open. Something amazing might come along when you least expect it," she says, a soft smile on her lips.

"You mean like the unexpected guy who stops by to help you when your truck is broken down and ends up driving you home?" I ask, referring to how BJ and Numbers first…started out.

She barks out a laugh. "Exactly like that. I even let him try to look under the hood, as if I didn't already know what was wrong with it. He was a true knight in shining armor."

"You two are so cute," I say just as my name is hollered from the living room. "Uh oh, I better go see what's wrong."

Carefully, I set my paint roller down in the tray and grab a damp cloth to wipe my hands off as I walk to the living room. There stand my two brothers, as well as my sister, and they're smiling. "What's going on?"

"Well, we know how uncomfortable it can be to sleep on an air mattress, so we brought your moving truck," my brother, Duncan, announces.

"What? But…we were going to move all my stuff later in the week."

Waylon shrugs. "Yeah, but we called the cousins to help finish loading your stuff, and now it's all here. Mom said the apartment is about ready for some of it, so we thought we'd help you move in what you need tonight. Then, we can come back when you're ready for more of it."

My eyes fill with tears as I stare at my family. "Wow, thank you," I state, walking over and giving them each a quick hug.

"And don't worry about going back and cleaning the old place. We've got it," Mom states, looking to Lyndee and Madelyn, who both nod.

"So, all my stuff is…here."

"Downstairs," Duncan confirms.

I glance around the apartment I'll be calling home for the time being, and even though I want all my things brought up right this second, there's still so much more work to do. I'm replacing the carpet and tile because what's here is from the seventies and have a bit more cleaning to do. It's all so overwhelming, especially when I partner it with the bar updates I'm making downstairs.

"If I may make a suggestion," my dad says, stepping forward and placing a comforting hand on my wrist. "Let's bring up your bed, and we can get that set up in the middle of the bedroom. This way, you can sleep there tonight and not on the air mattress. That'll be easy to move when it's time for the carpet in the bedroom."

I nod in relief, grateful for his guidance.

"We can bring up the couch and TV too, because those are also easy to move out of the way to accommodate flooring. Your kitchen table can wait in the truck and the rest of your bedroom suite and living room stuff. We'll bring up a few boxes with necessities too because most of that stuff you'll need sooner rather than later."

My eyes fill with tears once more. I feel like I've been on the verge of a good cry for days, as the emotion of what's been happening threatens to overwhelm me. I see the flash of panic in my dad's eyes as he watches me, waiting for a response.

"That's a great idea. Thank you," I tell him.

He steps forward and gives me a quick hug and a kiss on the forehead. "We got you, Lou," he whispers quietly before clearing his throat and turning toward my brothers. "All right, yahoos, let's bring up her bed, but be careful. The walls in here and the bedroom are wet. You get it all over and you'll deal with your mother, you hear me?"

Duncan and Waylon both offer a mock salute. "Yes, sir, drill sergeant, sir," Waylon states.

Dad rolls his eyes. "Why are all my kids smart-asses?"

"Umm…apple? Tree?" Mom states, making everyone laugh.

"I'm gonna run downstairs real quick and check on things," I say as they prepare to bring up some of my belongings and furniture.

"I'll come with you!" my sister insists, anxious to see the rest of the building.

We manage to slip down the stairs without getting run over by one of our brothers and make our way to the doorway that leads to the bar. "This is so cool," Emberlyn announces, taking it all in. "It has this retro vibe I'm digging."

"Retro because it hasn't been updated in forty years?" I ask with a giggle.

The music hits me first, which is a welcome change over the musky stale cigarette smoke smell that used to hit me. I recognize several of the regulars at the bar, all chatting and watching a baseball game on television. When my eyes land on Collin, my heart does this weird little leap, like a graceful ballet pirouette in my chest.

"Hey, it's Lizzie!" Tom hollers, grabbing everyone's attention, including Collin's.

I'm greeted with a variety of hellos, as well as a comment from Jarrod, "Who is that lovely young lady?"

"This is my younger sister, Emberlyn. Em, this is everyone," I state, watching as my sister waves to those sitting at the bar.

"Well, hello, Em. Would you like a drink?" Tom asks, a hint of humor glistening in his dark eyes.

"Are you buying?" my eighteen-year-old sister asks with a big grin.

"Of course! Collin, my good man, bring this young woman a Coke on me."

I can't help but laugh, because I'm pretty sure my sister was expecting something with alcohol in it.

Collin looks to my sister, the hint of a grin on his lips as he waits for my sister's permission. When she nods, he fills a cup with ice and pours Coke from the soda gun. "Thank you, kind sir," Em says, accepting the drink from Collin and giving Tom a smile. "Okay, show me around."

She follows me as I start to tell her all about the changes we made, mostly today. "We cleaned the windows and scrubbed the walls. I'm going to paint them too and try to save all the vintage beer stuff hanging up."

"I love those old signs," she says, taking it all in.

"Eventually, I'll get new stools too. The ones here are pretty rough, and some don't even sit level."

"But the old bar has a cool retro look," she tells me, walking over to the corner, away from where the others are sitting and running her hand across the wood before taking a sip of her Coke.

We move around the room, talking about the tables and chairs, the pool table, and additional changes I want to make, including refinishing the floors. Eventually, I'd love to update the lighting too, only because it's older than I am, and since I live here too, I'd feel better if an electrician came and made a few updates. But that's down the road for me, after the business starts making money.

"And I love the name. It's so you," Em announces after checking out the bathrooms, both of which are on the list for some needed improvements.

"Thank you. Didn't Aunt Beej do an awesome job on the signage?"

"Of course she did, but I wouldn't expect anything less from her. Speaking of Aunt Beej, I was wondering," Em starts, glancing around to make sure we're alone.

"What's up?"

"So, do you remember when we were little and talked about getting tattoos together?"

I can't help but smile. "Of course I do."

"Well, since I'm eighteen and will be leaving for college in a few months, I was hoping you'd consider getting something this summer, before I go."

"I'd love to!" I tell her, instantly pulling her into a hug.

"Yeah? We have to decide what we want," she says, practically bubbling with excitement.

"Do you even need to ask? I thought we already talked about that," I state, remembering the tattoo we always said we'd get together.

Her eyes fill with unshed tears. "Really? You'd get that? I mean, we talked about that when I was like eight."

"And I still love that idea," I insist, recalling the simple daisy flower with the word sister written within the stem.

"Me too." She beams at me before jumping up and down. "I'm gonna run and ask BJ to put us on the books. Be right back," she states, handing me her Coke and taking off running toward the back entrance that leads to the apartment above us.

With a chuckle, I make my way to the bar where Collin stands.

"Everything okay? Is there a fire somewhere?" he asks, clearly having witnessed my sister run out of here.

"Yeah, everything's fine. She's off to schedule our first sisters tattoo with our aunt," I reply, shaking my head. When he seems confused, I add, "My aunt who painted the mirror and the sign is an amazingly talented tattoo artist. When Em was like eight and I was eighteen, I was going to get my very first one. She was jealous and wanted one too, because she was my little copycat. Well, we said we'd get one together when she was legal. Since she's eighteen now and leaving for school in the fall, we decided to get one before she goes."

Collin nods. "Very cool. My twin and I have matching tattoos," he states, pulling up the sleeve of his shirt and revealing the two linked puzzle pieces on his forearm.

Leaning forward, I notice the intricate details in each of the puzzle pieces. "This one's for you," I state, placing the tip of my finger on his flesh and feeling the sizzle of attraction with that single touch. I jerk my finger back, but if he notices my reaction, he doesn't let on.

"It is," he confirms with a smile. "The Hap Arnold Wings symbolize the Air Force and the flames for the firefighting career I was pursuing."

"Very cool," I tell him, studying the amazing detail of the ink. "So, your brother was also in the military."

He nods. "Marines. This is the EGA symbol, or Eagle, Globe, and Anchor."

"What's this?" I ask, pointing to the bricks with some sort of device in front of them.

"He was a combat engineer," Collin states. "He was in charge of a lot of things but mostly structures within a combat zone. He helped build, maintain, and destroy obstacles so our troops could do what they needed to do. He did a lot of work on mines, which is what this is," he states, pointing to the small device. "He has a lot more experience with setting or deactivating them than any of us will ever know."

My eyes are wide, I'm sure, as I listen to him talk. "Holy shit, you two are both badasses."

He barks out a gravelly laugh, and I have to admit, it's the sexiest sound. It travels through my veins and lands firmly between my legs, causing heat to pool. "Well, I don't know about that, but we both found our callings in the military. I'm a full-time firefighter, and Cade works for a construction company, building roads this time instead of wrecking them."

"Well, I'm impressed. Beautiful pieces," I tell him, feeling a little lighter having learned something so incredibly personal about Collin.

"Thank you. Most of my ink was done by the same artist, but I do admit, some of my early stuff was done near where I was stationed in Texas."

"So, you have more tattoos than just what's on your arm," I find myself saying, and instantly wishing I hadn't. It sounds like I'm flirting with him, which I'm not. I'm just…curious.

"I have a few more," he informs me with a little grin and a glint of something that resembles mischief in his blue eyes.

I stand up, preparing to walk away and end this conversation, when he asks, "What about you? If you were getting one at eighteen, that means you have at least one tattoo."

Clearing my throat, I set my sister's half-full plastic glass on the bar. "I have three, actually. BJ did them all."

His eyes slowly scan me from head to toe, lingering a bit longer on my chest area than I'd expect. "Well, I don't see any tattoos," he teases with a grin that could make a nun turn in her habit.

Crossing my arms over my paint-splattered T-shirt, I lift my chin and reply, "Well, they're not visible right now."

The corner of his mouth ticks with a slight grin. "Interesting."

I walk behind the bar and dump out my sister's drink, so Collin doesn't have to. As I move past him, I lean in and whisper, "I'd have to take off both my shirt and my pants, and I'm certain that's not appropriate bar etiquette."

Not to mention employer and employee etiquette, but I'm not getting into that right now.

When I reach the hallway, I glance over my shoulder and find Collin still standing there, a knowing smile on his lips.

A smile I put there, which is a heady feeling.

Is that flirting?

Probably.

Flirting with someone I shouldn't be?

Definitely.

If I'm not careful, I'll be flirting with disaster.

CHAPTER SEVEN

Collin

I DOUBLE-CHECK THE FRONT ENTRANCE IS SECURED AND FLIP OFF the lights as I make my way to the back of the bar. It's just after nine, and thanks to an afternoon baseball game, everyone cleared out a little after eight, so closing down at nine was a piece of cake.

But it hasn't been quiet.

Apparently, there's been a herd of elephants moving in above this place because the amount of foot traffic on the back stairs and the heavy feet on the floor have echoed through the bar, despite having some classic country playing from the jukebox. But, oddly, the noise has been…settling. Probably because it reminds me of home, back when I was younger. Four kids all under one roof, and most of the time with friends in tow. To say it was chaotic every now and again is an understatement.

Grabbing the money bag with tonight's drawer, I slip it in the safe in the small office and head for the back exit. I always go through the rear entrance because it's closer than returning to the front door to leave. As I make sure the lock is secured and step outside, I smile when I realize quickly I'm not alone.

"Jeez, Way. Can you not pick it up and walk normal?"

"Fuck off, Duncan. I'm the one going backward down this ramp, and this couch is fucking heavy."

I stop and smile, watching as two guys struggle to get a couch out of the back of a moving truck. "You know, if you take off the cushions, you'll be able to grip it easier without having the extra fluff in your face."

The two guys stop and practically drop the couch in a start. "Who the hell are you?"

"Collin. Bartender."

"Ahh," the taller of the two says, adjusting his hold on the couch and trying not to drop it.

"You could be a peach and help my brother. He's apparently a wimp and can't lift shit," the slightly shorter one announces, earning him an eye roll.

"Fuck. Off. Duncan."

The other brother just snorts a laugh as they carefully remove the couch from the truck and head toward me. Before I can reopen the door for them, it flies open and out comes Emberlyn. "I've aged three years while waiting on you dorks!"

I can't help but laugh. Emberlyn reminds me of my own sister.

"You could help, Em," one of the brothers hollers as they juggle the couch up the broken concrete steps.

I realize instantly they're going to need some assistance getting this couch through the doorway and up the stairs. It's a pretty big couch, with what looks like oversized cushions and a chaise lounge on the end. "Uhh, why didn't you remove the lounge?" I ask, dropping my stuff on the ground and grabbing one of the corners.

"Because my stupid-ass brother didn't think we needed to," the brother I'm standing beside grumbles. "Notice who *didn't* grab this end?"

With the lounge attached, we have to hold the back of the couch up higher to keep it from hitting every step as we ascend. It's not easy, that's for sure, but we make it work. Now, getting it through the apartment door takes some shimmying and pushing—and a little bit of cursing—but we manage that too.

"Why didn't you take the chaise off?" one of Lizzie's uncles asks as they watch us try to get the piece of furniture into the living room.

"Ask the dumbass," the brother standing next to me states, sounding a little breathy.

"Hey, it worked, didn't it?"

"Why must you always do things the hard way?" Lizzie's mom asks, shaking her head. There's no missing the humor dancing in her green eyes.

"Because they're both boneheads," Lizzie announces as we're carefully placing the couch on the floor. As soon as I stand, our eyes meet and it's like a jolt of electricity through the air, a lightning strike you don't see or hear, but you sure as hell feel it.

"Lizard, we can take this couch back downstairs," the bigger of the two brothers announces.

If it's intended to be a threat, she's not scared. Lizzie rolls her eyes. "I'm pretty sure you wouldn't make it out of the living room with it," she sasses, hands on her hips and with a little splatter of paint streaked across her cheek.

She looks beautiful.

"Boys, stop fucking around," Walker states, crossing his arms and narrowing his eyes at his sons.

They both just gape at him. "What? Lizzie is name-calling and not at all appreciative of our free manual labor."

The corner of my mouth ticks up.

Yep, definitely a lot like my family.

Their dad doesn't reply. He just stares at them.

"Come on, Waylon. Let's go downstairs where we're appreciated for our muscles and ingenuity."

When the boys walk past, they snatch a pizza box off the counter and dive in to what's left inside.

"Sorry about that," Lizzie says, walking over to where I stand. "And thanks for your help."

"No problem. They seemed to be struggling a little, so I thought I'd help before the couch took a tumble down the stairs," I tell her.

She shakes her head. "I told them the couch came apart."

I take a quick look around at the apartment above the bar. I've never witnessed someone living up here.

"It still needs a lot of work," she says, following my line of sight and looking around. "New carpet and floors are first on the list, and then I'll have to update the bathroom."

I nod. "I came up here two or three times, but it was always in the kitchen."

"Want a quick tour?"

"Sure," I reply, feeling oddly anxious to spend a few extra minutes with her.

"We did a deep clean this afternoon, but it still needs so much work," she informs me, moving toward the hallway. I dutifully follow, eager to see the rest of the building.

She opens a closed door and steps inside. "I was going to make this into a second office, but my aunt Lyndee talked me out of it. My work should stay there, and even though I technically live there too, she recommended I use it for something personal. If I need to get paperwork done, it isn't that far to go to the office."

I nod, understanding where her aunt is coming from. "What will you use it for?"

She grins slightly and looks at the empty, dark space. It definitely needs an overhaul, but it does have some potential. "Besides a small guest bedroom for my sister, I'm going to use it as a small library," she starts, opening her mouth and closing it fast.

"And…"

Lizzie shakes her head and glances away, a rosy hue tinting her cheeks. "It's silly."

"Doubtful," I find myself saying, hoping she'll tell me the rest of her thought.

"I, uh, like to sew. So, I'll set up a small desk for my sewing machine, but I want to bring in a comfy chair too where I can do other stuff."

"Like?"

She meets my gaze and states, "I enjoy counted cross-stitch and have been learning to crochet."

"Yeah? That's cool," I tell her, even though I really don't know much about either. I remember my grandma making stuff when I was little, but I don't know if it was crocheting or knitting or something else.

"Thanks. I sat on my couch in my old apartment, so it'll be nice to have a designated space to create and work."

"I agree," I tell her, thinking about my guest room, which contains home workout equipment and a collection of autobiographies. "What do you like to read?"

Her cheeks turn a deeper shade of red. "Uhh, romance mostly."

I nod, trying to block the image my brain conjures up of Lizzie reading a steamy romance novel in bed, touching herself when the scene gets hot. It doesn't work, of course, because my mind not only watches the scene play out, but it also invites me to join her on the bed. I look away and start to count backward from one hundred.

"Do you read?" she asks, her voice soft in curiosity, yet so fucking sexy at the same time.

"Yeah," I state, clearing the desire from my throat. "I read autobiographies mostly. My favorite are musicians."

"Really? I just finished Ozzy's latest. The one he did before he passed."

"No shit? I just finished that one too," I tell her.

"My uncle Tank is a musician, even though he probably doesn't consider himself one. He sings and plays guitar."

"At the bar, right? I've heard about that," I confirm, earning a smile.

"Yeah, he has quite a following, even after all these years. Anyway, come on and I'll show you the rest of the apartment."

We exit the small, unfinished space and walk across the hall. I can tell right away it's her bedroom, and not just because of the queen-sized bed sitting in the middle of the room. It's freshly painted and already feels like her. It's bright and cheerful, and even though it still needs work, I can tell she's putting herself into the room.

"Aunt BJ is finishing up the second coat of trim," Lizzie states when the woman on the step stool turns our way.

"Last wall," she confirms. "You could probably move your bed tonight, but if it were me, I'd just leave it in the middle until tomorrow."

"Makes sense," Lizzie replies. "New carpet will be installed soon, and that'll help it feel a little cozier. My dad and uncles ripped up all the carpets earlier because they were nasty."

"I can imagine."

We exit the bedroom and stop at the other door in the hallway. When she opens it, I almost shudder. "Bathroom needs...work."

It's a small bathroom straight out of the seventies. "Yikes."

She giggles and shakes her head. "Avocado green and some shade of gold. Not only that, but they're in pretty rough shape. Chuck said he had the water shut off up here for decades, so it didn't cause problems. It was all pretty dirty and a little stained, so we cleaned it the best we could for now, but eventually, it all needs replacing."

"It all takes time," I state, stepping out of the small space. Not only does it smell like her, but I catch sight of her personal items, like her shampoo, bodywash, and razor in the shower, and her hair brush and small bag of makeup sitting on the vanity.

I need to get out of here. Even with her family stuffed in practically every corner of the apartment, my thoughts are less than appropriate. "Well, I'll let you get back to it. I put the deposit in the safe and the drawer in the cubby hole. I assume that's still where it's all supposed to go?"

Lizzie nods, following me into the hallway and toward the kitchen. "Yes, for now. I might look into some changes a bit later, after I get a new computer system, but everyone knows the process and it works, so why change it?"

"All right, well, I'll leave you to it." I head for the door, feeling everyone's eyes on me as I go.

"Oh, can we talk soon about your work schedule? Everything is set through Wednesday, but after that, I'm on my own," she replies with a chuckle. "I want to make sure I understand your other job."

"Uhh, sure. I'm off tomorrow."

"Great, can you drop by? I'm working all day tomorrow, since Guy has some appointments."

I nod. "I can do that. See you then." To the rest of the group, I offer a quick, "Good night," which earns me a round of returned well wishes as I head out.

The moment I hit the cab of my truck; my phone vibrates in my pocket. I pull it out and smile when I see my friend's name.

> **Wyatt: Whatcha doing?**
>
> **Me: Just leaving the bar.**

I set my phone on my leg and start my truck, cranking up the heat. The late-April air holds a chill but also the promise of warmer days and nights to come. Before I can put the truck in reverse, my phone vibrates with his reply.

> **Wyatt: Come out. Just started a little fire.**

I snort when I read his message. If I know Wyatt—and considering we've been friends since grade school, so I know him pretty well—there's nothing small about it.

> **Me: It's been a long day, man.**
>
> **Wyatt: Bullshit. Get your ass over here. Don't make me come lookin' for you.**

I sigh and drop my phone on the console before pulling out of the parking spot. When I reach the four-way intersection in the middle of downtown, I consider just heading for home. My own bed, an action movie on TV, and thoughts of a certain new bar owner plaguing my dreams, both awake and while sleeping.

As if on my own, I turn the wheel in the opposite direction, heading toward one of my oldest friend's place. Not that I want to go to some bonfire gathering on a Sunday night, pushing ten o'clock, but I know Wyatt well enough that he'd just drive to my place and bang on the door until I opened it.

I'm not sure what to expect by going to Wyatt's, especially at this point of the night. He's not a huge partier. Hell, none of us really are anymore. Most of us seem to have gotten that out of our systems in our twenties. That doesn't mean we don't enjoy a rowdy night every now and again. You know, the night where you're relaxed enough, comfortable enough, and the drinks are flowing. However, we always have someone who stays sober to make sure no one drives who shouldn't, even in a small town like Cooper Town, where you can walk from one end of city limits to the other in a short amount of time.

Wyatt: Don't be a loser. Get your ass over here.

I shake my head and make my decision, heading toward his place.

It doesn't take long and I'm pulling into his long driveway. Wyatt lives just outside of town on six acres. It's a small farm, a mixture of a little livestock and a patch of timber he uses for hunting deer, squirrel, and turkey. I head to where the fire is burning strong, the orange glow lighting up the night sky.

When I park my truck next to his, I climb out and say, "Sure it's big enough?"

Wyatt chuckles. "Never," he responds, pointing his beer at me. "I did call for backup."

I reach into his cooler and grab a bottle of water. "I'm not on duty, and I don't work for this department," I remind him, even though it falls on deaf ears.

"Anyway, what's up with you?" he asks, returning to his seat on a log near the fire.

"Not much. Just finished working," I confirm, taking my own seat on another stump positioned near the blaze.

"Sorry I missed Charli's birthday. We had a couple of cows get through the fence, so after Billy and I wrangled them, we spent some time fixin' the damage." Billy's his brother, who was in Charli's class in school. Together, they own a decent number of acres in this area and farm corn and soybeans.

I nod in understanding. When you have a farm, even a small one like this, it's not your typical nine-to-five job. Things happen after hours. "No problem. We'll catch you next time," I tell him.

"So, tell me about the hottie."

My eyebrows raise, and even though it's dark, I can see the mischief in his eyes as he stares at me. I don't ask who he's talking about, because that would be an insult to both of our intelligence. Besides, we've known each other too damn long for that crap. "She's interesting."

"How so?"

I shift in my seat, suddenly feeling the heat of the fire more so than before. "Well, she's not like I expected. She's funny and caring. She seems to listen to what everyone is saying, and even though she wants to make the bar her own, her changes aren't terrible. She named the place The Tipsy Lizard."

When I look at my friend, he's smiling. Widely. With a cocky glint in his eye.

"What?"

"You like her."

I shrug and take a drink of my water. "She's not so bad."

"No, I mean *like* her. Like, you want to strip her naked and douse her flames with your fire hose."

"Jesus, man," I state with a laugh. He's too much.

Wyatt just lifts his shoulders and smiles. "It's true. I can see it in your eyes."

I don't reply. I can't.

Because at the end of the day, I *do* like her. I don't know how or when it happened exactly, but being near her today confirmed it. She's really not as bad as I expected, and I find myself anxious to see what else she has planned for the bar. Not just the bar, but her apartment too. Will I get another look at it after the floors and the bathroom are done?

I sure as hell hope so.

And that's a bit of a problem. I don't *want* to want to see her apartment, because not only do I find myself wondering about the updates and changes, but being there seems to also bring focus to her bed, and that's the last place I should want to be.

Yet, I do.

"I see you're arguing with yourself about the lovely Lizzie Meyer," Wyatt says, grabbing my attention. "I haven't met her yet, but everyone's talking about her and has positive things to say. Especially about her looks," he states, waggling his eyebrows suggestively and making me growl. Wyatt barks out a laugh. "I knew it."

"Knew what?"

"You've already staked a claim."

I snort. "I've done no such thing."

He laughs. Hard. "Cade was right. You've already pissed on her leg."

"Gross," I reply with my own bark of laughter. "That's fucked up."

"Maybe, but the fact remains: you like her." He pauses for dramatic effect, because my oldest friend is that kind of guy. "If you like her, go for it."

I shrug, not confirming nor denying anything he's saying, because my mind is swirling right now. His words have caused a tornado of thought and emotion in my head, all fighting against each other. The tug of war is intense, the feelings of wanting her and knowing I shouldn't.

I like her and have no clue what to do about it.

"Come on, man," he states, breaking the silence and standing up.

"Where are we going?"

A wide grin spreads across his face, and I can already tell he's got a wild hair up his ass. "To cut down that big oak tree."

"Tonight?"

"Of course, tonight. What could possibly go wrong?"

CHAPTER EIGHT

Lizzie

I'M SMILING AS I JOT DOWN ANOTHER IDEA IN MY NOTEBOOK, knowing in my heart these are great options. My plan is to make a list and then choose my favorite two. From there, I'll incorporate other ideas, depending on the success or failure of the first two. But I feel it in my bones. These ideas are going to be hits. I know it.

I glance down at Burt, Tom, and Earl, who is a new patron. Well, not new. New to me, considering I haven't met him yet, but he informed me he comes in a couple times a week, while his wife is at ceramics with some of her girlfriends.

"You gentlemen doing okay?" I ask, ready to refill drinks if needed.

"Sure are, Lizzie," Tom replies with a smile.

"I'll take another Pepsi," Earl states, sliding his glass toward the edge of the bar.

His request sparks another thought. "So, no beer for you?" I ask, using the gun to refill his glass.

"Nope," he replies. "Never really had a taste for beer, even though I tried a lot when I was younger. And that hard stuff turned me into a person I didn't like. So, I stick with soda." He nods in a salute before taking a drink from the straw.

"Nothing wrong with that," I tell him.

"Coming here is about seeing my friends and getting out of the house for a little bit. I don't have to drink to have a good time."

I can't help but smile. "I agree. Believe it or not, I'm not a huge drinker."

"Nothing wrong with that," he states with a smile, repeating my words.

"It's funny, right? I grew up at the bar and restaurant my dad and uncles own, but it was more than just drinking to me. I enjoyed the people, the good times, the music. The alcohol is always a distant second to me."

"You're wise beyond your years, Lizzie," Tom says.

"You know, I was thinking of having a daily special, like the bucket of beer or a specific mixed drink. What if I also had a featured nonalcoholic option too?"

"That's a great idea!" Earl announces.

"Just as long as you keep my beer on tap," Burt adds with a chuckle.

"Always, but I am adding two new ones," I tell them, even though I haven't made the announcement yet. When your family owns Crüe Brewery, and the beer is awesome, you make room at your own bar to sell it. And not just cans and bottles, but drafts of their two most popular flavors.

"Whatcha adding?" Tom asks, completely interested in the conversation, as if he's getting the scoop.

"Well, I know the owners of Crüe Brewery pretty well, and I signed a contract to sell their products. I'll be adding Night Crüe and All American Crüe on tap."

"Nice," Tom replies with a nod. "I've heard a lot about those beers."

"Well, I'm a little partial, but they're pretty good, if I do say so myself," I reply with a chuckle. I don't need to tell the guys who my dad and uncles are, since they got to meet them yesterday. Dad enjoyed getting to know some of the regulars at the bar I now own and told me he felt like I was in good hands.

"Some additional nonalcoholic options is a great idea, Lizzie. You're doing well," Earl tells me, offering a friendly, grandfatherly smile.

"Shirley Temples all around!" Burt announces jovially as the front door opens.

I expect to see one of the regulars joining the small Monday afternoon group, but that's not who enters. I open my mouth to greet Collin, but I instantly realize that's not who's here. There's a lightness in his steps and his smile is quick and a little disarming. Definitely not Collin.

It's his twin, Cade.

"Well, hello there, beautiful lady," he announces when he reaches the bar and flashes me a wide grin.

"Hi, Cade," I respond, moving to where he stands. "What can I get ya?"

"I'll have a Pepsi with cherry, please," he states, sliding onto one of the stools. It shakes, one leg missing the protective end on it, and causing him to look up at me.

"Those are getting replaced soon," I tell him, pouring the pop into the cup and adding a dash of cherry juice. Before I place it on the old, stained coaster, I plop a cherry and a straw in the liquid and hand it off.

"I knew I'd get your cherry," he states, not missing the mischievous grin on his handsome face.

I snort and shake my head. "Sorry, friend. That ship sailed a long time ago," I reply.

"Figures. No one saves themselves for marriage these days," he says, shaking his head and taking a drink.

"Oh? So I take it you're saving yourself, patiently waiting for the right woman to come along?"

Cade barks out a laugh, making me smile in return. "Oh, my sweet, sweet Lizzie. How would I know what woman is the right one for me unless I sample them all first before deciding?"

I shake my head and laugh. "That's kinda gross."

Cade shrugs and winks. "But honest. Guys are gross, Lizzie."

"Well, I'll give you that," I state.

"What's that?" he asks, pointing to my notebook.

"A checklist of changes I want to make, and some ideas I've had."

"Ideas? I'm an excellent man to bounce ideas off," he states, holding out his hand and making the gimme motion.

I consider what's inside the book and quickly realize there's nothing personal written down. Not in that notebook, anyway, so what would it hurt to run the list past him? He might actually have solid advice for me.

Sliding the notebook his way, I say, "Knock yourself out."

He snorts and grabs the book. "I might, if this wobbly stool gives way."

I can't help but giggle. "You're so dramatic. You won't fall."

He just levels me with a look. "You've never seen me in here four whiskey sours deep at closing time." With a wink, he turns his attention to my notes.

I almost walk away, to give him time to read over everything, but honestly, I want to gauge his reaction. He looks up at me, his eyes just as bright blue as his twin's. "Uhh, little black dress night?"

"Well, women love getting dressed up. I was thinking a fun ladies' night with hors d'oeuvres, drink specials, and maybe like a piano player or something equally as relaxing and enjoyable."

Just as I finish talking, the door opens and in walks Collin. Our eyes meet, and a shiver sweeps down my spine. I quickly look away, only to have my eyes slam into Cade's wide ones. "What?"

He glances back to his twin as he approaches and takes the seat next to him at the bar. "He quits!" Cade bellows, pointing to his brother. "Hire me. Please!" he proclaims, drawing out his plea.

"What?" I ask with a laugh. "Why?"

He turns his attention to the newcomer at the bar. "She's having a little black dress night, man. Tons of single ladies all on the prowl. That's right up my alley," he insists. "So, I'm gonna need to work your shift that night."

I reach for the book and take it off the bar top. "These are just ideas," I counter.

"Well, that one's a good one! That should be moved to the top of the list," he declares, making me laugh once more.

"You're nuts," I say.

"I've been telling him that for years," Collin grumbles, his personality so very different than his brother's. It's kinda crazy to see two men who look identical and yet they're so very opposite in every other way.

"You're just jealous because I got all the good looks and the sparkling personality in utero."

Collin shakes his head and levels me with a look. "I apologize for him."

I flash a smile and wink at Cade. "He's nothing I can't handle. Guys like him are a dime a dozen. All looks and no brains."

Shock flashes in Collin's eyes before he barks out a laugh.

"Hey!" Cade bellows. "That wasn't nice."

"Neither is wanting to work ladies' night so you have the pick of the room to continue your manwhore ways."

Collin looks so much lighter, so happy as he laughs. "She totally has your number."

"You're mean," Cade announces, standing up from his seat. "I'm going to the other end of the bar to cry in my popcorn."

I shake my head, watching him walk down to where Tom, Burt, and Earl all sit. He jovially takes a seat beside them and dives into a bowl of popcorn I made not too long ago. "Did I insult him?"

Collin chuckles. It's low and gravelly and vibrates straight through my veins to my clit. "Cade? Hell no."

"Well, I kind of pegged him for that lighthearted, can take a joke as good as he gives them kind, but I've been wrong every now and again."

"No," Collin insists, meeting my gaze. "In fact, he'll be back soon, having forgotten all about you calling him dumb."

"I didn't call him dumb," I insist with a giggle.

"You didn't?" he asks, smiling.

"Well, rest assured, you didn't offend him, I promise. Cade is very easygoing."

"Unlike you, huh?" I ask, leaning my elbows on the bar.

He shifts in his seat but doesn't avert his gaze. "Yeah, unlike me."

"Anyway, Chuck and Guy have both filled me in a little about how the schedule is usually done, but I thought I'd speak with you directly, just in case things have changed." Of course, I'm referring to the verbal arrangement we made, where I requested he give me a month and if he wasn't happy, then he could quit.

He levels me with a look that causes my heart to beat a little faster and my breathing to become shallow. "Nothing's changed."

I release a deep breath. "Okay. Good."

"I work two days on and then have four days off. So it's not the same from week to week."

"I understand," I assure him, making a note in my book. "Chuck said he tried to use you in the middle of your four-day break so you could prepare to head back to the firehouse or catch up on sleep when you're coming off a shift."

He nods. "He did. That worked best."

"Well, I'll do what I can to continue that practice," I reply, adding that detail to my notebook.

"What are you doing?"

I look up and find him watching me. "Making notes?" It comes out a question, since I would have thought it was pretty obvious.

"No one uses notebooks anymore. Everyone utilizes their phones for that kind of thing," he replies without a hint of judgment in his voice. It's as if he doesn't quite believe that I'm hand writing something instead of using the app on my phone to take notes.

I lift my shoulders and set my pen down. "I've always been more of a physical notetaker. My dad used to do that behind the bar, and I think it just stuck."

"May I?" he asks, pointing to the open book.

"Sure."

He reaches for it and starts thumbing through the pages. He lands on the doodles I made with name options and logo designs, even though I knew I was going to turn the latter part over to Aunt BJ. It was still fun to tinker around with ideas and put them down on paper.

"Is this where your logo was born?" he asks, pointing to one of the designs.

"It is. I'm not an artist, obviously, but it was a rough draft to give BJ a starting point."

He nods in understanding and flips a few more pages. When he lands on the list of ideas I've been coming up with to draw in a bigger crowd, especially the ladies' night, he looks my way. "This is what my brother was talking about." It's not a question.

"It is."

He scans the list. "What's a paint night?"

"A night where customers can come in and paint a canvas, usually with a predetermined design. I thought about offering it monthly, with a different theme."

Collin seems to consider the idea. "That might be kinda cool."

"And guys can do it too, if they wanted. I'd have drink specials and maybe some snacks too. I've also considered a wine and cheese night, karaoke, and even live music on Saturdays. It's a huge draw at Burgers and Brew."

His eyes sparkle a little as he looks up. "And little black dress night?"

I feel my cheeks heat up a bit as I nod. "I might incorporate that with the wine and cheese night. Like a charcuterie board type of thing."

"A char-coochie-what?"

The bubble of laughter slides easily out of my mouth, and I lift my hand to cover it. "Oh my God, not a coochie. A charcuterie board. A board with lots of different meats, cheese, fruits, nuts, and chocolates."

His eyebrows pull together in confusion. "I don't know if that sounds better or not?" he replies, shrugging his shoulders and making me giggle even more. The way he furrows his brow in concentration, yet his eyes hint with mischief and his mouth teases something dirty, makes me suddenly very hyperfocused on his nearness. There's a bar between us, yet we could reach out and touch the other if we wanted to.

And damn, do I suddenly really want to...

Clearing my throat, I add, "It was just an idea I had."

He holds my gaze for several seconds before replying, "These are good. I think you should give them a try."

"Hey, Lizzie, mind if I get another when you got a sec?" Tom hollers, pulling my attention away from Collin.

"Yep!"

Just as I turn to move to the other end of the bar, I hear, "Even the little black dress night, but only if you'll be wearing one too."

I pause and glance over my shoulder at the man sitting behind me. He smirks, knowing exactly what he said and not at all embarrassed by it. It's a heady feeling and it leaves me torn on what to do about it. On one hand, he's my employee. I know it's frowned upon to date coworkers or employees, and while I've managed to avoid it to this point, it's not a rule I set for myself. Not like my dad did back in the day. Well, until my mom and I broke through his defenses and his rules.

And there has been all this sexual tension between us. I noticed it right away, last Monday night, when I dropped by the bar before the closing date when I got the keys. It wasn't until he found out who I was that his own defensive walls were slammed back into place, and he made his displeasure with me very clear. However, before that, there was a spark.

I felt it.

He felt it.

Now that spark seems to be alive and well, growing as the minutes pass by.

As I pour a draft for Tom, I think about all the possibilities and the repercussions. There are plenty on both sides of the coin. The fact we work together, and if we started something and it went south, what would that mean for our working relationship? Then there's his job. Not the fact he's a fireman and has a dedicated work schedule, because let's face it, my schedule right now is a little wacky too. It's the fact he's a first responder. A very brave, noble career, but also scary too, especially on this end of it. He puts himself in danger, in the line of fire on the daily. Can I deal with that?

Of course, I'm probably getting way ahead of myself here. Just because we've flirted a little bit doesn't mean we're headed for a relationship.

In fact, the best thing I can do is to just hang back and let it play out. Be me. Don't jump with both feet but have my eyes open to the possibilities, all while keeping my head focused on the major life-changing things I've set out to do.

I sigh, setting the fresh beer down in front of Tom and marking his drink with a tally on the sheet of paper, while offering the customer a smile.

Maybe considering a *thing* with Collin is a bad idea. I have way too much going on in my life to add nurturing a new relationship into the mix. I didn't come here looking for love. I moved to Cooper Town and purchased this old bar as a way of setting out on my own, paving my own path. It's been my dream for as long as I can remember, and getting tangled up in the sheets with someone who works here might jeopardize everything.

But then my eyes seek him out, completely on their own. His brother moved back down to where he's sitting and leans in to say something to him. When he does, Collin looks up and our eyes slam together once more. There's a sexual charge hanging in the air, waiting to devour, and I have no clue what to do about it.

I can't turn my back on it, so what does that mean?

I guess time will tell.

CHAPTER NINE

Collin

"WHAT'D YOU DECIDE ABOUT CHUCK'S PLACE? YOU STILL working there?" Gio asks, pulling my attention away from the rig we're washing.

"Yeah, for now. The owner requested I give her a month before I make any big decisions. It seemed like the appropriate thing to do," I tell him, putting a little extra attention to scrubbing the front fender of the rig, even though it doesn't really require any extra work.

"Seems fair," he states, walking over and grabbing the hose to start rinsing.

"What about you? How'd it go with Clara?" I ask, realizing in the first twenty-four hours of working together, he hasn't brought it up. Probably because we've been busy with calls, but still. That's unlike him.

He sighs. "We decided to end it for good."

I stop what I'm doing and turn my attention to him. "Sorry, man."

He shrugs, not meeting my eyes. His focus is on cleaning the suds off the truck, as if it's the most consuming task he has. "It is what it is. You were right. The constant up and down is hard, and it's not fair to either of us."

I swallow hard, hating the hurt I hear in my friend's voice. I feel even worse for not asking before now, but to be honest, we haven't been alone since we started shift together. I'm grateful I didn't ask in front of anyone else, especially now, after knowing they ended it again. Of course, they could be on once more next week, but I don't think so. There's something different, something heavier in his eyes. It feels final.

"Hey, if you ever need to get away for a night or two, my door is always open."

He lifts an eyebrow and stares at me. "Like, on your lumpy-ass couch?"

I bark out a laugh. "I got a new couch about six months ago, but if you're gonna complain, I recant my offer."

"I just can't believe you're not offering to share your bed, man. You have a king. Some friend you are."

I laugh, mostly because I know he's joking.

At least I think he's joking…

Just then, our razzing and teasing is halted by the blare of the alarm. We move everything aside, Gio making sure all the soap is washed off the rig before we run for our gear. The call is playing through the speaker, a multi-vehicle MVA with entrapment. EMS in route.

I try to push everything out of my mind, focusing on the job. An MVA, or motor-vehicle accident, with multiple vehicles and victims requires complete concentration. As a first responder, we see people on their worst days, and that's why we train as hard as we do. I'm the light in their darkness, to help in their time of need.

Jumping into the truck, we take off out of the bay, two of our four trucks are en route to the scene of the accident. I finish securing my gear as reports start coming over the radio. Semi-truck and two vehicles, one on its roof and smoking. Passengers trapped and lifesaving measures already beginning at the scene.

As we arrive, my heart thumps hard in my chest and I do a few deep breathing exercises to calm myself. The moment the truck stops, we're all out. Captain Howard starts barking orders, and we quickly fall in line and head for where we're needed. Gio and I, along with Roger and Franci, move to the car wedged near the back axel of the semi-truck. I do everything I can not to focus on what's directly before my eyes.

The woman in the mangled driver's seat has her eyes closed, her breathing coming in sharp rasps. "Ma'am, can you hear me?" I ask, crouching down beside the car as my team works to free the other occupants.

"My babies. Save my babies," she whispers.

I risk a glance looking into the back seat, and that's when I see the two young boys trapped in the back. I do everything I can to stay focused on my job, to free the driver so she can be transported for urgent care, but my eyes bounce a few times to where her sons are motionless in the mangled mess of metal behind her.

I suck in a greedy breath of oxygen and double down my efforts to free the family. We use the Jaws of Life to cut into the wreckage, finally freeing the driver first, followed quickly by her two young sons. Paramedics jump in, doing everything they can to help the victims of the accident, and even as I walk away to gather our tools and return them to the truck, I see them. Their faces will forever be etched in the recesses of my brain.

All I can do now is pray they make it.

I haven't slept hardly at all in the last forty-eight hours.

Certain things stick with you, and the accident two days ago was one of those things. Every time I close my eyes, I see their faces. Sometimes, it's just fucking impossible to compartmentalize the bad we've witnessed and move on. Sometimes, things stick with you, and this is one of those times.

I've been home since this morning, and even with Mom trying to talk to me during my drive, my focus wasn't there. She talked, but I barely listened. When she finally asked why, all I had to do was tell her there had been an accident and it was weighing heavily on my mind. I didn't tell her the outcome because, frankly, saying those words out loud makes them real, and I wasn't ready to deal with it.

I'm still not sure I am, but I know I need to.

I slip my feet into a pair of running shoes and angrily lace them closed. I've never been a huge fan of distance running, but cardio is an important part of my job, so I do it anyway. Usually, I run on one of the treadmills at the firehouse, but I need something extra tonight to help burn off this overwhelming pent-up anxiety and frustration.

When I step outside, it's a bit chillier than it was this morning. The early May air is still crisp when the sun goes down, leaving a layer of goose-bumps on my arms. But I don't go in and grab a long-sleeved shirt. After a few minutes, I'll be sweating my ass off, so while I might be cold now, I know it'll be short-lived.

I stretch a bit in my front yard, grateful for the night sky overhead. There's a streetlight across from my neighbor's house, so it's not direct light illuminating me. When I have my legs and back stretched out good, I take off at a slow jog with no destination in mind.

Running the streets of Cooper Town, I try to push all thoughts of work out of my head, but it's impossible. Even when I get to the corner of Elm and Hobart, where I had my first fender bender at seventeen, I don't chuckle as I recall everything that happened that fateful night. I won't go into all the details, but it might have involved a girl and her hand down the front of my pants. Came in a little too hot to the stop sign and rear-ended the car in front of me.

Try explaining that to the responding officer, who just so happens to be good friends with your parents…

I should note that everyone was fine in the accident, including the driver of the car in front of me. He knew something was up, could read the guilt written all over my face when I stammered and tried to lie about why I was so distracted. And the girl who was riding shotgun in my truck? After being checked out by the responding ambulance, she went off to meet her friends and ended up in the back seat of someone else's car later that night.

Oh well. You live and you learn.

I jog through the intersection and make a left, heading toward down-town. Since it's pushing eight, everything is closed, with the exception of the small grocery store, which is getting ready to flip the sign at the top of the hour, and the bars. I spot the bright, flashing lights of The Tall One and recognize a few of the vehicles parked nearby. The place is pretty popular, but mostly with the younger crowd. The loud, upbeat music filters through the crevasses, oozing into the streets and the quiet night sky.

While I don't negate their success, it's just not my thing. Even when I was younger, I preferred the quieter, subtle vibe of Chuck's Place over the lively atmosphere offered at the other end of our downtown. That's why I panicked when I heard Chuck sold it. I was afraid Lizzie was planning to transform my favorite little dive bar into something catered to the younger generation, like The Tall One.

Now, don't get me wrong. She may still come in and make changes I'm not a fan of, but so far, that doesn't seem to be the case. She's making updates, but keeping the feel the same, and while I respect her business sense and wanting to grow, she seems keener on creating her own vibe and holding true to that than competing with the other bar down the street.

I don't even realize I had stopped running until I'm standing directly in front of The Tipsy Lizard. The new sign makes me smile, especially after seeing her notebook and discovering how much thought and time she's invested in the rename and logo design of her business. The windows are clean, something else that's a positive change from what it was before, and the light reflecting outside is comforting and inviting.

Reaching for the handle on the old door, I slowly pull it open and step inside, not worrying about the fact I'm in shorts and a T-shirt and am a little sweaty.

"Hey," Jani greets when I step inside. She's wiping down the small round tables scattered around the outside of the room and straightening the chairs.

"Busy night?" I ask, moving in her direction. I glance around and spot a handful of the regulars at the bar, all who turn and throw me a wave, but also a few new faces too.

"Not bad," she replies, walking toward me and glancing back to make sure the customers were still okay. "What are you up to?"

"I just went for a run," I tell her, omitting the part about my legs automatically carrying me to this very place.

"It's still a little chilly out there, but I can tell the warm nights are right around the corner."

I nod, but before I can reply, I hear what sounds like a loud thud overhead. My eyes slam to the ceiling and my feet start moving toward the rear of the building.

"She had her new flooring installed today, and I think she's been trying to move things around up there. I found her earlier pulling stuff out of the moving truck out back," Jani says.

"I'll go check on her and see if she needs any help," I insist, giving Tom and Larry each a squeeze on their shoulders as I walk past.

"We all offered to help, but she refused," I hear Jani state, but I keep moving.

I push through the back door and head for the stairs, taking them two at a time. When I reach the landing and find the entrance wide open, I step inside the apartment and lift my hand to knock on the doorframe.

Before I can hit the wood, my eyes land on the motionless woman lying on the floor. She's sprawled out, looking like one of those chalk outlines you see after they remove a dead body. My heart hammers in my chest and panic fills my entire body.

"Jesus," I holler, practically running toward her.

Her eyes fly open and smash into mine as I drop to my knees beside where she lies. "What are you doing here?" she asks, her words a little breathy.

"What am I doing here? What are you doing on the floor?"

The corners of her lips turn upward as she replies, "Feeling the carpet."

All I can do is stare down at her and blink. "Are you serious right now? I heard a loud thud and thought you had fallen, and then when I came up here and saw you on the floor like this, I was almost afraid to feel your pulse."

Lizzie giggles but doesn't get up. "You have to feel this carpet, Collin. It's magnificent."

"Excuse me?"

She reaches for my arm and tugs. "Lie down."

I do as instructed, lying on the floor beside her.

She moves her arms and legs, and when I glance her way and see her eyes are closed, there's a smile on her perfectly kissable lips. "This feels so amazing. I don't ever want to get up."

My cheeks relax as my own grin slides across my mouth. "It's carpet."

She turns her head and opens her eyes, leveling me with a look of outrage. "The most perfect carpet ever!"

I can't stop my chuckle. "If you say so."

"I do," she insists, looking back up at the ceiling. "They installed carpet in my bedroom, the second bedroom, and living room today, and they'll be back tomorrow to do the kitchen floors."

"What about the bathroom?"

She groans and shakes her head. "I can't do them until I figure out what I want to do about the rest of the room. It needs everything, and my dad thinks it would be best to wait on the flooring until the bathtub, vanity, and toilet are being replaced."

"Probably smart," I reply, realizing how comfortable I am. Not just the carpeting—which *is* nice, by the way—but just lying here and chatting. It's...relaxing.

"I was moving the couch and knocked over my sofa table."

I turn my head. "What?"

"That was the thud you heard. I wasn't falling, though I do appreciate your knight-in-shining-armor theatrics."

"Theatrics?" I ask, fighting a grin.

She snickers and turns to face me. It's the first moment I realize how close our faces are. We're practically shoulder to shoulder, and it wouldn't be too difficult to shift my position and take her lips with my own. "It was very noble."

"Next time I find you sprawled out on the floor, I'm just leaving."

Lizzie bites down on her bottom lip, sending every ounce of blood in my body to my crotch. Considering I'm wearing athletic shorts, it's a reaction I won't be able to conceal if she happens to glance toward my groin.

Grandma, grandma, grandma…

"You wouldn't," she says, slowly starting to sit up, so I quickly do the same. "It's not in your DNA."

"True," I reply, bringing my knees up and resting my arms on them.

"So, what brought you here, besides your desire to rescue a damsel in distress?"

"I—" The images that plague my brain come back, playing out the traumatic scene all over again. "Uh, I was out for a run and stopped by the bar. We heard the crash, so I thought I'd come check on you."

She nods and glances around. "I was being all brave and independent and decided to move some of my living room stuff up from the moving truck."

"Want some help?" I blurt out, knowing I should just head home but not wanting to.

A look crosses her face. "Oh, I don't want to take you away from your run."

I shrug. "I hate running," I confess, carefully standing up and reaching my hand toward her.

She gently places her hand in mine, which causes a bolt of electricity to slide through my veins. She must feel it too because her beautiful green eyes widen, and her delectable lips form the cutest little O. She quickly clears her throat and glances away for a brief moment before returning her gaze to me. "I, uh, am not exactly a fan of it myself. I don't think I've run since high school."

"Then you understand my pain," I state easily with a lift of my shoulders. "What do you need to bring up?"

Again, she nibbles on her bottom lip as she thinks. "Not much, but I'd love to bring my end tables up. My brothers offered to come this weekend and help bring the heavier stuff up."

I already have my phone out and start typing. "What kind of heavier stuff?"

"Uhh, a recliner, the rest of my bedroom furniture, and maybe a few more boxes."

> **Me:** Can you come to the bar and help me take some of Lizzie's furniture up to her apartment?
>
> **Cade:** What are you doing at her apartment?
>
> **Cade:** *Insert waggling eyebrows emoji*
>
> **Me:** Helping her move furniture. You know what, never mind. I'll ask our little brother. He's probably stronger anyway.

I know that'll get a response. I crack a smile as I wait for his answer.

> **Cade:** Fuck off. I'm already out the door.

Slipping my phone back in my pocket, I say, "Help is on the way."

"What?"

"I messaged Cade. He'll come help me move that stuff up here for you," I tell her.

"But…it's, like, eight at night," she informs me, glancing down at her watch.

"And it won't take us very long to bring up what you need."

"But I don't really need it now," she insists.

"Yeah, well, now you won't have to worry about it anymore," I reason, knowing unless it's something oversized, it won't take much for my brother and I to move it upstairs. Between our own moves, my sister's, and even Camden's recent move, we're pros at this. I'll help my boss and then finish my run.

I'm sure I'll be heading back home in no time.

At least, that's what I keep telling myself.

CHAPTER TEN

Lizzie

I CAN'T STOP STEALING GLANCES.

There was no missing the way he got hard while we were lying on the floor, and even though I did my best to keep my eyes above his waist, I admit I looked.

Twice.

"You really don't have to stay and help."

Collin shrugs his shoulders and leans against the wall. "I have nothing more pressing to do at the moment."

Something flashes in his eyes. It's a guarded mixture of hurt and anguish, and even though I should probably let it be, I can't do it. "Are you okay?"

He holds my gaze, giving nothing away. The man's poker face is top-notch, that's for sure, but there's this underlying hint of discomfort, and that's what has me concerned. "I'm fine. Just a...uh, it was a rough shift."

"You worked today?" I ask, thinking back to the schedule he texted me. If I recall correctly, he was off earlier this morning.

"Until eight," he confirms. "But..."

I don't push him. If he wants to talk about it, I'll listen. I consider him a friend, even if we haven't known each other very long. Even if I ignore the sexual tension that seems to surround us whenever we're together. I can push that all aside and be a friend first and foremost.

Noticing the internal battle he seems to be engaged in, I throw out a comment to hopefully make him smile and keep things light. "Hey, I'm a bartender. I'm like a therapist, only cheaper."

The comment does the trick, and he flashes me a small, grateful smile before sobering and straightening his spine. "There was an accident a couple days ago. It was pretty bad. Nothing we haven't seen or done before, but this one was…different. I was tasked with freeing a driver—a mother—who had two young boys in the back seat."

Something passes through his eyes, and suddenly, I wish I wouldn't have pushed. "Oh no," I whisper as a lump forms in my throat, making it hard to breathe.

"Yeah. We were able to get them all extricated, but…" He stops and looks away. "The mom and one of the boys ended up passing away."

"Oh," I reply, tears filling my eyes, partially for people I don't even know, but also for Collin. I know it's his job, but I can't imagine being a first responder in a situation like that and having it not affect me. "I'm so sorry."

He swallows hard and levels me with a gaze. "It's been weighing on my mind since it happened."

"I'm sure it has," I reply, taking a step closer, needing to be near him. "I can't imagine what you see and do on a regular basis."

"It usually doesn't affect me as bad as this, but when it's a kid—"

"I honestly couldn't do what you do."

"Sometimes it's a pretty heavy job."

I nod and take another step forward. He's now within reach, and even though I shouldn't touch him, I'm overwhelmed with the urge to provide a little comfort in his time of distress. Placing my hand on his arm, I take one additional small step and hold his gaze. "What you do is very admirable, but it's heavy. You see some of the worst things possible."

He nods. "Usually, I can compartmentalize it, which isn't always the healthiest way to deal with what we see and do, but we have to. But sometimes," he says, taking a deep breath, "sometimes, it sticks with you."

"I can see that," I reply gently. "I'm sorry you had to witness something so tragic, especially the loss of a young life. I can't imagine what the surviving child and father are going through and will for probably the rest of their lives. It's not something anyone should have to deal with. We expect to lose loved ones later in life, but when it happens to a child and young mother, it's unimaginable. It's traumatic, honestly. For everyone."

"Yeah," he replies, giving me the faintest smile.

"Listen, I know we don't know each other very well, and this might not be the manliest way to handle it, but maybe you can talk to someone? Professionally, I mean. Not that you can't talk to me and I'd listen, but someone who can truly help you."

"We have a department doc," he states, surprising me.

"You do?"

He snorts. "We do," he confirms. "Not everyone likes or wants to see him, but others find it helpful. I've been a few times over the years."

"Oh, well, good."

"I've already decided to give him a call in a few days if I'm still struggling to sleep."

"Good," I repeat, still a little shocked to hear they have a department doctor to help them deal with the heavy stuff. A lot of people don't like to talk to a therapist, and most definitely won't openly talk about it.

"But, if I'm being honest, being here has helped me."

Okay, now I'm super surprised. "What? How?"

He shrugs his shoulders and glances over toward the door. "I don't know, really. You have a calming way about you."

I can't help but snort. "A calming way. Sure. I'm sure my family would be rolling after hearing that," I reply, shaking my head.

"No, you do. You listen without judgment, and I see nothing but kindness in your eyes. And you're right, I'm not the only one who is going to struggle with this one. Children can be both the best and worst victims.

I've had some smile and hug me. One even invited me to his birthday party the next week."

I chuckle at the image he creates in my mind, of kids being rescued from a burning building or extracted from a car accident and smiling in appreciation on the other side. It's a much better image than the one he's dealing with in his head. "Did you go?"

"Hell yes," he replies, grinning from ear to ear. "A couple of us dropped by with gifts. There was a fire truck cake, and we were the guests of honor, along with the birthday boy."

We stand here, smiling at each other, and I can't help but realize how good it feels.

"Thank you."

His heartfelt words make me pause. "For what?"

"For listening. For offering me words of comfort. For being…you."

My cheeks heat a little, but I don't look away. His words spoken and even the ones neither of us speak hang heavy between us. The moment is broken when the sound of heavy footfalls echoes up the stairs.

"I hope you're not naked!"

Collin closes his eyes briefly and shakes his head.

When Cade reaches the top, he stops in the doorway and glances between the two of us. We're still standing close, but nothing that would be considered scandalous. He flashes me a charming grin and adds, "Well, unless it was you, Lizzie. You can be naked anytime I come over."

I bark out a little laugh and state, "You wish."

Collin's eyes widen moments before he bursts into a fit of laughter. "Guess she told you."

Cade gapes at me, as if I just told him I saw Bigfoot, and covers his heart with his hand. "You wound me."

I can't help but roll my eyes. "Something tells me you'll get over it."

"Never. I'll carry this pain for the rest of my life." There's no real emotion behind his words, and I know he's just clowning around, probably to get a rise out of his brother.

"Are you done being a goof and ready to help?" Collin asks, stepping away from me and moving to the entryway.

"If I must. Used and left alone. It hurts, Lizzie. Really, it hurts." Then he flashes me a megawatt grin and claps his hands together. "Lucky for you, I get over pain pretty quickly, so let's do it." But then he looks my way and gives me a lopsided grin. "Not literally, my lady. That ship has sailed. You had your chance. I'm nothing more than muscle to you. Unless you really do want to do it, then I'm in."

I can't stop the giggle as Collin rolls his eyes hard and pushes his brother through the doorway. "Let's go, Romeo."

"You've always been a cockblocker," Cade states to his twin before moving down the stairs.

I follow behind, ready to show them what needs brought up. I still feel bad they're both here on a weeknight, moving furniture, but Collin wasn't taking no for an answer. And at the end of the day, I told them it wasn't necessary today, so the fact they're doing it right now was their decision. Or it was Collin's decision.

It doesn't take them long to bring the rest of my living room furniture up the stairs, and when they get that into place, they set their sights on my dresser and nightstands. My old place had decent-sized closets, so I was able to hang a lot of my clothes. Unfortunately, the closets in this apartment are pretty small, with only a single bar for some hangers. I'm going to have to use the tiny closet in the second bedroom to hold some of my things. Maybe I can rotate my wardrobe based on the season. Like, in the summer, keep my heavier, winter wear in the other closet and then switch it in the fall.

"What are you thinking so hard about?" Collin asks, startling me, since I didn't realize he had approached and was standing beside me. "Sorry, didn't mean to scare you."

"You're fine. I was just trying to think of where I'm going to put all my clothes," I reply with a little chuckle. "I'm kind of a clothes whore."

He runs his fingers through his hair and pins me with a look of concern. "Uhh, do you have hidden closets up there somewhere?"

I snort and shake my head.

"Well, then, I suppose you found a use for that smaller bedroom." His blue eyes are dancing with humor as he adds, "A walk-in closet."

"What the hell? It's not break time!" Cade hollers from the truck, hands on his hips like a disciplining father.

"Zip it!" Collin retorts.

"You know, that's not a bad idea," I reply, though I really had hopes of creating my private library/sewing room. However, it just might not be in the cards for this apartment. Maybe, someday down the road, I'll be able to afford a place big enough for walk-in closets *and* a library/sewing space.

"Don't give up on your dream space just yet," he states, as if reading my mind. "You might be able to create some extra closet space and still be able to have your other area."

I nod, wondering if that's true. The second bedroom is pretty small and would have fit my bookshelves and sewing supplies easily, but some sort of extra wardrobe or extended closet for my clothes? I'm not so sure about that.

I carry a few smaller boxes up, placing them in the second bedroom, even though that room has a long way to go before it's set up. For now, it'll be a good spot to keep the things I need to sort and put away so I can get the moving vehicle back sooner rather than later.

"What else?" Cade asks, glancing around the truck, which is now well on its way to being empty.

"I think that's all for tonight. This was a huge help, thank you."

"Are you sure? Besides the kitchen table, you really only have boxes left," Collin states, glancing around.

"Yeah, but most of that is kitchen stuff and more clothes, décor, and some holiday stuff I have to figure out what in the world I'm going to do with," I grumble, my head starting to swim a little. I have way too much stuff for a woman who downsized her living space.

"How long do you have the rental truck for?" Cade asks.

"Well, I was being really ambitious and hoping to have it emptied by the end of the weekend so I'm not charged another week's use. I knew all the rooms wouldn't be ready to put everything away, but I grossly mis-judged the amount of stuff I had versus the space. I guess we could stack all the kitchen stuff in the living room," I state, hating that thought. I really wanted to have the living room set up and livable without having to trip over mountains of boxes, but I guess that's just not feasible.

"I have an idea," Cade states, glancing over to Collin. Even though he doesn't say a word, I swear I see something like communication pass between them. Honestly, it's a little freaky, because Collin responds with a nod. "Okay, so I have a small trailer I'll bring over. What you don't have room for upstairs can be stored there until you're ready to sort and what-not. Then you're not under any pressure or timeline."

"I can't do that," I insist.

"Why not?" Collin asks.

"Because...that's...it's..." I take a deep, calming breath. "I don't know."

Cade grins from ear to ear. "Exactly. Plus, it'll save you a few bucks from having to rent the truck another week."

"I can pay you," I blurt out, needing to feel like I'm contributing something.

"Fine. You can buy me a beer."

I roll my eyes. "That's not enough."

His smile starts slow and lights up his entire face. "You can make me the guest of honor during little black dress night."

I bark out a laugh and shake my head. "You're incorrigible."

"That I am, Miss Lizzie. That I am."

"Are you sure there is nothing else you need tonight?" Collin asks, his seriousness so very different than his brother's playfulness.

Looking at the remaining boxes, I shake my head. "No, I think that's all for tonight."

Collin flips off a small lantern my brothers had used on Sunday, bath-ing the small space in darkness. Reaching up, he grabs the pull strap and starts to lower the door on the back of the truck. I don't miss the way his T-shirt rides up, exposing the hard planes of his muscular stomach. Even in the darkness, only illuminated by a security light on the back of the building, I can see the light smattering of dark blond hair below his belly button. The happy trail, as it's so often called, that leads straight to...

"You're drooling," Cade mumbles near my ear, causing me to startle.

His laughter fills the space, causing his twin to turn around. "What?"

"Nothing!" I blurt out, praying Cade keeps his damn mouth shut and doesn't mention the fact he clearly just busted me perving on his brother.

"Nothing," Cade singsongs, unable to contain his smile. "All right, I'm outta here. I'll bring the trailer over later this week and can help you get everything transferred over if needed."

"Thank you," I reply, my throat a little thick with emotion. I had plenty of family and friends back in Stewart Grove, but to already have found some so quickly after moving here feels pretty amazing. These people don't know me, but they're willing to help me.

This is what I love about a small town.

"Later," Cade hollers to Collin, holding out his fist for a bump. Then, he disappears around the buildings to head home.

Turning my attention to Collin, I realize we're standing outside in the cool night air. I open my mouth, prepared to invite him inside—for what, I'm not sure—but before I can, he says, "I should head home."

I nod, knowing he's right. "I really do appreciate your help. And for running to my rescue when you thought I was in trouble."

He cracks a smile and walks toward me. His gait is strong, his gaze piercing with each step he takes. Reaching up, he brushes hair off my forehead and whispers, "Good night, Lizzie."

"Night," I reply, my pulse pounding in my ears.

I remain where I stand near the back entrance, watching as he heads the same way his brother went. Just when he reaches the corner, he stops and turns back. "Get inside."

I lift my chin and sass, "You're not the boss of me!"

He grins. "Get your ass inside, Lizzie. It's cold."

"Yes, sir," I holler, unable to hide my own grin.

I feel his eyes on me as I slowly spin around and move to the back door. I close the heavy door and make sure it's double locked before leaning back against it and closing my eyes.

Why this man?

I still don't have it figured out, but he seems to have pushed his way through my defenses without even trying. Not that I have all these walls built around my heart, but a girl is definitely more careful after having her heart broken a few times.

Especially when it comes to someone I work with behind the bar.

Realizing the time, I push all thoughts of Collin as far from my mind as possible and head for the bar. Jani should have just closed down for the night, and since I'm right outside the back entrance to the business, I might as well slip inside and check on her.

Then, I'll be able to take a quick shower and get ready for bed, where I'm almost certain all thoughts will return to a certain firefighter with a kind heart and the most alluring blue eyes.

It just might be another sleepless night for me…

CHAPTER ELEVEN

Collin

"H EY, LOSER!"

I turn around and find my sister walking through the back gate, where I'm currently doing some spring yardwork. "Hey," I reply, setting the rake against the small fence and turning my attention to her.

"What are you doing here?" I ask, pulling work gloves off my hands and walking the few steps over to where I left a bottle of water.

"I was out and about. Thought I'd drop by and see my favorite brother," she replies, flashing a quick grin my way.

I roll my eyes. "What do you want?" I ask, knowing it's something. Not that I care. I'd do anything for my sister—hell, we all would—and she knows it.

"I brought you something," she says, a playful little smile on her lips as she extends her hand.

"What's this?" I ask, taking the card and flipping it over. It's a small four-by-six envelope with my name written across the front with big, fancy letters.

"I don't know," she states, looking like she's about to burst with excitement. "Someone dropped it off for you."

Without opening it, I look up. "What?"

She shrugs. "I was with a client in my room when someone dropped it off at the front desk for you." Charli's a massage therapist at the local salon.

I'm so confused right now. Why the hell would someone drop something off to my sister's work? "Did she say who it was from?"

"Jenn didn't recognize the woman, and you know between her and Lila, they know everyone in this town. She said she was young, blond, and *busty*."

I roll my eyes. "Is this a joke?" I ask, not taking my eyes off my sister for a second.

"Of course not!" she bellows with a laugh. "I'm dead serious."

I glance down at the card and toss it into the brush pile I've been working on.

"What the heck? You aren't even going to open it?" she hollers, reaching down and grabbing the card.

"Nope," I reply, turning my attention back to cleaning up along the fence line. It catches all the leaves and crap that I don't get cleaned up before winter hits. Not to mention the sycamore tree in the middle of the yard that drops big leaves and sticks all the damn time. It's a messy tree, but it's huge and provides shade for a big part of the yard, so I don't complain too much.

"Well, I'm gonna," she states, ripping open the sealed envelope and pulling out the card.

I keep my eyes focused on what I'm doing, but admit I stop and turn her way when she bursts out laughing.

"Oh my God, this is the best pick-up card I've ever read!"

"A what?" I ask, afraid to hear the answer.

"*My dearest Collin, roses are red, violets are blue, firefighters are hot, that means you. I'd love to get to know you better. We met once before about six weeks ago. My pussy cat was stuck in a tree, and you rescued her. Now, I have another pussy that needs a little attention.*' Oh my God! This is so scandalously nasty!" my sister bellows through her laughter, and now I really wish I had lit the card on fire before she had a chance to read it. "*'Please meet me at Station Street Bistro at ten o'clock Friday morning. I'll be the woman in red. Love, Cherie.'*"

Charli doubles over laughing, tears streaming down her face. "Holy shitballs, Col. This was better than I could have expected. I wish Cade and Cam were here," she states.

"I'm glad they weren't," I mutter, thankful for small favors. Why I thought I should let my sister read it was beyond me. I knew whatever was inside was probably trash, and I was definitely right. Believe it or not, fire-fighters do receive all sorts of random mail like this. Police too. It's worse on the internet. All it takes is one woman snapping a photo of you in your turnout gear, and suddenly you're an internet sensation to be fawned over by horny women around the world.

It's been a while since we've received anything of this nature at the firehouse, but it happens. Hell, there's a whole cabinet of notes from over the years. Some have accompanied baked goods, and most are simple shows of appreciation. However, there are times where a woman steps forward with a firefighter fantasy and she expects us to fill the role. It's fucked up.

But what's more fucked up is the fact this wasn't left at the firehouse like any other note. This was hand delivered to my sister's place of employment. That means, she not only knows my name, but she knows where I live—and who my family is.

I rub my temple, a headache already forming. Extending my hand, I wait for her to hand over the card.

She shakes her head. "I'm keeping it," she replies, slipping it beneath her arm.

I move, fast, practically tackling her to get the note away. "You're not keeping it. You'll show it to everyone," I insist, shoving my fingers into her side, which I know will get the result I'm looking for.

Charli squeals and squirms, opening her arm and allowing me to grab the card. "Dirty trick, Collin."

I shrug and slip the card into my back pocket. "You know I can't let you leave with it."

She giggles. "It's fine. I have it memorized already anyway."

I exhale deeply, wishing I hadn't been so stupid as to allow my sister to open the card. "Whatever."

"Do you know who it is?" she asks, her face straightening as she gets past the words on the card and finally understands the seriousness of the situation.

"No clue. I'm sure I can look back over the calls I've responded to, especially if her cat in the tree story was accurate."

My sister tries to fight a smile but fails. "You mean…her pussy."

I sigh loudly. "Go away."

"Fine, but I'll see you later," she says.

"You will?" I ask, mentally running through my calendar.

"Yep! I heard Lizzie is considering doing a paint night, and I want to support her and sign up."

I run my hand through my hair, knocking some debris loose. "Do you really think they're as big as people say?"

Her eyes widen in shock. "Are you kidding me? Paint nights are huge. I'm surprised Cooper Town hasn't had more of them."

A single eyebrow shoots upward in question. "If you say so."

"I do. I bet she'll sell out, and me and my girlfriends will be there," Charli states emphatically.

"Well, I guess I'll see you there later then."

"Yep. Maybe I'll call Cam to see if he wants to come up and have a drink with me," she says.

I shake my head. "Two of you?"

She barks out a laugh and walks over to where I stand, pecking a kiss on my cheek. Of course, in order for her to do it, I have to crouch a little. "Behave, or I'll call Cade too."

"You wouldn't dare!"

She turns and heads for the driveway. Just before she's out of sight, she glances over her shoulder and announces, "Try me."

Of course when the heavy door opens and I see my sister walk in, I groan at the sight of both of my brothers and a couple of friends trailing behind.

"What's wrong?" Lizzie asks, turning her attention from reorganizing the shelves beneath the bar.

"The riffraff just got here," I state, narrowing my eyes at my sister, who is smiling from ear to ear.

She stands up and smiles the moment she spots my siblings approaching the bar. "Hey!"

"Lizzie!" they all seem to holler in unison.

"What brings you all in tonight?" she asks, noting the larger than normal group.

"I came to talk to you about your paint night, but I gathered the troops to come bother that big lug," Charli informs Lizzie, throwing her finger my way, as if to make sure she knows I'm the lug.

"Oh! I just confirmed the date and time," Lizzie announces, moving closer to my sister.

"I can't wait. I know my girlfriends and I will be here."

"The art teacher is going to teach the class, which will be next Saturday evening at six. I'm going to have some snack foods and drink specials. I'm really excited," Lizzie replies, her energy palpitating from where she stands. I can't help but just watch.

"Me too. Sign me up, and I'll text my friends now and see who is going to join me."

Lizzie nods and moves her notebook across the counter. "Go ahead and put your name and cell number down on the list. She'd like to keep it to under twenty, so I'm having people sign up, first come, first serve."

"Yep, I'm in. I'll have more for you by the end of the night," Charli states, pulling out her phone and letting her fingers fly over the screen.

Lizzie chuckles. "Don't you want to know the details?"

Charli shrugs. "They won't care. We're always looking for fun things like this to do together, so the cost is irrelevant. But you should totally have people prepay to reserve their spot. This way you can fill the event and don't have to worry about no-shows who took spots from paying customers."

"Yeah, but I was worried about asking for money right away, considering I'm new to the area."

Charli waves off her statement. "You're a business first and foremost, and anyone who doesn't understand that probably wouldn't have signed up and shown up anyway."

I crack a smile at my sister's very diplomatic, businesslike reply. I remember what it was like with her starting out her massage business at twenty-three. She had tons of no-shows and that affected her bottom line, because those spots were filled with names, taking the spot of another potential paying customer. She implemented a two-strike no-show policy, in which you get charged fifty percent of the cost of your massage if you no-show a second time.

"Are you gonna get us a drink or just stand there and make googly eyes at the pretty girl all night?"

I turn my attention to my twin and narrow my eyes. "Why are you here?"

He grins widely. "You mean besides the fact you are?"

I sigh, already knowing my sister opened her big fat trap and told him what was on that card dropped off to her. "What can I get you? If you're going to take up space, you're going to buy something."

"Just a Coke for me. I'm babysitting the kids tonight," he replies, obviously referring to our youngest brother and his friends, Quinn and Robby.

"I'm not babysitting," Alex, one of Cade's and my friends, announces, ordering a draft beer. "Wait, you have Crüe beer in stock?"

I nod, pointing to the sign over the bar that announces the very recent arrival of two of the Crüe's most popular varieties. "Just bottles right now, but she's on their list for draft soon."

"Sweet!" Alex proclaims, choosing a bottle of All American Crüe, the lighter of the two options.

Camden and Robby come over and order beers before making their way to the pool table to rack the balls. I glance up at Cade. "You paying?"

"Nope. Just because I'm babysitting doesn't mean I'm buying too. Just put it on their tab and the kids can pay at the end of the night," he replies, taking a sip of his soft drink. His eyes glance over to where Lizzie and Charli are still talking. "They seem to be getting along well."

I shrug and take money for his Coke. "Charli becomes fast friends with everyone."

"That's true. She's a lot like me. Unlike you."

Ignoring his comment, I set his change on the counter and take the five-dollar bill. "Tip."

He points at me. "That's all you get. Quit stealing my hard-earned money."

I laugh and shake my head. "What do you think I'm doing here?" I ask, holding up the money.

"Thanks again, Cade, for letting me use your trailer. I got everything moved over from the rental to yours, and I promise to get it cleared out as soon as possible," Lizzie says, coming up to stand beside me. She smells like a mixture of flowers and the harsh cleaner she was using beneath the bar. But I admit, it really looks good. She painted all the shelves and covered them with some sort of grippy stuff that's removable and washable.

"No rush," my brother replies. "I won't be needing it until Memorial Day weekend."

Her green eyes seem to sparkle just a little more. "What happens then?"

"I ride that weekend," he says, referring to his four-wheeler.

"Tell me more," Lizzie insists, leaning forward and hanging on his every word as he explains the large off-road park in Indiana he goes to every year with a group of friends. I've been a handful of times, but with my work schedule, I don't get to go every year.

"It's pretty awesome," he says, after telling her all about the property. "We camp for two nights and then come home Monday morning."

Lizzie nods. "Sounds like fun."

"You should come!" Cade insists, catching Charli's attention, and of course, I realize instantly what's about to happen.

"Oh, I couldn't. I'll have to work."

"No, you have to come! It's such a great weekend. Even if you can't come both nights," Charli insists, inviting Lizzie directly into our inner circle. "Collin's work schedule is always a little jacked up, so sometimes he only comes for one night. You can come with him." To me she adds, "Didn't Chuck usually close down for Memorial Day?"

I don't reply, because I don't want to insert myself into this conversation any more than I already have. Besides, how Chuck ran the business and how Lizzie will aren't the same, and the last thing I'd want to do is step on her toes when it comes to making business decisions.

Lizzie shrugs her shoulders. "I haven't thought that far ahead, but I know my dad's place is always closed on major holidays like Memorial Day. Everyone's at home, cooking out and drinking beer there. It does make sense."

"Yes! Exactly! So, promise you'll consider coming. I'm sure you can find coverage on Sunday."

"I don't have a four-wheeler," Lizzie states, but like my sister always does, she has an answer for everything.

"You can ride with Collin."

The blonde with big curls and the most alluring green eyes I've ever seen snaps her attention to me. I shrug, not saying a word, because if Charli wants something bad enough, she'll fight tooth and nail until she gets it. And right now, she wants Lizzie to be her friend, wants her to go with our family and small group of friends to ride four-wheelers at the off-road park.

I smell a matchmaker at work...

"We don't have to decide anything right now," I state, grabbing one of the sanitizing cloths and starting to wipe down the section of bar we're standing by.

"No, of course not, but I want my new friend to know she's more than welcome to come for the weekend. It's so much fun. We tent camp in this big circle and sing 'Kumbaya.'"

Since I'm stealing glances at Lizzie, I don't miss her reaction to that one. "What?" she asks, laughing.

"No, I'm kidding. We sing George Strait and Eminem."

"Nice."

"All right, I'll let you get back to what you were doing, but the invitation is there. We'll talk more as it gets closer. Oh, and you can even stay with me and my friends in our tent." With that, my sister turns around and heads toward the pool table to join the rest of our group, leaving me, Cade, and Lizzie standing here.

"Notice how she completely monopolized the conversation?" I say to my twin.

He snorts and takes another drink of his soda. "As she usually does."

Lizzie laughs and shakes her head. "Pot? Kettle?"

Now it's my turn to laugh. "She has your number, little brother."

Cade narrows his eyes. "Five minutes. You're five minutes older than me."

"Older is older," I state with a shrug and toss the cloth into the bucket.

"I'm gonna head over and make sure the kids behave," Cade says, but turns his attention to the woman standing close enough I can smell her. "But just to add on to what my sister said, you're definitely welcome to come. We get completely filthy and then sit around the fire, eat tons of food, and drink a few beers. It's a lot of fun and a great way to unwind."

With that, he heads to where the rest of the group is teasing Cam and Quinn for losing the first game, jumping right in to harass the youngest Miller as if he had been a part of it the whole time. We never neglect an opportunity to dive headfirst into some sibling razzing, no matter who the recipient is.

"Your family's pretty great," Lizzie says softly beside me, her gaze locked on the antics on the opposite side of the room.

"They are," I confirm. "They can be a lot, but it comes from a place of love."

She snorts and shakes her head. "Oh, you don't have to explain the fine line between obnoxious and love to me. My family straddles said line daily."

I offer her a smile before noticing it's time to refill some drinks down at the end of the bar. Before I walk away, I say, "Charli can be kinda blunt and opinionated, but it all comes from a good heart. She's also a good judge of character, and if she's inviting you into her inner circle, it's because she truly likes you and wants to get to know you. She wouldn't be wanting to hang out otherwise."

Lizzie regards me closely, considering my words and the meaning behind them. My sister has a handful of very close friends, but she's not afraid to invite outsiders in if she feels like it. And for some reason, she seems to really like the woman in front of me. I get it. They're actually quite similar in many ways, including coming from a large, loud family who doesn't know the definition of personal space.

I start to make my way to the other end, grabbing a couple of bottles of beer as I go. Just before I reach my destination, I hear, "Thanks, Collin."

I nod, opening the bottles and setting them on the bar, tossing the empties in the recycle can.

Just as I return to wash the few dirty glasses gathered beneath the bar, I hear, "So, tell me about this *pussy cat* stuck in the tree."

CHAPTER TWELVE

Lizzie

I LOOK AROUND AND SMILE.

This place looks amazing!

It's been incredibly hard over the last three weeks, since I took over Chuck's Place and turned it into The Tipsy Lizard. I've poured myself—and every penny I had saved—into this building. I've spent countless hours updating what I could and prioritizing what I couldn't yet. My lists are long, but what I've been able to check off them is fulfilling in itself.

Guy opened the bar for me today so I could get everything set up for paint night. I had planned to rent banquet tables and chairs, but when the Miller clan heard, they insisted I borrow their tables and chairs. Apparently, Collin's parents host enough gatherings that they have enough eight-foot tables and chairs to seat thirty-two people. I don't need that many chairs, but the table space will come in very handy for holding easels and painting supplies.

"This place looks great, Lizzie."

I spin and offer Guy a big smile. "Thanks."

"And I'm not just talking about the decorations you added for the paint night. This place looks…" He glances around at the space, where walls have been cleaned and painted, the stools have been repaired and all sit level until new ones can be purchased, and the floors have been sanded and refinished.

My dad and Uncle Jameson might have helped, but I was right there, doing a lot of heavy lifting.

"Thanks, Guy," I reply, unable to hide my excitement.

"And you kept the same vibe. That comfortable, laid-back feel that's always been present at Chuck's. It's like Cheers. Everyone's welcome and everyone knows your name."

That's what I wanted.

"I told you all," I tease the man I've come to get to know and respect.

"Yeah, I know you did. It was nothing personal, Lizzie. We're small-town, sometimes small-minded people. We don't like change."

"Hey, I don't judge. I'm from a small town," I remind, even though I'm certain he's well aware, considering he was here one of the days my dad and Jameson made the trip here to help me with the barstools.

I think Guy was a little starstruck when it came to having two of the four owners of the well-known Burgers and Brew in house for the day. Guy took full advantage, talking to them both about the industry and what's changed over the last couple of decades. When my dad left, he hugged me tightly and seemed incredibly grateful once more I have a seasoned team behind me that's both knowledgeable and have my back.

The front door opens and in walks my additional bartender for the night. Collin looks…good. Too good, if I'm being honest. He's wearing a black T-shirt that molds to his arms and sports the logo for my business on the front, jeans that make me want to cry as I mentally peel them off his legs, and well-loved work boots. His hair is freshly cut, but his jaw is left a little rough, as if he hasn't found time to shave in the last day or two.

"Hey," he says, slipping behind the bar and offering greetings to the regulars. When he reaches where we stand, he stops and takes a look around. "Wow, this place looks great."

A grin spreads across my lips. "Thanks. I love how the floors turned out," I reply, knowing Collin hasn't worked since we refinished them.

"I love it. It still looks rustic but…cleaner."

I chuckle and nod. "Yeah, I think I removed four decades of spilled alcohol off them."

"At least," he replies with his own snicker. Taking in the tables, he adds, "Full house tonight?"

"Yep. I can't believe the first class filled up so fast with twenty. Some of the names on the list I don't know. They must have signed up when I wasn't here," I say, remembering the handful of names I didn't recognize.

Something flashes in Collin's blue eyes, but whatever it is vanishes quickly when the door opens and we all turn our attention that way. In walks his sister and her two friends I have yet to meet.

"Hey!" Charli hollers the moment she steps inside. "Oh my God, look at this place! These floors are killer!" she bellows, heading our way.

"Thank you," I reply, again, grinning ear to ear.

"I don't know if you've met Lila and Sommer. Lila is the best nail tech in the area and works at the salon with me, and Sommer is my sister from another mister. We've been besties since kindergarten. Ladies, this is Lizzie, the new owner of our favorite establishment."

I greet the two new faces in front of me and welcome them to paint night. "Go ahead and pick your spots. Anita should be back any minute," I tell them, referring to the woman who is going to conduct tonight's paint class.

Just then, the door opens and in walks the woman herself. Anita is the art teacher at the local high school and incredibly easy to work with. She presented me three painting options for tonight, and I picked a wagon wheel and lilacs in an open field. Of course, if someone wanted to paint a different flower, they're more than welcome. That's one of the things I like about Anita. She seems very easygoing and willing to allow the paint-ers a little freedom with the design. I'm really hoping tonight's class goes well and the attendees enjoy her, because I can definitely see a continued partnership in the future.

"Hi, ladies," Anita greets, approaching with a smile and a paint smock. "Are you ready to paint?"

"We are," Charli replies.

"Everyone else should be arriving soon. Go ahead and get a drink and help yourself to some of the snacks," I tell the small group.

I have my food handler certification, thanks to my time at my family's restaurant and bar, and after meeting with the health department, I was granted a food certificate and all other necessary documentation in order to serve food at The Tipsy Lizard. Right now, my plan isn't to do anything big, but to be able to offer things like appetizers during the events I plan is a huge plus.

Collin moves behind the bar and jumps right in to serving drinks. Some are alcoholic and some are not. I'm featuring a Blueberry Smash non-alcoholic drink this week, which is a combination of blueberries, simple syrup, sparkling water, lemon juice, and rosemary. It's pretty tasty, if you ask me, and I'm happy to see some of the ladies attending tonight order one.

Just as I turn to check on the food, the front door opens again. The group of four who enters has me stopping in my tracks, my mouth dropping to the floor. My eyes burn with unshed tears and the four women I love most in this world rush toward me. "What—"

"You didn't think we'd let you host your very first paint night and not attend, did you?" my mom asks, smiling so wide and proud it causes a few of those tears to fall.

Aunt BJ laughs. "I called that hottie behind the bar and asked him to make up four names so you wouldn't know. We actually got the last four spots."

"It's amazing how fast it filled up," Aunt Madelyn adds, looking around the room as she reaches up and touches the delicate pearls around her neck she always wears. I take a quick glance at her appearance and hold back a smile of my own. She's in pressed navy slacks and a gorgeous rose-gold blouse with nude ballet flats. This is her dressing down, and the best part is, even knowing she's likely to get paint on her clothes, she still wears them.

Man, I love her.

All of them.

"I'm so happy you're here," I tell them, pulling each into a quick hug. "Let's get you all a drink and then you can claim your spots. I think that far table is still open."

"You ladies get the drinks. I'll go reserve the table," Aunt Lyndee states, moving to where I pointed to claim those four available spots.

"What can I get you?" I ask, slipping behind the bar to get my family a drink.

"I'll have an All American Crüe draft, please," Mom requests.

"Same," BJ adds.

"I'll have a white wine, and Lyndee would like that Blueberry Splash you've been promoting on social media," Madelyn orders.

I turn to pour the beers from our newly installed draft system, which now features the two most popular varieties from our brewery, and then set out to pour a white wine and make the nonalcoholic drink. I place the drinks on the bar and wave off the card presented.

"No, you're not giving us free drinks," my mom chastises, thrusting the card farther toward me.

"You're not paying. Not tonight. Tonight is…special. A celebration." I don't know why I'm so choked up. I can barely get the words out. Having them here, it's everything.

"We'll see about that," Mom announces as she slips her card back into her pocket and grabs her beer.

I roll my eyes. "There are snacks back on the table."

"Well, hello, lovely lady. You must be this one's sister," Gus says smoothly, making my mom chuckle.

"Mother, actually."

"I don't believe it. You're too young to have a daughter her age," Gus practically sings.

"Stop hitting on my mom, Gus," I demand without any fire behind my words.

He gasps, "Would I do that?"

Collin, who happens to walk up to grab the bottle of white wine sitting directly in front of me, says, "Of course you would. Probably to get some of those snacks."

I bark out a laugh. "I already told you I made extras for you guys. No need to hit on my mom just to get a plate of food."

"Well, I heard that, Gus. Come on with me and we'll get some food," my mom states, taking her beer over to the table and setting it down before making her way to the food table.

Gus jumps up off his stool, as do Larry and Burt, and moves in that direction.

"They don't pay," I say to Collin as I watch my aunts take their drinks to the table and then go make a plate of the snack food.

"You're the boss," he replies, pouring his glass of wine. "Need this still?"

"Nope, I'll put it away," I reply, taking the bottle and replacing the topper before slipping it inside the cooler. When Collin finishes his order, he turns his attention my way, so I add, "Thank you."

"For?"

I nod to where my mom and aunts are having a seat at the table, their plates full of snacks as they prepare for tonight's painting class. "Them."

He shrugs. "Hey, I just made up fake names so you wouldn't know it was them," he replies with a chuckle. The gravelly timbre of his voice sends waves of something dirty straight to the apex of my legs and makes my nipples tight.

"Well, it was the best surprise."

"Good. And the smile on your face was worth it."

I look his way, still grinning. An electrical charge seems to fill the space around us, sucking all available oxygen from the room. Everything and everyone just fades away. It's as if we're the only two people left remaining in the world. It's both exhilarating and scary all at the same time.

"I, uh, better go check the food," I reply, clearing my throat. Glancing at the bar and finding the regulars enjoying a heaping plate of snacks, I add, "I made plenty. Probably too much. Help yourself."

He nods once and keeps his eyes glued to me. "Thanks."

I slip away and check everything on the table. I made a large crock-pot of meatballs, as well as a charcuterie board of meats, cheeses, crack-ers, dips, fruits, and nuts. Plus, a variety of desserts I purchased from the bakery inside the grocery store. All in all, I know I overdid it, but I wanted to make sure I had enough. Once I have the first event under my wing, I'll be able to plan a little better for the next one.

But something tells me there won't be as much left as I think. Most of the ladies are snacking, but I imagine they'll restock their plates as the night goes on. Not to mention the guys at the bar and Collin. I had planned for them to snack too, even if they aren't attending paint night. They're still paying customers, and I'd never tell them they couldn't have something I was serving to other guests in the same building.

At exactly six o'clock, Anita starts her class. I stand off to the side and watch as she goes through the steps of creating tonight's painting. There's a completed one at the front of the room, and she'll be painting another along with her twenty students. All I can do is watch it happen.

"Well, is it everything you wanted it to be?"

I don't startle when Collin steps up beside me, because I could smell his woodsy soap or whatever he uses before he started talking. "Yes."

"Good."

I can hear the smile in his voice, and when I glance his way, I catch it on his lips. "Did you eat?" I already know he did, but I like talking to him and find myself wanting to drag out any conversation I can.

"I did, thank you." After a beat he adds, "Tonight went well, I think."

"I agree."

"I, uh, wanted to apologize."

That gives me pause. "What? Why?"

"Because I was wrong." His blue eyes bore into mine and steal my breath. "This place looks better than I could have imagined, and the things you're doing are bringing in new customers. Not just that, you're bringing in the right kind of customers. Well done."

The pride I feel swelling in my chest is intense. It's as great as hearing my family praise me for what I've accomplished in such a short amount of time on a budget. It's validation I made the right decision moving here and starting my own place. I wanted this. Something to call my own. Something I could be proud of.

It hasn't been easy. My savings is basically gone, and some of the other projects I want to do are on hold for a while, like the bathroom upstairs. It's not pretty, but I won't complain. I have running, hot water and a roof over my head that doesn't leak. Eventually, I'll save up more money and be able to check more repairs off the list.

I know it.

"Lizzie!" My attention is pulled to where Anita stands. "Come on, we're going to take a group picture with our masterpieces."

Smiling, I look to Collin and say, "Excuse me," before practically skipping to where the group is gathering with their paintings. I stole a few photos throughout the evening, capturing the work in progress. I feel like I'm floating on cloud nine with how well tonight's event went, especially after seeing the finished paintings and the smile on each of the ladies' faces as they gather for a photo.

I snap a few pictures of the group proudly showing off their paintings when Collin steps up behind me. "Get in there."

"Yes!" everyone hollers, inviting me to join them for another group photograph.

They part down the middle and make a spot for me to slip in right beside my mom. Collin takes a few shots of the whole class, and when everyone starts to disburse to clean up their area and get more food and drinks, I turn to my family and ask Collin to take one more picture of me with my mom and aunts. I don't even care I have tears in my eyes as I smile happily for the camera.

I'll print that photo and put it in my office—my first official successful event and the four women who mean the most to me.

The rest of the night progresses quickly, and before I know it, my family is heading back home to Stewart Grove and I'm closing down the bar with Collin. He's quiet as he locks the front entrance, and the room suddenly feels too small. Too quiet. Moving to where the old jukebox is mounted, I select a few classic country songs to fill the silence. Alan Jackson starts to sing about life next to the Chattahoochee River, and I find myself smiling and humming along.

I let Collin do his thing behind the bar, while I work on tearing down the remnants of the paint party. I was a little nervous painting over the floors I just refinished, but at the end of the day, this place has life and reflects the good, the bad, and the ugly that is life. If paint got on the floor, then so be it. I'd clean it the best I could and move on.

Fortunately, I don't see anything damaging and continue on with my business. I get everything torn down and start moving the tables to the back hallway. Cade dropped them off earlier this morning and said he'd come back tomorrow for everything.

"Let me help," Collin says, jumping in and helping me carry the tables. Of course, he grabs one in each hand, and the job is complete pretty swiftly.

"I really appreciate your family letting me borrow their tables," I say.

"No problem. Better than renting them from some company or buying new," he states with a shrug.

"Very true. And these plastic ones are fairly lightweight and durable." I wipe my hands down my pants. "Plus, I love that they fold in half. Sure makes moving them easier."

My heart rate is elevated, and it's not because of a little extra exertion. I moved and set up the tables with ease, so I know it's not that.

It's Collin.

I don't know why he gets under my skin the way he does, and it's not in a bad or annoying way. It's simply…him. His scent, his powerful gaze, his uncanny ability to get me without even trying. I can sense his nearness, and my body reacts. It gravitates toward him all on its own.

"You okay?" he whispers, his mouth surprisingly close to my ear.

I don't know when he moved to stand before me, but he's right here, and it takes every ounce of control I have not to lean into him. "Yes," I reply, my voice breathy and at a higher pitch than normal.

Our eyes meet, and I swear I can see the flames dancing in those sapphire pools. It reflects his desire, his raw need. It's alive, clawing to the surface like a tangible being. Or perhaps that's just the reflection of every-thing in my own eyes dying to be unleashed.

I need to walk away, to put some distance between us before I do something I might regret later.

Like throw myself at him.

Because let's be honest.

I'm his boss.

End of story.

And anything happening between us would be unprofessional, right?

Right.

That's what I tell myself. Problem is, I don't think I believe it.

Especially when I turn to excuse myself, and I'm met with his mouth pressed firmly against mine.

Suddenly, kissing him feels like not only the best idea ever, but the only one.

I am all in, even if it's going to cost me.

CHAPTER THIRTEEN

Collin

I'M WELL AWARE KISSING MY BOSS IS PROBABLY THE WORST IDEA I'VE
ever had, but the moment my lips meet hers, I don't give a shit. Every
reason, every excuse I've been telling myself anytime she's near just
evaporates, leaving me with only the thoughts of a man hypnotized by a
woman he's incredibly attracted to.

And I am.

The more I watched her tonight, the more I wanted her. With every
minute, every second that passed, I grew closer and closer to the edge of
control. For a man who prides himself on remaining calm and collected
under pressure, I sure as hell did a crappy job of hiding it. Conceal, don't
feel…or whatever that line is from the *Frozen* movie.

Not that I've seen the movie, just to be clear.

That damn song played on every station for months.

And then it won awards and played some more.

But here I am, my mouth pressed to Lizzie's, and it's the best damn
feeling in the world. And what's worse? There's no going back now. Not
after tasting her lips, hearing the way her breathing hitches and she mewls,

or the feel of her body pressed against mine, her fingers gripping the back of my shirt as she anchors to me.

My tongue slides out, tracing the seam of her lips until she grants me entrance, and when she does, I take. Our tongues clash in a fury of need, and my fingers itch to explore. Instead of letting them drift beneath her shirt, I move them to her hair, tangling in those long, blond curls that have been hypnotizing me since the first time I saw her.

Lizzie presses her chest against mine, her fingers gripping tightly to my shirt, and as much as I want to progress this kiss into something more, this isn't the time or the place. I refuse to be the asshole who takes this farther in the middle of a bar, despite wanting her bad enough I could in a heartbeat.

When I gently apply the brakes, she sighs against my lips. That one sound goes straight to my balls, making them ache even more than they already do. Closing my eyes, I rest my forehead against hers and whisper, "I should apologize for kissing you like that, but I'm not sorry."

"I wouldn't accept your apology if you were to give one," she replies, the faintest smile crossing her kiss-swollen lips.

I run my thumb over her lips, committing the feel of them to memory, before stepping back and creating space between us. "That wasn't… appropriate." I have no idea what else to say.

She shrugs and places her hands on her hips. "Felt very *appropriate* to me."

We both smile, lost for a moment in the recollection of the kiss. Clearing my throat, I reply, "I meant it wasn't appropriate to do at work."

"No?" she asks, cocking her head to the side just a touch. "But if we were out of work, it would have been appropriate then?"

I consider her words, knowing it's probably not very appropriate any time, any place, considering we work together. But I also know it's damn hard to keep fighting this attraction I feel for her. She's like a magnet, her force too strong to keep fighting, and for the life of me, I can't think of one reason why I should. Well, beyond the obvious.

Except, there is a reason I hesitate…

"Listen, we don't have to make this weird," she says when the silence draws on too long. "It was a great kiss."

The corner of my lip ticks. "It was."

She levels me with a flirty, yet serious look. "We could do it again."

"We could."

"Maybe not here, since the whole work thing seems to be a hang-up for you. And I get it, don't get me wrong. My dad supposedly had this no-dating rule at work before my mom and I entered his life. He tells me he was a goner from that moment on." Lizzie inhales deeply. "And I get it. Work is work, and while it can be fun, it still needs to hold some sense of professionalism. I'm your boss. There should be boundaries and lines we don't cross," she continues, taking a deep breath. "But to be honest, I enjoyed that kiss far more than I worry about said boundaries."

All I can do is stare at this gorgeous woman. She's smart and driven, yet thoughtful and considerate at the same time. She's completely unlike anyone I've ever known, and the more I get to know her, the more I like her. "You surprise me."

Her head cocks to the side just a tick. "How so?"

I don't know how to put my thoughts into words, but I give it a shot. "You're just different than anyone else I've ever known."

She pins me with a look of skepticism. "I'll take that as a compliment?"

I crack a smile, wishing I were kissing her again. "Most definitely."

Nodding, she glances around the room. "That'll be enough for now. How about we get this all finished up and get out of here?"

"Then what?" I find myself asking, because I know what I'd like to happen. I just don't know if she feels the same.

"Well, I'm exhausted, so you can walk me to my door and maybe kiss me goodnight. After that, we'll have to see. I'm not opposed to *this*, whatever *this* is, Collin. I like you. I enjoy spending time with you, even though most of that has been here."

I step forward, invading her personal space once more. "My schedule can be…challenging." That's the only way to describe it. On for two days, off for four isn't ideal, especially when you're hoping to spend time with a woman who owns a business and works most days of the week.

Lizzie shrugs. "I don't mind a challenge."

I snort, realizing she probably has no idea. I'm not the easygoing Miller twin. The one who smiles and laughs easily, though I find it a little easier to do when she's near. I have scars and baggage I seem to carry, despite trying to get rid of them years ago. I carry the weight of past mistakes on my shoulders, see it, even though it's invisible, when I look at myself in the mirror.

"Tell me what you want," I find myself stating, needing her to spell it out for me.

"We spend time together and let things progress or not naturally."

I nod, my mind already replaying that kiss and anxious to walk her to her door. "I can get on board with that."

"Good," she replies with a grin. "Now, what else needs to be done?"

"I have to count the register."

She grabs a broom from the hall closet while I move to close out today's register. When Chuck owned the place, he had a woman who came in three days a week and closed up. Mostly sweeping and mopping, and the occasional dusting of alcohol bottles and whatnot. However, Lizzie decided to do it herself as a way to save money. The bartenders always take out the trash at the end of the night and clean up as much as possible, especially behind the bar. She doesn't require us to sweep and mop at the end of the night unless there's something spilled, choosing to do it herself in the morning.

When I have the drawer counted and the closing sheet filled out, I take it into the office and put it all away. Then, I grab the trash bags placed at the back door and go throw them in the dumpster. Just as I come in, Lizzie is putting the broom away and offers me a tired smile. "At least part of it is done. I'll mop in the morning before I open."

"Come on then, Cinderella," I state, reaching out my hand. "You look like the carriage is about to turn back into the pumpkin."

She chuckles as she flips off the storage room light and places her hand in mine. I turn off the remaining overhead lights downstairs and escort her to the back entrance. She engages the lock for the bar and gazes up at the stairs leading to her apartment. "How come you know so much about Cinderella?" she asks just before she yawns.

"Charli. She was obsessed with all things Disney when she was little. I remember watching that movie a million times. Cade and I hated it."

She giggles the sweetest sound as we ascend. "I bet you both were great big brothers."

"We loved her, but she used to follow us around all the time. It bothered us when we were younger, because no one wanted their little sister underfoot when they were playing with their friends, but soon we became used to it. She was just part of the group most of the time, and none of our friends seemed to mind. She was one of us."

Lizzie unlocks the door to her apartment and turns to face me. "My brothers were all boy and rarely wanted to play with me, but by the time Em came along, I had a sidekick for life." Something crosses her beautiful face. Even in the dim light illuminating the stairway, I don't miss the sadness in her eyes.

"You miss her."

She sighs. "I miss them all, but I definitely miss her. She'll be going off to college in a few months, and with me here, I don't get to see her nearly as much as I used to. I'm hoping after her high school graduation, I can get her here for a few days or a week. I'll have to work, but she really wants to come and just hang out."

"I only got to spend a few minutes with her, but I enjoyed meeting her when she was here with your family," I say, reaching up and giving a gentle tug to one of her curls.

"She's feistier than I am," Lizzie states with a cheesy grin. "She's all Walker Meyer."

I chuckle at the image she paints. "Well, thankfully she looks more like your mom than your dad."

"She's the perfect mixture of both in every regard," she replies just as another yawn erupts.

"All right, I've kept you out here longer than I should. You're exhausted."

She nods. "Yeah."

Stepping into her personal space, I keep her fingers entwined with my own, just so I'm not tempted any more than I already am to take this further than a kiss. Then, I move in, pressing my lips to hers and feeling that smoldering layer of desire ignite once more.

But somehow, I rein it in. I taste, but I don't devour. If I do, I'm liable to throw her over my shoulder and extend our night together inside her apartment. While that's what I'd love to do, that's not taking this slow, the way we just discussed downstairs. So, I keep my wits about me and the kiss from escalating to steamy.

Instead, I savor. I revel in the feel of her lips, the slide of her tongue. My unoccupied hand comes up to cup her cheek, my thumb caressing the smooth line of her jaw. When I let it trail down her neck, she shivers, and I can feel the goosebumps on her skin.

"I'll see you soon, Lizzie," I murmur against her lips, placing one more chaste kiss to her skin.

"I'll be here," she whispers, her fingers gripping the side of my shirt as if it were the anchor she needs to keep her grounded.

Pulling back, I give her a slight smile, release her hand, and turn to head down the stairs. "Lock up."

"I will."

When I reach the base of the stairs, I glance back and say, "Now, Lizzie. Lock up now."

"Yes, sir," she states with a mock salute that makes my cock twitch in my pants.

She waves before slipping inside her apartment and closing the door. I listen for the sound of the locks engaging, and only when I hear the distinct sound do I push out the back door. I check the handle to make sure it's also locked, and only then do I shove my hands in my pockets and make my way to my truck.

When I slide inside the cab and start the engine, I smile. I can still feel her against my lips, taste her on my tongue. As I throw the truck into reverse and pull from my parking spot, I realize I'm in trouble. Not the kind of mischievous trouble I found myself in when I was younger. This trouble causes a rapid beat in my chest.

That kiss wasn't enough.

No, there's no going back now.

I'm completely addicted to Lizzie Meyer.

I shut off the mower and leave it in the yard. Not because I'm lazy and don't want to put it away, but simply because if I don't go up to my deck and find out why Cade is here, he's liable to sit there and drink all my beer without a care in the world.

"What's up, dickhead?" I ask, dropping onto the Adirondack chair next to him.

"This the only beer you have?" he asks, making a face.

"You tell me. You were in my fridge." I wait a few seconds before adding, "You know it's barely eleven."

He shrugs. "It's five o'clock somewhere."

I grunt in response and survey my backyard. It was one of the reasons I picked this house when I was looking. It's spacious, has a firepit, and ample space for entertaining. "I thought for sure you'd come up to the Lizard last night," I state.

He takes another pull from the bottle of beer. "I was gonna but found a friend to…entertain." He waggles his eyebrows, as if I needed any further clarification as to what he meant.

I snort and shake my head.

"What? Just because you live a monk lifestyle doesn't mean I have to," he counters, a wolfish grin on his face.

"I date," I argue, even though it's a loose argument.

"Having sex twice in the last year is not dating, Collin."

My eyes narrow. "Did you forget Sam?"

He barks out a laugh, clearly at my expense. "You mean Sam, who broke into your house and stole your clothes?"

I knew I shouldn't have brought her up.

Shifting in my seat, I reply, "Yeah. Her. She might have been a little... different, but I still dated her."

He laughs, practically in my face. "Different. Yep. We'll go with that. And I probably wouldn't be boasting about her. She took all your socks."

I have no response, because the fact remains, she did steal my socks. And my boxers, and my T-shirts. Though, apparently, just the dirty ones of those. When I saw her wearing the shirt I had slept in the night before I had to work, knowing full well I left it in my laundry, I called her on it, and she confessed to borrowing it. Then proceeded to show me the socks and boxers she was also wearing.

That was the end of my relationship with Sam. Not only did she invade my personal space after only a few months of dating by somehow jimmying the lock on my back door, but she also slept in my bed and took my shit, as if she had a right to be there while I wasn't.

"You should ask out Lizzie."

His words make me pause. I take a second to school my features so they're neutral, but it's too late. My twin—the person who knows me better than I probably know myself—just smiles that shit-eating grin of his. It's cocky and full of self-righteousness, because the asshole knows he has me.

"What happened?"

"I don't kiss and tell," I counter, which is a complete lie. At least where he's concerned.

Like I said, no one knows me better than Cade.

"So...you kissed her. Nice."

I exhale deeply, only to be greeted by his cocky laughter once more.

"Don't stop now. Tell me everything."

"I didn't tell you anything to begin with," I state.

"Maybe not with words, but it was what you didn't say," he replies like the cocky bastard he is.

"There's nothing to tell." *Not yet, anyway.* "I kissed her. We agreed to keep it professional during work."

"But after work..." he says, leaving his statement wide open, and for good reason. Like I said, he knows me well.

"We'll see what happens."

"I'll tell you what better happen," he retorts. "I better not have to explain it to you."

"You don't," I blurt out, hoping to end this conversation.

I've never had a problem talking to my brother about women, but it feels different now. I want him to know all about how amazing I think Lizzie is, but he doesn't need to know all the dirty details. Not that there are any of those...

Yet.

"So, what's your plan for the rest of the day?"

"Yardwork," I reply.

"After."

"I don't know."

"Let's go up to the Lizard. You can buy me a beer," he says.

"Because drinking all of mine at home isn't good enough for you?" I ask, even though I secretly love the idea.

"Because getting to watch you fawn all over the hot girl is going to be better than drinking all your beer."

I exhale and shake my head. Something tells me he's going to make this as uncomfortable as possible. I don't care about him giving me a hard time, but I definitely don't want him upsetting Lizzie. Or her thinking I blabbed to my brother about what happened last night.

"If we're leaving, you have to help me with my yardwork before we go," I state.

"Fine, but you better bring me another beer."

And that's how I get roped into going to The Tipsy Lizard with my bonehead brother on a Sunday afternoon.

CHAPTER FOURTEEN

Lizzie

E VERYTHING SHIFTS THE MOMENT HE WALKS THROUGH THE DOOR. Without even looking up to confirm, I know Collin is here. There's a sudden electrical charge in the air, and my body responds instantly. A shiver sweeps through me, and as much as I try to pretend it's because my hands were just inside the cooler, grabbing two beers, I know there's another reason. It's the memory of his mouth, his hands on my body—despite keeping them outside of my clothing—that has me on total edge.

"Lizzie!"

I smile. "I should have known double trouble was here."

Cade's hand covers his heart as his mouth falls open in mock insult. "That's cold, Lizzie Lou."

My eyes narrow at the nickname as I rest one hand on my hip. I do everything I can not to look at Collin, because I know the moment I do, I'll feel weak in the knees and want to throw myself at him again. With a bar full of customers, that's the last thing I need to do.

The twins take a seat at the bar after hollering their greetings at the regulars positioned just down from them. "What can I get you?" I ask, dropping a new coaster onto the bar top.

"Nice," Cade states, picking his up and checking it out. It's nothing fancy. Just a basic pulpboard coaster with my logo printed on it.

"Thank you," I reply, waiting for their order.

"I'll have an All American draft, please," Cade requests. "This guy has terrible beer at home. Did you know he buys a national brand, Lizzie Lou? Can you believe it? Can't even support the family."

A single eyebrow shoots upward, and I risk a quick glance at Collin. He's just shaking his head, as if apologizing on his brother's behalf. "Family?"

"Well, yeah. I mean, I know they're *your* family, but this place is practically one big family here, so that makes them *our* family. Get what I'm sayin'?"

"Not really," I reply, earning a chuckle from Collin.

He sighs. "You two are perfect for each other. Both thorns in my side."

I bark out a laugh and turn to retrieve his beer. Once it's poured, I place it on the coaster and turn my attention to Collin. "And for you?"

"Same as the idiot," he replies with a hint of a smile on his lips.

Lips I want to kiss...

Just as I turn to grab a second frosted mug from the cooler, I hear Cade ask, "Are you sure you want to hang out with this loser, Lizzie Lou? I'm undoubtedly the better choice. I know you turned me down before, but I'd give you a second chance, because you obviously weren't thinking clearly the last time we talked."

I can feel Collin's eyes on me as I deliver the second draft to the bar. Placing my elbows on the hard top in front of Cade, I lean forward and whisper, "The loser kisses like a dream, so I'm all set, thanks."

Collin barks out a laugh and slaps Cade on the shoulder. "Second place, my friend."

Cade stands up and grabs his beer, sloshing a bit over the rim of his glass. "I'm going to go cry in my beer over there."

With that, he takes off toward the regulars, instantly jumping into conversation. "Clearly he's devastated again."

Collin snorts in response and takes a drink of his beer. "Clearly." Then he adds, "I didn't tell him anything...about us."

My eyebrow draws upward in question once more.

"He just...knew. I know that's probably hard to believe, but I swear, I didn't say a word about last night. He just guessed. Accurately, I might add."

I shrug and move over to where he sits, leaning forward on the bar. I don't miss the way his eyes drop to the hint of cleavage flashing in the neck of my shirt. "I'm not embarrassed, Collin."

"I'm not either, but I don't usually kiss and tell. Well, at least I didn't in this case."

"Noted," I reply.

The door opens, causing us both to look that way. When I see his youngest brother, Camden, walk in with a group of friends, Collin sighs. "I'm going to apologize in advance."

"For what?"

The group instantly runs toward Collin, yelling loudly until they reach where he sits. Then, as if he weighs nothing, they hoist him up above their heads, carrying him off toward the pool table. I'm left standing here, my mouth hanging open in shock.

"Crap! I missed it," Charli states the moment she walks through the door less than a minute later.

"What was that?" I ask, my wide eyes still glued to the group of guys who have finally set Collin on the floor and are harassing the hell out of him. The only thing that keeps me from intervening is the fact Collin is smiling, so I know it's nothing nefarious.

"Collin had a rescue Thursday night at work," she says, the pride evident in her voice. "Apparently, he told Mom when she was talking to him Friday morning on his way home."

"Oh, that's cool."

She grins and nods. "He doesn't like to tell people about those times though, and Mom let it slip. Apparently, he and his coworker, Gio, saw a man trapped on the second floor, hanging out of a window. They got there just in time to catch him when he jumped."

"Wow," I reply, picturing the scene and the harrowing rescue, as I glance toward the man himself.

"I heard the guy who jumped suffered a few minor burns and smoke inhalation, but for the most part, he's okay. He could have really hurt himself jumping out of the window if it hadn't been for Collin and Gio."

I nod, still staring across the room at Collin. As if feeling my eyes, he glances my way and offers a slight smile. I can tell he hates the attention, but there's also a sense of pride in the way he grins and accepts the accolades from his friends and family.

I end up buying a round for the bar in honor of Collin, which he hates, mostly because of the extra attention it garners. He accepts the toast his twin makes, even if his cheeks are a little pink throughout it.

I also get to meet his core group of friends, the ones he's close to and grew up with. I can definitely tell why he likes them. They're a rowdy bunch, but they all seem to click. It makes me long for those I was close to back home, even if the majority of those people were my family and extended family.

Now, the place has cleared out as the nine o'clock closing time approaches. Collin and his group left around six to eat and probably crash early, thanks to the few drinks they enjoyed throughout the afternoon. I smile as I clean and prepare the bar to close. I sweep and mop, make sure everything is wiped down, and haul the garbage to the back door. When the clock strikes nine, I flip off the open sign and lock the front door. It was dead almost the entire last hour, thanks to a rare Sunday evening with no professional ball games on TV. Plus, it was such a gorgeous weekend— one of the first real warm ones in May—and it appears everyone chose to be at home, probably cooking out or doing whatever else they do around here during the summer. If there's one thing I know, the hot, humid days are coming soon.

Summer is stretching her legs, preparing to hang out for a while.

I don't mind summer. It's the humidity that gets me. When you have curls in your hair, humidity is the worst thing in the world. It doesn't matter how much product you put in your hair, it's a frizzy ball of fuzz that looks nothing like the infomercials for haircare products.

I get the register counted and the tip jar emptied. I'm shocked to see as much cash as what's in there, but I suppose it was pretty hopping this afternoon. Collin and his crew hung out for several hours, shooting pool, listening to music, and generally harassing each other like friends do. It was actually a really good time. Charli came to the bar and sat with me numerous times, and the more I get to know her, the more I like her. In fact, I'm going to call the salon next week and schedule an appointment for a massage. I've never had one, but with the way I've overworked my body these last few weeks, I could definitely use one.

Just as I put the deposit and cash drawer in the safe, I hear the back door open. Since that one is locked from the outside, I know it's someone with a key to get in. A zing of anticipation slides through my veins, and my nipples harden at the thought of Collin being here. Then, he's there, filling the doorway to my office with his confidence and charisma.

"Hey," he says softly, the deep timbre of his voice rumbling through my core like a freight train.

"Hi," I reply, locking the safe and turning my full attention his way. "How was dinner?"

He smiles and holds up a container. "It was good. I brought you something to eat. I wasn't sure if you got to eat anything this evening."

As if on cue, my stomach growls, making us both chuckle. "No, I haven't eaten yet. What'd you bring me?" I ask, stepping closer.

He grins. "Come on. You can head upstairs, and I'll throw the trash in the dumpster."

"I can do it," I respond, not wanting him to think I'm not capable of getting two trash bags inside the trash receptacle outside.

"I know you can, but then these French fries will get cold. Might as well eat them while they're still hot, because cold fries are nasty," he says, and I realize it's a losing battle. Not just because I'm hungry, but simply because he would never stand around and watch me take out the trash and hoist it up and into the dumpster. He's not sexist. It's chivalry, considerate.

Taking the food container, I head for the stairs, while he locks the back door for the bar and grabs the garbage bags, easily lifting them up and heading out the back door to discard them. My mouth waters as I catch a whiff of the contents of the container, and even though I only know of fries, I can't wait to dive in.

Unlocking my apartment door, I slip inside, leaving the door open for Collin. I set the container on the counter and finally open the lid, practically drooling over the delicious smelling food. I grab the bottle of ketchup from the fridge and move to the small kitchenette table. Squirting a blob of ketchup onto the lid, I dive into the fries as the back door opens, closes, and footfalls echo up the stairs as Collin heads this way.

"Oh my God, where did you get this?" I ask, taking a huge bite of the juicy cheeseburger.

"The diner. They were closing, so I had to kinda take whatever I could talk them into."

After swallowing, I state, "I should feel bad for them having to make food at closing, but this is amazing."

"Yeah, I get their smashburger anytime it's on the menu. I wasn't sure your thoughts on grilled onions and pickles, but I figured they'd be easy enough to pick off if you don't like them."

"Pickles? The more the merrier, and I don't mind onions," I tell him between bites.

Collin washes his hands, then retrieves two bottles of water and joins me at the table, setting one in front of me.

"Is that where you guys ate?" I ask, coating a fry in ketchup and popping it into my mouth.

"Naw, we went to the Mexican restaurant. Charli has a love affair going with their queso."

I nod. "Anytime you can eat cheese, especially in dip form, is a good day."

He chuckles. "You sound just like her."

After a few minutes of sitting in comfortable silence while I eat, I wipe my mouth off and ask the question I've been wondering. "So, the save... the person is gonna be okay?" Even though Charli told me what she heard, I want to hear it from him, if he's willing to talk about it.

"He will be. He would have been if he would have had to jump, but he would have been in a lot worse shape." He holds my gaze and asks, "I assume you heard about it from Charli?"

I nod and take another bite. "She explained why Camden and your friends came into the bar and did what they did. I was about ready to run over there with my broom and start whacking them."

He barks out a laugh. "You were going to rescue me...with a broom?"

"Well, there were a bunch of them, and they were bigger than me. I'm not going to show up empty-handed. I've worked in this industry long enough to know words aren't a very powerful weapon when you're talking to drunks in a bar."

He cracks a smile. "They weren't drunk."

"Not this time, but still. It didn't happen too often at Burgers and Brew because it's built a reputation of not dealing with bullshit. They have a no tolerance policy. You act up, you get thrown out. No exceptions. My uncle Tank has been in charge of security since they opened, and no one fucks with him."

"I can see why," he replies, just sitting there, watching me.

"Anyway, it did happen on occasion, but I never had to actually get between two guys about to come to blows. Women, however, were a different story."

"Really?" he asks, so I tell him all about the chick fights that would occasionally break out, always over a man.

By the time my food is almost gone, I'm stuffed. "Want the rest?"

"No thank you," he replies, his penetrating gaze locked on me. "You good?" he asks, grabbing my container and tossing it in the trash. "Get enough to eat?"

"Too much," I confirm, realizing it wasn't very ladylike to devour a burger and fries the way I did, yet not really caring. I was hungry, and I'm not about to starve just so I don't eat in front of a guy.

Turning, he leans against the fridge and asks, "Tired?"

I shake my head.

"What would you like to do?" he asks, pushing off the fridge and stalking toward me. Yes, stalking. That's the only way to describe it. It's like a lion watching the gazelle, moving slowly and quietly to get in the perfect position to pounce.

"We could watch a movie," I suggest with no real desire to do that.

"We could."

"Or we could play Uno."

When he reaches my side, the corner of his mouth ticks upward. "Uno?"

I shrug. "I grew up with family game nights. There's no friends in Uno though. I'll throw a Draw Four at my mom and laugh the whole time she's picking cards."

He chuckles, extending his hand. "Good to know."

When I stand, I wrap my arms around his shoulders and slide my fingers along the column of his neck. "Or we could do...*other* things."

"Other things besides movies and Uno? Keep talking..."

I'm not the most direct person out there, but I don't shy away from being bold. Leaning forward and pressing my chest to his, I move to my tiptoes and kiss just below his jaw. "What I have in mind involves a lot less clothes and zero sleep."

I feel his already hard cock jerk in his pants, and he hums and swallows. "Not exactly the taking things slow we talked about last night, Lizzie."

"No, but I'm not going to ignore the fact I want you. Bad."

His gaze is pure fire as he peers at me. "You're sure? Because we really can play Uno or watch a movie."

I snort and shake my head. "We'll call that Plan B."

"So, this Plan A...what exactly does it entail?" he asks.

"Orgasms, Collin. Lots and lots of them."

A pained groan erupts from his mouth moments before it slams into mine. This kiss turns feral in less than a second, and I find myself climbing him like a tree. My legs are wrapped around his waist, my arms around his neck, and I still don't feel close enough. The need I feel for him explodes like a bomb, incinerating every part of my soul and leaving me raw and yearning for more.

We're moving moments later, his long legs eating up the space between us and my bedroom. Just as we cross the threshold, he rips his mouth from mine and says, "You can stop this at any point."

"I don't want to stop," I insist, rolling my hips against his erection.

"Fuck, do that again and this might be over before it really begins," he mutters, closing his eyes.

"What, this?" I ask coyly, rocking once more and grinding myself along his cock.

"Christ, woman," he mumbles, spinning us around and gently depositing me on top of my bed. His eyes burn like fire, those blue orbs a navy ring of desire. "Strip."

"You're awfully bossy," I start, standing up and toeing my athletic shoes off my feet.

When he doesn't say a word, I look up and find him watching me. Suddenly, I realize what he meant. He wants me to strip so he can watch.

A fresh wave of desire races through me. I've taken off my clothes in front of men before, but I've never felt this…seen. Raw. Aroused.

Slowly, I grab the hem of my T-shirt and lift it over my head. Taking a quick mental inventory, I'm so grateful to have slipped on a prettier set of undergarments. The light blue satin set isn't super sexy, but at least it's not made just for comfort.

When I drop the shirt onto the floor, I glance up and watch as he devours me with his eyes. He scans my chest and licks his lips, resulting in goosebumps peppering my entire body.

Dropping my hands to the fly of my jeans, his eyes follow, watching, waiting. I flick the button open and slide down the zipper before starting to shimmy out of my blue jeans. I feel the burn of his eyes on me every moment I step out of my jeans and kick them to the side. After adjusting the waistband, I slip my socks off and finally stand up. Our eyes meet in a flurry of reckless need.

"On the bed," he states, reaching down and pulling his T-shirt over his head.

I do as instructed, breathing harder than I should be as anticipation races through my blood. He takes off his boots and socks before releasing the button and zipper on his jeans. I'm sad, however, when he doesn't remove those too. Instead, he climbs onto the bed, still wearing his jeans.

"Aren't you going to take those off?" I ask as he positions his body between my spread legs, lying between them.

He looks up and shakes his head. "If I take them off, I'm liable to rush this, and I'm not going to do that." He sets his sights at the wet satin between my legs. "You hold all the cards, Lizzie. You say stop, I stop."

"While I understand and appreciate the sentiment, if you don't hurry up, I might die."

He chuckles, moving his fingers and lazily dragging them across my wet panties. "That seems a little extreme, Lizzie. Die of ecstasy, maybe," he states with a little smirk.

"Well, that has yet to be proven."

His eyes flare as my challenge is laid out. One I can already tell he accepts, and if he has anything to say about it, will succeed over and over again. Collin's intensity is evident, and something tells me he's not a quick hit it and quit it kind of guy. Not by a long shot. I have a feeling I'm in for quite a ride. "Reach up and grab the headboard."

I look over my head, taking note of the wood slats of my headboard. When I hesitate, he removes his finger from my panties and demands, "Headboard. Now."

The firmness laced with arousal has my body responding. My nipples are so hard they ache, and a fresh wave of wetness floods my core as I quickly wrap my hands around the slats and look down. I don't even realize I'm holding my breath until he gently instructs me to breathe.

"Sorry," I murmur, taking a few deep, calming breaths. Once I do, I feel his finger return to the apex of my legs.

Collin slides his thick index finger across my folds before gently slipping it beneath the satin. "I've been thinking about this. A lot. More than I should admit."

"Me too," I reply, his touch fueling the flames.

"What have you been thinking about?"

"You want a detailed list?" I tease.

"That would be great, thanks," he says, lazily dragging his finger through my wetness and creating even more.

I lift my head and meet his gaze, instantly realizing he's not joking. He's waiting on me to list out all the things I've been daydreaming about him doing to me. "Well, let's see. Since we've already stripped—well, mostly—I suppose I can skip that. I thought about your mouth between my legs."

"What is my mouth doing?"

My heart is hammering a million beats per second as I close my eyes and let the sensations wash over me. Just the simplest touch feels so fucking good, so fucking right.

His finger stops moving. "Tell me, Lizzie."

I open my eyes, trying to figure out what it was I am supposed to be telling him. Then it hits me, and I feel my cheeks flush even warmer. "Licking me."

"Like this?" He bends down and slides his tongue from the bottom of my clit to the top.

"Umm, yeah, just like that," I reply through a gasp. Reaching down, I thread my fingers into his hair, causing him to stop.

"Hands on the headboard."

I immediately do as instructed, even though I'd much rather be touching him.

I feel his warm breath against my core as he whispers, "Good girl. Now hang on tight."

CHAPTER FIFTEEN

Collin

ER TASTE EXPLODES ON MY TONGUE, AND I HAVE TO GRASP AT
every ounce of control I possess so I don't just say screw this and
take her hard and fast. But that's not how I want our first time
together to go. She's not just some quick fuck to scratch an itch.

She's…more.

Sliding my tongue through her pussy, I listen as her breathing hitches
and feel as she tenses beneath me. "What else?"

"Fingers," she murmurs softly, keeping her hands positioned above
her head.

"One or two?" I ask, already slipping the tip of my thumb at her
entrance.

"Start with one. It's, uh, been a while."

I revel in the thought, of knowing no other man has been here, tasted
what I now consider mine, for some time. "How long?"

I'm met with silence, so I lift my tongue from her pussy until she answers, "About a year."

I groan. My balls ache. It's been about a year since anyone tasted or touched this pussy, and I'm about to blow in my damn pants.

"Where's my reward for answering the question?" she asks, lifting her head and glancing down at me with a smirk.

"Yes, ma'am," I reply before lowering to her clit and sucking it hard into my mouth. As she gasps from pleasure, I slide my thumb into her hot, wet pussy. I can feel the tightness, feel her muscles already pulsing. I can't wait to experience the taste of her release. It's all I can think about.

All I crave.

I keep my tempo steady as she starts to relax around me, alternating between sucking on her clit and licking. Her body is starting to move, her hips rocking as she seeks out more of that sweet friction. When she's ready, I slip a second finger inside and feel her stretch around them.

"How do you get off, Lizzie? On that list of yours. What makes you come?" I ask, watching her chest rise and fall rapidly as I flatten my tongue on her clit and apply pressure.

"Fingers and mouth. Both. Together."

Your wish is my command.

I thrust both fingers inside and curl them upward. Her gasp fills the room and triggers a fresh wave of wetness. Her pussy is getting tighter, and I know she's close. I need her to come on my fingers, on my mouth, more than I need air, and I'm determined to give her everything she needs before we take this any further.

"Oh, God," she whimpers, gyrating against my mouth and chasing her release. "So close."

"Come, Lizzie. I want to feel it. Taste it."

And she does. As if triggered by my words, she detonates beautifully. She squeezes my fingers so hard I can barely move them, but I keep my mouth on her clit, drawing out every last drop of her orgasm she has left. Her legs are pressed firmly against my face as she cries out, riding the waves of pleasure.

When her body is sated, she goes limp, making me chuckle. "You all right up there?" I ask, gently drawing my fingers out of her pussy, which spasms around me.

"Dead."

"Mmm, but what a way to go," I murmur, nuzzling the soft hair above her pussy with my nose. I'll commit the feel of her, her scent, everything about her to memory and pull it out on the nights I'm alone and needing her.

"Can I move my arms?"

"Yes." When she does, I add, "Good girl." Reaching for them, I rub her forearms, helping make sure the blood is circulating once more. "You okay?"

She gives me the most breathtaking smile I've ever witnessed. "Are you kidding? I'm great."

I rise to my knees and take her in once more. Her panties are stretched, her pussy bare and wet. She's a dream, and for now—for tonight—she's mine.

Taking her hand, I help her stand. "Let's get this off, shall we?" I reach for the clasp of her bra and release the closure.

She drops the bra onto the floor and quickly shimmies out of her panties, discarding them on the floor too. She stands before me, completely naked, and every bit the fantasy I've envisioned since the moment I met her. "You're stunning," I say, drinking her in.

I don't miss the blush on her cheeks or the way she doesn't shy away from me. "May I?" she asks, stepping forward and reaching for the opening of my jeans. When I nod, she grabs the waist and starts to push them down.

The moment my cock pops free, her eyes zero in on my erection. She wraps her soft hand around my hardness and gives it a gentle squeeze. Precum oozes from the tip as I fight not to thrust in her palm, desperate to find my own release.

She looks up and locks eyes with me. "May I?"

I have to swallow over the dryness and lump in my throat as I nod in approval. I'm in complete awe as she drops to her knees and looks up at me. My pants are still around my knees, but I don't give a shit. I'm transfixed on the beauty before me as she leans forward and swipes her tongue across the head of my cock. Precum oozes and strings from point A to B, and I swear I'm about to blow right now.

Her green eyes locked on mine, she moves forward, drawing me inside her warm, wet mouth. A groan erupts from my soul as I watch her make slow, steady strokes of her hand, while licking and sucking me. My hand wraps around her ponytail, mostly to give me some form of leverage. I feel like I'm teetering on the edge of a cliff, one tiny move away from falling. Her hair is soft, those blond curls like silk in my palm.

I wonder what her bare ass will feel like against said palm.

Her pace picks up, and I try to compartmentalize the sensations, but it's hard—no pun intended. I realize all too quickly I'm growing dangerously close to exploding inside her mouth. She sucks hard, drawing me farther down her throat and twisting her hand against the root of my dick.

I'm on the verge of coming.

But not like this.

I pull back, dislodging my cock from her hot mouth. She gapes up at me with wide, wild eyes so full of lust. Reaching out, I cup her jaw and gaze down at her. "I'm not coming in your mouth. At least not the first time."

She gives me a sassy grin as I help her stand. "I'll look forward to that next."

I crack a smile myself, my cock twitching with anticipation. "Me too. Now, turn around," I state, all evidence of my smile gone. With my hands on her hips, she moves to face the bed. She's about to climb on when I add, "No, right here."

When I know she's going to stay, I step back and remove my jeans and boxers, grabbing a condom from my wallet before kicking them out of the way. I make quick work at covering my dick with protection, feeling her eyes on me as I go. Finally, I'm ready.

Oh, I am so fucking ready.

She meets my eyes as I ask, "You're sure?"

Standing up straight, she reaches back and slides her hand in my hair,

steering my mouth down to hers. I can still taste her cum on my tongue as she whispers, "More than sure."

"Then lean forward," I instruct, holding on to her hips as she places her hands on the bed.

My view is absolutely perfect. Her ass, the curves of her hips, her blond hair pulled away from her face in a ponytail. I cup the globe of her ass cheek before reaching down and lining up my cock with her pussy. She takes a small step to the side, giving me a little more space to slide to her entrance. I'm there, ready. With my hands holding her hips firmly, I ask once more, "Ready?"

Her answer is to push back, taking the head of my dick inside her body.

With that, I move in one slow, steady push forward. I don't thrust, even though my body craves it. I make sure she's okay and adjusts to the invasion first. When I'm fully seated inside her, the muscles of her pussy already starting to grip me, I stop.

"No, don't stop," she whispers, rocking her hips to try to create more friction.

"I need to make sure you're okay," I insist, gripping her skin and holding her still.

"Please, Collin." Her plea is raw, a whimper in the still of night.

Pulling back almost completely out, I thrust, filling her a second time with a little more force. Our mixed groans and the sound of my hips hitting her ass fill the room. Both are the fuel we add to an already raging inferno.

I start to pump, letting my hands slide around to the front of her hips. Lizzie lifts her torso and throws her hands over her shoulders, grasping my head. Her nails dig into my scalp as I pull her back against my chest. Sliding my right hand up, I cup her breast, holding it in my palm and pinching the tip of her nipple. She gasps and drives against me, her push to my pull.

My mouth finds her neck, licking and sucking on her sweet skin. My first thought is to mark her, to let everyone know I was there.

That she's mine.

She cries out, bucking hard back against me, riding my cock. She's

chasing her release, as am I. I feel her muscles start to tighten, gripping my dick with their pleasurable force. My balls draw up, but I will not come unless she's with me.

"Come, sweet Lizzie. I want to feel your pussy squeeze my cock."

She whimpers as I roll her nipple between my thumb and index finger and reach down between her legs with my other hand. I find her clit and swipe my fingers over the hard, swollen bud. My mouth sucks on her neck, and I feel it happen. The moment she comes on me, against me, for me.

She tightens so much it's almost hard to move, but I do, triggering my own release. My spine tingles as I come hard, driving inside her body and emptying myself in the condom. I feel every ripple of her muscles, milking every drop of my release. She shivers against me before leaning forward, her hands moving from my head to the bed as she sags forward.

I do the same, pressing a kiss to the back of her neck, her shoulders, her spine. My hands move over her slick skin before landing gently on her hips. I carefully pull out, even though I don't want to. I'd much rather remain exactly where I am, buried deep inside her and ready for another round.

But that can wait...

When I stand up and take in the sight of her, I feel something shift in my chest. It's not just from great sex, but for the simple fact it's her. She's felt different all along, and tonight just proves it. I don't feel the urge to run away, to offer a quick thanks for the good time. Instead, I want to crawl into bed beside her and hold her close. I want to talk and get to know her even better, learning about her past and her dreams for the future.

I want more than just this one night, and I hope she feels the same.

"I'll be right back," I say, needing to get rid of the condom.

Quickly slipping into the hallway, I step inside the bathroom and close the door. I look at the reflection in the mirror, surprised by what I see. Not a man with a wounded soul and a jaded past, but one who's smiling and anxious for more. Sure, more sex, but also more Lizzie.

I make quick work at tossing the condom in the trash and cleaning up. I crack a smile at the floral décor, the stark opposite of the ugly vanity,

tile, and floor in the small space. She may not be able to change the appearance of this room quite yet, but she's doing her best to make it homey and inviting.

Grabbing a second washcloth, I wet it with warm water and exit the room. Returning to where I left Lizzie, I find her in bed, beneath the soft green and ivory bedding. "I brought you this," I state as I approach, holding out the cloth.

She reaches for it, but I keep it just out of grasp. Instead, I pull back the bedding and set out to help her clean up. The only light in the room filters through the window and the hallway, but even then, I can still see the remnants of her arousal. I hate to clean it off, but I don't want her to be uncomfortable when she tries to sleep.

As I finish wiping her off, she wraps her arms around my neck and pulls me down to cover her. I go willingly, careful not to squish her as I cover her body with my own. I toss the cloth onto the floor and let my fingers glide into her hair. Our kiss is gentle, tender even, yet still causes life to stir inside me once more.

I roll to the side, pulling her with me. She tosses her right leg over mine and cuddles into my side. Her fingers dance against my chest as she brushes her lips across my stubbly jaw. Finally, I reach down and pull the bedding up to cover us. "Is this all right?" I ask.

"Of course," she replies, relaxing into my embrace as she rests her head on my shoulder and glides her fingertips along my neck. "You're kinda bossy," she murmurs, a hint of humor in her voice.

"Is it too much?" I'm not domineering, but I do like to be in control, if that makes sense. I've always liked to take charge, but don't have to have it to get off.

"No," she replies immediately. "I liked it."

All I feel is the touch of her skin against mine. It's relaxing, comfortable. "Good," I whisper, leaning forward and pressing a kiss to her forehead. "The truth is, I like to take control in the bedroom, but don't let that scare you. In reality, you're the one in control. I would never do anything you didn't want me to."

"So, I'm the boss downstairs, but you're the boss up here?" she asks, smiling coyly at me and making me grin in return.

"I like the sound of that," I state, feeling my body truly relax with her snuggled against me.

"Me too," she agrees through a yawn.

After a beat, I ask, "Is this okay?"

As if completely understanding what I mean, she says, "Yes. I like you here."

Here in her bed, in her arms, in her life. I hope she means all of it.

"I do too," I murmur softly.

"Good night," she whispers, those two words already heavy with sleep.

"Night, sweet Lizzie."

I know the moment she falls asleep in my arms. Her breathing evens out and her body grows limp. And as tired as I feel, sleep doesn't find me right away. I just lie here and enjoy being with her. I notice every twitch of her body, every soft murmur as she sleeps.

I think about what this means.

We agreed we'd take it slow and just see where it goes, but after only one night with her, I'm ready to jump into the dark abyss of the unknown with both feet.

It's hard for me to wrap my head around that, honestly. I've been pretty closed off for the last eight years, thanks to the betrayal of the woman I loved. I've dated over the years, but looking back, I know I kept them at arm's length. Lizzie's the first one I've *wanted* to draw in, to let her get closer than anyone before her.

She holds all the cards and has the ability to destroy me if I'm not careful.

But I can't get over the feeling of her right now, in my arms. It's not just having *someone* there.

It's her.

And as much as that scares me, I refuse to hide from it. I make a living out of running into the flames when everyone else is running out. So, like we said, we'll take this day by day and see where it goes. It doesn't mean I'm falling for her or ready to jump into marriage, but it does mean I'm keeping my eyes open and staying out of my head. It's pretty simple, really. A simple request to just stay present.

Just feel.

And if I start to feel something more?

Well, we'll cross that bridge when I get there.

CHAPTER SIXTEEN

Lizzie

I RUN MY HAND OVER HIS BARE CHEST, LOVING THE WAY HIS BLOND hair tickles my palm. I let my hand slowly trail down his abdomen to where his hard cock is resting. My fingers glide down that hard, yet soft, skin before I wrap my fingers around the appendage.

"Well, good morning to me," he murmurs quietly, his voice so sexy when it's full of sleep.

"Hi," I reply, squeezing and stroking.

He grunts and bucks his hips. It feels quite powerful, as a woman, to have this much control over a man with the slightest touch. I shift to my knees, keeping my hand on him and moving. Lowering my mouth, I swipe my tongue over the tip, tasting his arousal. He jerks in my hand, that simple little touch causing such a reaction.

Painstakingly slow, I suck him into my mouth, holding his gaze as I do. There's no hint of sleep in his blue eyes now. He's wide awake, those sapphire orbs burning with need. Just as I start to bring him back out, an idea hits me. Kissing the tip of his cock, I firmly state, "Grab on to the headboard."

His eyebrows shoot up in question, humor suddenly dancing across his features. "Excuse me?"

I completely release my hold on him, letting his cock flop back onto his stomach. "What's good for the goose is good for the gander. Grab the headboard. Now."

He openly smiles, reaching behind him and grabbing the headboard. "Good boy," I coo, mirroring much of what happened last night when he was in control.

He chuckles, holding on to the slats behind his head. "Do your worst."

Taking him back in my hand, I stroke him from root to tip. "Oh, I plan to do my best."

Then, I lower my mouth to him and get to work. His entire body is tense as I twist my hand and bear down on him. I bob my head, taking him as deep as I can without gagging. It doesn't take long before his entire body is shaking, his release looming. I feel him swell even more in my hand. He's close.

"If you don't want me coming down your throat, pull back now."

His statement only fuels my need to finish him off down my throat. Twisting my hand, I reach down to cup his balls, sending him over the edge. He comes hard, his body jolting and spasming as I swallow. Only when he stops moving and sags heavily against the bed do I stop.

Sitting up straight, I can't help but feel pretty proud of myself.

"I know you're smiling," he mutters, taking a deep breath. Opening heavily hooded eyes he grins and says, "And you should be. That was pretty fucking amazing."

"Happy to hear you enjoyed it," I reply.

"Oh, I did," he confirms before reaching out and grabbing my arms. As if I weigh nothing, I'm moving through the air and positioned over his head. "Grab on to the headboard."

My eyes are wide as I glance down. His blue ones are full of determination as he watches me. "What are you doing?" I ask, even though I'm pretty sure I already know the answer.

He just grins wide and licks his lips. "I heard breakfast was the most important meal of the day, so I thought I'd go ahead and eat mine right now."

And he does…

"What are your plans for today?" Collin asks, watching me over the rim of his coffee cup. When I jumped in the shower, he walked down to the coffee shop and grabbed us a couple of drinks and muffins. Now, we're sitting at the dinette and finishing off our breakfast.

I shrug, popping the last bite of banana chocolate chip muffin into my mouth. "I'm not sure. Guy works today, so I'm not needed there until four. I really need to catch up on laundry."

"What if you start a load of laundry, and then come with me?"

I look up into his piercing blue gaze. "Where?"

He lifts his shoulders. "Out. It's supposed to be a gorgeous day, and you're still fairly new here. I can give you the grand tour, and the best part is, since it's a Monday, most everyone will be at work."

Shifting in my seat, I ask, "Don't you have stuff to do today? You work tomorrow."

"Naw, I'm good. I have a little laundry to do and pack for work, but I can do that later."

The thought of exploring Cooper Town does offer a little extra excitement to my day, especially with Collin as my tour guide. I know where all the basics are—the grocery store, the bank, and other local retailers—but I've never really been able to just drive around and discover all the wonderful little things that make this a great small town. You know, the parks, cute homes, and schools.

"Are you sure? I'm sure you have something better to do than chauffeur me around town," I insist, even though I really want to join him.

"I'm sure. What do you want to see?"

My eyebrows shoot upward. "Everything?"

He chuckles and nods. "All right then. If we're going to see everything, we should get ready to head out soon. Unless you want to go back to the bedroom and let me have *breakfast* again." He waggles his eyebrows suggestively, making me giggle. I've never seen this carefree and relaxed side to him, and frankly, I like it. A lot. Broody Collin is sexy, but this playful version is downright sinful.

I finish getting ready for the day, which consists of a little makeup and splashing on some of my favorite perfume. I leave my hair down, the curls somewhat tame, and grab my crossbody bag and a pair of sunglasses.

"You don't mind if we swing by my place so I can run through the shower quick and change, do you?"

I turn around and find Collin standing in the doorway of my bedroom, leaning against the jamb. He's wearing yesterday's clothes and manages to look positively delicious, despite them being wrinkled from being tossed on the floor. "Of course not. I assumed you would want to."

He nods and pushes off, stalking toward me. When he reaches my side, he gently slaps me on the ass and says, "Let's go, woman. I'm wearing yesterday's socks, and I *hate* that."

I giggle and open my top dresser drawer. "I have a pair you can borrow." Holding up the white ankle socks, I flash him a cheesy grin.

"No thanks," he replies, grabbing the socks and tossing them back in the drawer. "Socks are the first thing I change when I get back to the firehouse after a call. I remember being at basic military training in Texas, and I felt like my feet were always wet from sweat. I can't stand it now. I walk around barefoot almost all year when I'm home. My toes like to breathe."

I glance down, but he's wearing his boots already. "Makes sense," I agree, and together we head for my door.

We move down the stairs after making sure the door is locked and push out the back. The sun is shining high in the sky, the air warm and promising. "It's going to be a beautiful day," I note unnecessarily.

He takes my hand in his and smiles. "Agreed."

I climb inside the cab of Collin's truck and together, we make our way to his place. He lives on Oak Street, several blocks from where the bar is. I take in our surroundings: the streets, the houses, the people. "I love small towns. I've only ever lived in a bigger city for college, and I couldn't wait to get back to Stewart Grove when I was done. I can't imagine living anywhere else."

He glances my way for a brief moment before returning his eyes to the road. "I agree."

"Where all did you live when you were in the Air Force?"

"I started in Texas, at Lackland Air Force Base. I went through training there before being sent to Goodfellow Air Force base then to Fairchild in Washington state. It was pretty cool, except I hated winters there. But I learned a lot. We did a lot of air refueling and supported the West Coast tanker fleet."

I watch his facial features, and even from the side can see the emotions crossing over his face. Pride, fondness, and even stoicism. "Thank you for your service," I find myself saying and meaning it wholeheartedly.

He flashes me the hint of a smile before focusing on the road ahead once more. "After Washington, I was lucky enough to spend my last year in the UK at Lakenheath."

My eyes widen in surprise. "Seriously? That's amazing," I say, suddenly wanting to know more about his time overseas. "Tell me everything."

He snorts and keeps his gaze locked straight ahead. "After my time in Washington, I was given the opportunity to go to Lakenheath in Suffolk, England. Largest base in the UK and cool as shit. We flew a lot of aircrafts in and out of that place."

"Only a year?"

Something crosses his face once more, and it's gone almost immediately. If I hadn't been staring straight at him, I would have missed it. After a few seconds he finally nods. "Yeah, only a year. Overseas are usually shorter assignments. I got a year, and at the end of it, they asked me to stay." He swallows hard.

"But you didn't."

"Nope," he replies, turning into a driveway and parking in front of the garage. When the truck is shut off, he turns to me and adds, "I just wanted to be home. I enjoyed my time in the military and got to experience things

I never would have otherwise, but…stuff had happened back home, and my heart was heavy. I missed my family and all my focus was shifted."

I nod, understanding what he's saying, but at the same time, I feel like there's a lot more he's *not* saying. Reaching over, I place my hand on his and give it a gentle squeeze. "There's a story there."

He looks down at where we touch and keeps his gaze there for several seconds. When he meets my eyes, I have all the confirmation I need. "There is."

"Let me guess, it involves a woman?" I flash him a grin, hoping to keep the mood light.

"Doesn't it always?" He rewards me with his own small smile.

"Usually, yes. Or someone of the opposite sex, as I've come to learn. Being a bartender is the equivalent of an unpaid therapist, so I'm used to being an ear to bend when someone is going through something deep."

"It's a heavy conversation," he finally states, his voice low and his words raw.

"And when you're ready to share it, I'll listen. And not just because I'm a bartender. Because I want to know you."

His blue eyes are stormy as he watches me. "I want to know you also, and I get that means I need to share my past too." He swallows hard but doesn't look away. "I just don't talk about it. It's hard."

I release my seat belt and climb over the console of his truck. It's not easy, considering his size and the steering wheel, but I manage. My leg is wedged between his and the door and the steering wheel is lodged in my back, but at the same time, it's the most comfortable spot in the world.

Because I'm straddling him.

His hands slide around my hips and rest on my lower back. "I'll be here when you're ready. I don't know where this thing will go between us, but I'm enjoying my time with you. When you're ready to tell me about what causes that pain in your eyes, I'll listen. Without judgment." Cupping his cheek, I feel him relax beneath my touch. "But I make no promises on the bitch that hurt you. I'll definitely judge her. Maybe even throw hands."

He snorts out a laugh and pulls me hard against his chest. "You could definitely take her."

Wrapping my arms around his neck, I revel in the feel of his hard body pressed firmly against mine. "Oh, I know I could. I'm scrappy as hell."

His bark of laughter fills the cab and my soul. I love it when he laughs, mostly because I know they're more meaningful, since he doesn't do it often. "I don't doubt it." He presses his lips to mine in a gentle, chaste kiss. "What do you say we go inside so I can get ready?"

"That sounds really good," I reply, rocking my hips and feeling him grow hard.

He grunts, trying to shift his position to alleviate the discomfort of his sudden erection. "I was talking about my shower and change of clothes."

I slide my core against his length, watching as his eyes dilate and fill with desire. "Me too. I thought I'd help."

"I'll never turn down an offer like that," he replies gruffly.

"Then what are we doing in your truck, talking?"

Suddenly, we're moving.

Or, at least I am.

Just as I climb out of the truck cab and he goes to follow, we realize the issue. His seat belt is still on, and he's sort of dangling from the truck. I can't help but laugh as he scrambles to release the belt and shut the door. The moment he stands before me, all fits of laughter die on my lips. He looks…intense. Turned on. And ready to pounce.

"You laughing at me?" he asks, the only indication he's playing is the slight tick of his lip.

"No, of course not," I insist, fighting my smile.

His response is to scoop me up and throw me over his shoulder. It happens so fast, I don't see it coming. One second I'm standing here, and the next I'm staring at his ass and being carried to his house like he just rescued me from a burning building. "Collin!" I holler as he takes his back steps in one huge leap.

Without setting me down, he unlocks the door and carts me inside. There's no tour, no formalities. Just a man desperate to get inside a woman.

And, likewise, I'm all for it. I crave his touch, hunger to feel him moving inside me. I need it more than air, more than anything.

When we reach the living room, he finally lowers me to the floor. The moment my feet are planted, he threads his hands into my hair and kisses me. He kisses me like a man possessed by the very desire I evoked within him. Our clothes are flying until we both stand naked. Then, he reaches into his wallet and retrieves the last condom, quickly covering his erection.

The second it's in place, we move. He falls onto the couch, taking me with him. I'm straddling his legs, just like I was in the truck. Only this time, with far fewer clothes in the way. "I want to watch you ride me," he states.

I lift up onto my knees, and the second I feel his erection at my entrance, I slowly sit back down. Our joint moans of pleasure fill the room. There's no time for sweetness or for making sure I adjust to the invasion. When I'm seated completely on him, I lift back up and fall more rapidly. Our bodies lead. They do all the talking. I rock my hips, grinding against him, as he fills me hard and fast. It takes no time for my orgasm to build, and when I fall, he's right there with me, catching me as we go over the edge together.

It's magic.

Perfect.

Breathing hard, I fall forward, plastering my chest to his. "That was better than I imagined," he murmurs softly, his fingers dancing across my back.

"You've been imagining that?" I ask, cracking a grin.

"From the moment you slipped across my truck cab and straddled my waist." He presses his lips to my forehead. "Come on, Lizzie. Now we really do need a shower."

CHAPTER SEVENTEEN

Collin

I DON'T THINK I'VE EVER BEEN THIS COMFORTABLE—NOT AROUND another person, except maybe my twin, and definitely not a woman. I took her to all my favorite places and shared stories associated with them. We even ran into my good friend, Wyatt, who wasn't at the little impromptu thing yesterday, since he was finishing up getting the crops in. He took great pleasure in telling her as many stories of our younger days as he could fit in a ten-minute conversation. Thankfully, he really needed to get back to the field with the lunch he grabbed for his guys.

Now, we're walking through the downtown area, after having lunch at the diner. "That's where Charli works," I say, pointing to the white brick building across the street.

"It is? Is she there?"

"Actually, it looks like she is," I state, noticing her car in the lot. "The hair place is closed, but I know Charli will work some on Monday afternoons."

We cross the street, Lizzie's hand tucked firmly in my own, and head for her building. As luck would have it, Charli is finishing up with a client inside and is standing at the counter. She spots us and holds up a finger, asking us to wait a second.

When she completes what she's doing, she walks her client to the door and releases the lock. "Have a wonderful afternoon, Ginny."

"You too, Charlotte. Say hello to your mother for me," the older woman I remember from school states. She nods at me as she passes, but I don't miss the way her lips curl up in annoyance.

"What's her problem?" I ask when Charli steps aside and waves us in.

My evil sister barks out a laugh. "What? You don't remember?"

"Remember what?" I ask, suddenly very afraid of where this is heading.

"That's Mrs. Gilmore, the home ec teacher. You glued all her cabinets shut the night before the cooking class final. No one could get in to retrieve their utensils and pans."

I groan and shake my head. "I forgot about that. And technically, that was Wyatt, Cade, and Vic. I was just along for the ride."

Charli snorts and shakes her head. "Right. You were always the innocent one." Then, she turns her attention to Lizzie and gives her a hug. "It's so good to see you. What are you doing out and about with the ugly ogre?"

Lizzie grins before replying, "We just had lunch at the diner. He's been giving me a little tour of the town, since I really only know a few places."

"Well, don't blink or you'll miss it all," Charli chirps with a chuckle.

"This place is beautiful," Lizzie sings, glancing around and taking in the space.

"Isn't it? It was the old bank, and when Jenn bought this place, it had been an office of some sort. She completely transformed it into this gorgeous salon and spa. Aren't the ceilings to die for?"

"They really are," Lizzie agrees as my sister grabs her by the arm.

"Come on, I'll give you a tour."

I remain where I am and lean against the counter as they walk off, Charli chatting a mile a minute. I've already seen the place and take the opportunity to check out Lizzie's ass as she goes. I'm trying not to be a pig, but it's a great ass. I remember exactly how it felt in my palms as she rode my cock earlier this morning on my couch.

"Seriously, you'll love it, I promise," Charli says as they reenter the main salon.

"What will she love?" I ask, inserting myself into the conversation.

"A massage." My sister moves to her scheduling app on her phone and says, "What day do you have off?"

"It can vary, based on when everyone else can work," Lizzie says. "I don't go in until four on Thursday, but that's kinda last minute."

"No, actually, that's perfect," Charli insists. "I have an eleven o'clock that just opened up on Thursday."

"Okay, I'll take it."

"Great! And then when you're here, you can talk to Lila about getting on her schedule," Charli adds, referring to her friend who is also one of the stylists.

"Perfect," Lizzie agrees, slipping her own phone back into her pocket.

"I don't know why you have to pay someone for a massage," I say, mostly because I know it'll piss my sister off, and I love to push her buttons.

Charli rolls her eyes. "Because I'm amazing at my job and it feels phenomenal."

"I could give you a massage for free," I argue, looking at Lizzie, whose face is suddenly getting red.

"Oh, please! Men think they're these great masseuses, but I beg to differ. After thirty seconds of rubbing, they're hard and just want sex!"

Lizzie bursts out laughing.

"Not true. I could totally make it five minutes," I insist, my eyes scanning her sexy body. "Okay, maybe three minutes."

Charli waves her hand. "I rest my case. A woman doesn't want to be getting felt up while she's trying to relax."

"Why not?" I ask, clearly not understanding. "I would. I think a massage sounds amazing."

Charli rolls her eyes. "That's not relaxing."

"You're right," I confirm. "The relaxing comes after." I waggle my eyebrows to punctuate my point.

"Gross," my sister says. "I don't want to think about that. It's bad enough when a man gets an erection on the table. I don't want to know how he *takes care of it* after he leaves."

My mouth falls open. "What?"

Again, my sister waves off my outrage. "It's biology, Collin. Happens all the time. It doesn't mean they're sexually aroused with me."

I groan and run my hand down my face. "We need to go. I don't want to think about that." But then something else hits me and I stop, facing my sister. "You're safe here, right?"

She rolls her eyes dramatically. "Of course I am, big brother. Like I said, it's human nature, especially for men. Most pop boners easily when a woman is rubbing all over them, and the ones who don't get an erection are so tense from trying to stop it, they don't really enjoy the massage. Relax. Literally. I'm fine."

I close my eyes and shake my head. When I open them up, I turn my attention to Lizzie. "She's going to kill me. One day, my headstone will read *Died of a Heart Attack Thanks to Charli.*"

Lizzie giggles and reaches for my hand, threading her fingers in mine. "Well, I promise not to get a boner while she's giving me a massage."

My eyes narrow.

"Well, at least not a boner, boner. A lady boner is an entirely different thing," Charli announces.

"Come on, we're leaving. And you're never allowed to be around my sister ever again," I tell Lizzie, who is laughing and waving to Charli as we head for the door.

"Bye, you two little lovebirds. Have a boner-tastic day!"

The door closes behind us, and I don't stop walking until we're back at my truck. "She's a menace," I grumble.

Lizzie leans against the passenger door and offers a smile. "She really only said all that to get under your skin."

"She makes my eye twitch," I grumble, hating how easily she gets a rise out of me.

Wrapping her arms around my waist, she draws me against her body and smiles up at me. "That's what sisters do."

"Not just sisters. Cam is the same way."

"I get it. Three younger siblings, remember?"

Unable to resist any longer, I lean forward and press my lips to hers. Lizzie's mouth opens, her tongue darting out and colliding with my own. "How was your tour?" I murmur against her lips. "If we hurry back to your place, we have enough time for a massage before you have to head down to work."

A burst of laughter seeps from her mouth as she smiles up at me. She slides her thumb over my lips, which are turned upward like her own. "I like seeing you smile so much."

My heart is galloping in my chest. "I feel like I can finally smile when I'm around you." The confession is deeper than it should be, considering how new this whole thing is between us, but that doesn't make it any less true.

"Come on," she says, shifting to the side so she can open the passenger door. "I need to get ready for work."

My eyebrows arch.

"After, big guy. Massages after."

I've been sitting at the end of the bar, nursing a glass of Coke, for the better part of an hour. Watching her.

I need to head home, to finish laundry and pack for tomorrow morning.

But I can't seem to get up off this barstool and leave.

That's why I'm still sitting here when Cade comes strolling through the door. He throws a wave to some of the regulars at the other end and flashes a big grin at Lizzie while she mixes a rum and Coke before sliding onto the empty seat beside me. "I knew I'd find you here."

"Excellent detective work, Sherlock," I mutter, taking another sip of my Coke.

Just as I place it on the coaster, Cade reaches over and steals it, taking a drink. "Eww, there's no liquor in this."

"Some people act like respectful, responsible adults and don't drink when they have to work the next day," I state, even though I know that's not my brother. He's not a huge drinker, despite hanging out at this place off and on throughout the week. Frankly, he's a social butterfly and comes up for the atmosphere and the fact he's not at home, alone.

He scoffs at my comment. "Who are these people? Sounds boring," he states as Lizzie walks up. "Hey, Lizzie Lou."

"Hello, Cade. What can I getcha?"

"I'll have what this party animal is having," he says, flinging his thumb in my direction.

"Virgin Jack and Coke it is," she replies with a grin before spinning around to retrieve the drink. As she's scooping the ice into the glass, she asks, "No hot date tonight?"

"You know I'm a one-woman man, Lizzie," my twin replies, waggling his eyebrows suggestively.

Lizzie snorts as she pours the Coke from the soda gun. "Whatever," she sasses. "You couldn't handle me."

I keep my eyes forward, feeling my cheeks heat up in a blush. What the hell? I never blush. Of course, my brother notices right away and smacks me on the arm. "I don't know about that, Lizzie Lou. Good thing my brother is the spittin' image of me. We're practically the same person."

She chuckles and shakes her head. "You two may look alike, but you are as different as night and day." Tapping the bar, she adds, "I'll let you two catch up. Holler if you need anything."

I watch her walk away, because I can't seem to help myself.

Cade whistles. "Damn, you have it bad." He takes a sip before adding, "Never thought I'd see the day."

I know exactly what he's talking about. "Me neither."

After a beat, Cade asks, "Have you seen her?"

Keeping my eyes on the baseball game on TV, I confirm, "Here and there. Haven't spoken."

I don't have to tell him how badly it hurt to see her. Living the life we were supposed to have. Together.

But looking back now, I don't even really recognize that life or the person I shared it with. Hell, I don't even recognize myself. A lot has changed since then, and it wasn't until right now that I realize it's changed for the better. I feel more settled, more content than ever before, and to be honest, I could not care less about looking over my shoulder or what people are saying about me.

My eyes seek out Lizzie, who's standing by Tom and Larry, chatting it up. She fits in so fluidly here—with me—and never in a million years did I expect to say something like that. I never expected to find myself completely enamored with an outsider, someone who blew into town and turned my life on end. As badly as I anticipated her arrival in town and at the bar to be, it was anything but.

"Have you told *her* yet?" he asks, grabbing my attention once more. There's no question as to who the *her* is he's referring to.

"No."

There's a pregnant pause before he asks, "You gonna?"

I exhale, not wanting to have this conversation right now. Not when I'm sitting in the bar, my eyes locked on the one woman I can't seem to get off my mind. I don't want to talk about Whitney. Not tonight. Not ever.

But I know that's not logical. Talking—especially about your past—is a key element in any relationship. I just never really got to that point with any of the women I've dated since the whole Whitney mess. However, I can already tell Lizzie is different. I *want* to talk to her, get to know her, share things with her, and that means I'm going to have to share what happened with my ex.

When I'm ready.

"Yeah," I finally confirm, answering his burning question.

"Good. Doesn't have to be today, but if that dopey look on your face is any indication, you're already falling for this girl. Make sure she knows everything, especially since you know Whit. Chances are, when the Cooper Town rumor mill starts its thing, she'll hear all about you and your hot new girlfriend. She's gonna have to investigate."

"She needs to mind her own fucking business," I counter, my tone downright lethal.

"Agreed, but we both know that won't happen."

I grunt in response, because he's absolutely right. In fact, I'm surprised Whitney and her posse of bitchy friends haven't already come in to give their opinions about The Tipsy Lizard. Everything from the new owner to the décor to the updated name and logo are free game when it comes to busybody gossips like that group.

"Anyway, you've done well to tune out the chatter around you, but it might be more difficult now with her," Cade says softly, referring to the woman across the bar.

"I hear ya."

"Good. The last thing I'd want is for Whit to fuck up the best thing that's happened to you in the last decade," he replies. "You have any problems, let me know. I'll sic Charli on them."

I chuckle at the thought. My sister hates my ex with the passion of a thousand fiery suns. She has no problem letting her opinion of Whitney fly and doesn't care where she's at when she does it. Of course, the feeling's mutual, mostly because Whitney knows my sister is right in what she says and has the upper hand, and Whitney hates that.

"Anyway, I'm gonna head out. We've got a bridge deck pour in the morning, and the laborers I'm shoveling with are green as fuck, which means I'll be doing most of the work."

I lift my chin as he stands.

"I don't know what's going on between you two, but I can see the difference in you. I hope whatever it is, you just stay present. It's that simple. Don't let the noise in the background fuck up a good thing," he states,

159

turning and glancing at Lizzie. "And something tells me, she's good, man. Probably too good for your dumb ass."

I snort and grin, catching her attention. We stare at each other, a secret, knowing smile on her beautiful face. "She's definitely too good for me." Taking a deep breath, I return my attention to him and add, "It's still early days, but I like her. I like the way I feel when I'm with her."

He slaps me on the back, nice and hard, the way any good brother would. "Happy to hear that. And don't piss her off. I've seen her family, and I have a feeling you'd disappear, never to be heard from again."

I want to laugh at his statement, but to be honest, I can't. While I don't get mafia vibes from them, they definitely protect their own. I have no doubt if they wanted me to disappear, they could make it happen.

And then help everyone look for my body.

"Have a good day tomorrow. Be safe," he says, throwing his hand up to wave at Lizzie. "Night, Lizzie Lou! I'll have your side of the bed ready."

She rolls her eyes and shakes her head. "Good night, Cade."

I sit here, nursing what's left of my Coke for another hour, watching her and chatting when she makes her way down to my end of the bar. Unfortunately, I need to get home, or I won't have enough clean clothes to take with me to work. I always make sure I have three days' worth, because you never know when you'll have to change or stay late.

I pull my wallet out to leave a tip and realize we're low on a couple of the popular bottled beers. Dropping the cash on the bar, I get up and head toward the cooler. Just as I step inside and move to the cases I want, I hear someone enter behind me. "What are you doing?" she asks.

"Well, I was getting ready to leave and thought I'd help first." I grab two of the cases and turn to face her.

She's smiling. "I could have gotten them."

"I know, but I thought I'd do it quick."

She steps to where I stand, the beer separating us. "Thank you," she whispers before going up on her tiptoes and pressing her lips to mine.

There's no way to deepen the kiss, not with the cases between us, but that's okay. If I did, I'm liable to toss the beer to the side, say fuck it to the customers in the bar, and do very dirty things to her right here in the walk-in cooler.

"You're welcome," I reply when she pulls back. "I'll help stock these, and then I gotta take off."

She nods. "Okay. I'll see you when you get back to town."

I nod. "I might be able to call you," I find myself saying, surprising the both of us. "Or maybe text."

"Oh, okay. I'd like that," she agrees, offering one more smile. "Be safe."

"I will," I state, leaning forward and brushing my lips to hers once more.

We walk out together, her making sure the old door is latched firmly behind me. I don't miss the way the regulars smile when they see us, as if they know there were a few stolen kisses in that walk-in cooler. Kisses we said wouldn't happen while at the bar, but to be honest, it feels like the most natural thing in the world to kiss her—here, anywhere.

"See you guys later," I holler to those at the bar, throwing up my hand in a wave before I leave.

"See you in a few days," Tom replies with a wave.

Feeling Lizzie's eyes on me, I give her my attention one last time and wink. She grins ever so softly, and that one simple gesture goes straight to my heart. Like a fucking bow and arrow, it hits its target with a sharp punch.

I push out the back door, smiling as I walk to my truck, all while wishing I could stay.

Stay with her now.

Stay with her tonight.

It's literally been one day since we took our relationship to the next level. The fact I don't want to leave is awfully telling, if you ask me. For a man who kept everyone except family at a distance, I sure am eager to jump into the unknown with both feet.

My brother's right.

I do feel lighter, happier.

In just a short amount of time, she's turned my world upside down.

And do you know what? I like it.

I whistle as I climb into my truck and head for home. Tomorrow I'll have to focus on my job, but tonight, I'll let her consume my every thought and dream until then.

I'm already anxious to see her when I get back.

CHAPTER EIGHTEEN

Lizzie

Emberlyn: What are you doing this weekend?

Me: Working. What's up?

Emberlyn: I thought I'd come for a visit.

Me: You're always welcome. You don't have any senior last few weeks of school stuff?

Emberlyn: Nope. Prom is next weekend and then graduation. I can't believe I'm almost done.

Me: Me either, squirt.

Emberlyn: Don't call me that!

Me: Fine, fine. Anyway, I have to work Friday and Saturday night, but I'm all yours otherwise.

Emberlyn: Mom says I can drive over Saturday morning, but I'm gonna ask Dad if I can go Friday after my softball game. It should be over by seven.

Me: It's an hour drive here, Em.

Emberlyn: I know, Mom. I'll be fine.

Me: Well, if Dad says it's ok, then it's fine with me.

Emberlyn: Yay! I'll keep you posted!

Me: Sounds good.

I slip my phone into my pocket and climb out of my vehicle. I've been anxiously waiting for my massage appointment all week, and it's finally here. Add in the fact my sister is going to come for the weekend, and I'm all smiles when I pull open the door to the salon.

"Hey!" Charli greets exuberantly over the noise of a blow-dryer.

"Hi."

"Are you ready?" Her blue eyes twinkle like sapphires, much like her brother's.

"So ready," I proclaim, drawing out that first word.

"Follow me." As we walk toward the back room I know to be her massage studio, she says, "You're extra smiley today. Have you talked to my brother?"

"Umm, not since last night. We texted for a while, but then he got a call."

"Oh. I thought that smile meant you two were sexting or something."

My eyes widen at her comment, and I'm suddenly very happy for the hair dryer noise in the room. "Umm…"

"You know what?" she says, stopping and holding up her hand. "Let's not discuss *that*. I'm all for girl talk and all, but I draw the line at knowing anything about my brother." She shivers in disgust. "It's bad enough I had to hear Cade and Melissa going at it one night in his tent while we were camping." She makes a face. "Or was it Megan? I don't know. There's so many. He's such a whore."

She takes in my wide eyes and fast smile. "Not Collin though. He's always been the quiet, broody one."

"It's crazy to me how different they are," I say, stepping inside the room.

"It really is, yet so similar. They've always been best friends though. Okay, let's talk massage for a second before we dive back into my brother. Do you have any medical conditions or anything?"

"No."

"Do you know what type of massage you want?"

There are different kinds?

She laughs. "I can tell by the panicked look on your face you have no idea. That's okay. I recommend a Swedish massage, because it will relax the body, help with circulation, and ease muscle tension."

"That sounds perfect," I reply.

"Any trouble areas? Pain in your neck, back, legs?"

"Nope, all good."

"Okay, then I'll let you get undressed. You can get down to what you're comfortable with, but I recommend down to panties. You're under a blanket the entire time, unless I'm working on your back or an extremity. Privates are always covered, but I know most people are most comfortable in their skivvies. Any questions?"

"Nope, I think I got it," I reply, hanging my purse on the hook on the wall.

"When you're ready, climb under the blanket, face down. I'll knock before I enter."

And with that, she exits the room, leaving me alone to undress. I take a quick look around the space. It's comfortable, peaceful, and warm. There's soft music playing and a little waterfall on one of the shelves echoing lightly throughout the room. I strip down to my panties and climb beneath the blanket, placing my face in the hole. After a couple of minutes, there's a gentle knock on the door.

"Ready?"

"Yes," I reply, feeling the warmth beneath me.

Charli enters the room, quietly closing the door behind her, and says, "Let's begin." Her tone is serene, her footsteps light. "Are you comfortable?"

she asks. "If the bed gets too warm, let me know and I can turn off the heater."

"It's perfect," I reply.

"This lotion is hypoallergenic," she informs me before placing her hands on my back and moving. "This is called effleurage. It helps warm up the muscles and gives me a glimpse at your pressure preferences."

"It feels amazing," I whisper, practically groaning in euphoria already.

"The entire massage will be. Now, I'm gonna shut up and get to it. If you want me to increase or decrease pressure at any point, just say so. You control this. If you don't say anything, I'll assume what I'm doing is good and will keep going."

"Okay."

And for the next forty-five minutes, I'm in heaven. She massages my back, my legs and feet, my arms, and then my head and neck. She even rubbed my hands, which was practically orgasmic. It's pure bliss, and to be honest, I can't believe I've never had one of these before. In fact, I think everyone should have one.

Massages for everyone this Christmas!

"All right, I'm gonna step out and let you redress. Take your time and be careful getting off the bed. When you're ready, come out front." She exits the room just as quietly as she entered, leaving me lying on the bed and not wanting to get up.

Unfortunately, I know she has other appointments, so I slowly sit up and stretch. I feel amazing, my limbs loose and my body relaxed, and I have a soft smile on my lips the entire time I get dressed.

When I'm ready to exit, I open the door and find Charli waiting just down the hall. "Well?"

"Incredible," I reply.

"Oh, good. I want everyone to have the best experience, but when it's someone's first massage, I want it to be the best it can be." She hands me a small bottle of water.

"Well, it was. You'll definitely be seeing me again."

That makes her smile. "Happy to hear. Now, there isn't much

post-massage care to deal with, but make sure you drink lots of water. Technically, you should avoid strenuous activities for twelve to twenty-four hours, but I know you work in a bar and will be lugging those cases of beer and whatnot. Just try to rest as much as possible. Plus, I'm sure my brother'll be by after he catches up on his sleep. I don't want to think about what strenuous activities might be involved later, so we won't talk about those."

I can't help but giggle. "He told me he usually sleeps part of the day when he gets home from a shift."

She nods. "He does, especially if they were out all night with calls."

"All right, well, I'll get out of your way. How much do I owe you?" Reaching into my small purse, I retrieve my wallet.

"It's taken care of."

I glance up, meeting her gaze. "What?"

She smiles. "Someone covered it. He tipped too. I made sure it was a generous one," she states with a little chuckle.

My heart skips a beat in my chest. "Oh."

She winks and starts to walk me toward the front of the salon. "He's totally into you, if you didn't already know. He's never once—not ever—reached out to me and paid for someone's massage."

"That doesn't mean anything," I argue.

"Are you kidding me? It means more than you think, believe me. I know my brother, and this is very out of character for him," she says as we reach the front counter. "Oh! Do you want to talk about scheduling a hair appointment? I spoke with both Lila and Jenn, and both feel Jenn is a better fit for your hair type. Jenn is Curly Girl certified and is the absolute best for clients who have any and all types of curls."

"That's perfect," I reply, pulling out my phone and bringing up my calendar.

"Jenn told me just to schedule you for an extended appointment, and she'll talk to you beforehand about your hair. You can go to her Insta page and see her work, but I assure you, she's amazing."

I nod. "Sounds good. The thought of driving an hour back to Stewart

Grove just to see my usual girl doesn't sound all that convenient right now, so I'm willing to talk to Jenn and see what she can do."

My hair has loose curls, but curls, nonetheless. Anyone who has them knows you have to take proper care of them, or you'll have an uneven, frizzy mess. Ever since I can remember, I went to someone who is certified in caring and cutting those curls. My mom is the same, with long, loose curls. But all it takes is one bad cut to change everything.

"She had a cancellation next Wednesday at nine. Will that work?" Charli asks.

Tapping on the calendar app, I see Guy is opening that day. "Perfect." I add the appointment to my calendar.

"Great! We'll see you then."

"Thank you, again, for the massage. I'll definitely be back."

She flashes me a smile that reminds me of Cade. "You're welcome. Talk soon."

I wave to the others and make my way out of the salon, feeling relaxed and refreshed for the weekend ahead. Collin is working Friday night with me and Jani on Saturday evening. Things have definitely picked up on those two nights, requiring me to make the decision to staff two bartenders.

Tomorrow night is the first karaoke Friday, and I'm super excited. I found a great DJ locally who's got a great setup. He usually sticks to weddings, but we were able to come up with an agreement and schedule that didn't overwhelm him and offers a little bit of flexibility. Plus, the added bonus of a set schedule is great for marketing. We have a six-month agreement in place and will discuss changes or extending after we see how it goes.

Plus, next Saturday night, I'll have my first band. It's a local group of musicians in their forties who play a mixture of classic rock from the eighties and nineties country. When I spoke to their lead singer, he was thrilled with the prospect of playing at The Tipsy Lizard, stating he was turned down at playing at The Tall One across town, since they only wanted today's music for the younger crowd.

They don't know their ass from a hole in the ground, because what this band is offering is *exactly* what brings patrons out.

Not to mention my sister is coming over for the weekend, and I have the perfect project for her to assist me with. Not only do I need to make posts on social media for the band next Saturday, but I want her help finalizing my next paint night and the new book club night I want to add, and if I know Em, she'll be so excited to help plan it all.

When I climb inside my vehicle and start the air-conditioning, I pull out my phone and tap on the text app. His name is near the top of the list, thanks to our messages back and forth last night. I know he's probably sleeping, but I want him to see it as soon as he wakes up.

> **Me: What a wonderful surprise to find out someone paid for my massage. If you know who that was, let him know he's in for quite a thank you later.**

Smiling, I slip the device into the cup holder, but before I can back out of my parking spot, my phone rings. "Hi, Dad."

"How's my favorite oldest child?"

"I'm doing well. I just had my very first massage."

"Really," he replies, a hint of a smile in his voice.

Man, do I miss him.

"Uh huh. It was amazing. Have you ever had one?" I ask.

"Nope. The only hands I want all over my body are your mother's."

"Umm, first off, gross visual," I grumble, making him chuckle. "And second, I'm sure there are male masseurs."

"I don't know that's any better, Lou." He sighs. "Listen, your sister just stopped by the bar to tell me she's going to your place after her softball game tomorrow."

I can't help but grin. I can imagine my sister blowing in like a little tornado and telling him her plans, despite knowing he won't be a fan of them. "She mentioned something to the fact," I reply, keeping my stance neutral.

Dad exhales long and slow. "I'm not a fan of her driving there in the dark."

"I know," I reply. "But she *is* eighteen and graduating high school soon."

"Don't remind me," he murmurs, clearly having a hard time with the fact his youngest child is about to fly the coop. I don't say anything, because I can tell he's struggling right now. "Anyway, I'm not sure she needs to be on the road after her game. She could just as easily head over Saturday morning."

"I know that's what you'd prefer, but you need to consider Em. She's a good driver, and she's very mature. She's leaving for college in a few months, and then you won't be able to control what she does like you do in Stewart Grove. Like you told me when I went off to school. All you can do is hope you taught them how to be upstanding, levelheaded adults, and pray they don't mess it up. But if we do, you're only a phone call away, no matter the time, day, or reason."

I'm greeted with silence, but only for a second. "I sound much more responsible than I feel."

I snort a laugh. "You're the best dad in the world. You've taught us all well. Well, the jury's still out on Waylon."

His chuckle makes me smile. "Yeah, that boy...he's his father's son."

"We all are."

He sighs. "So, I should let her leave after the game to drive to your place."

"You should," I confirm. "And I'll be watching and waiting for her arrival."

"I know you will be. All right, she can head your way after."

"Good, I have a list of things for her to help me with," I tell him.

"Like?"

I tell him about the karaoke night starting tomorrow, and all about the band performing next weekend. "I was thinking of asking Uncle Tank to make me a platform. You know, for a stage. Something that can be moved if needed."

"Where are you thinking?" he asks, switching from the dad hat to the bar owner one.

"The back corner by the pool table. It can be pushed to the side to create space."

"Yeah, I see what you're saying, but still. Might be tight. And you want to make sure your stage is big enough to accommodate larger bands."

"I know."

"What am I talking about, of course you know. You're my daughter. You've probably thought this through a hundred different ways before coming to the conclusion you've settled on."

Smiling, I confirm, "I have."

"I'm sure Tank will be more than willing to help you."

My heart aches for the distance between us. I will never take my dad's hugs for granted. "I'd be disappointed if you didn't come with him," I add softly.

I can practically hear the smile in his words as he responds, "Try to keep me away."

"Never."

"Good," he states, clearing his throat. "Now, when she arrives tomorrow, how about you shoot your old man a text, letting me know she made it safely. Heaven knows she won't send one."

"Of course."

"Now, the other reason I called. What's going on between you and the firefighter?"

My face flushes bright red and my mouth drops open. "What? Who told you?"

Again, silence.

"Well, no one. It was a hunch, but now you've confirmed it."

I growl in frustration. "Walked right into that one."

"You did. Now, what's going on with you two. Is it serious?"

"I don't know. We're just…hanging out."

"I see."

"I'm fine, Dad."

"I know you are. Your mother raised an exceptional young woman."

I can't help but grin a little. "You had a hand in that too."

"Yeah, but she's the rock star. I was just lucky to be beside her through it all."

LACEY BLACK

"And it all started at work." I knew that will get him.

He groans. "Yeah, yeah." Clearing his throat, he adds, "Anyway, if this thing ever becomes more than just hanging out, I want to meet him."

"You've already met him."

"No, I want to meet him as the man who loves my daughter. That's different than meeting him as her employee."

"Dad," I groan, closing my eyes and taking a few deep breaths. This is not the conversation I want to be having now, especially since whatever this is with Collin is so new. We're having fun, not that I want to say that to my dad.

"I know, I know. I get it, believe me. Just…you've only ever brought one guy home, and it was the asshole right after college."

No need to ask who he's referring to.

The asshole is Jason.

"I'm not bringing this one home," I remind.

He huffs out a deep breath. "You're being difficult."

I bark out a laugh. "Just like my dad."

"Your mother," he mutters. "All right, I'll let you go, and I won't bring him up again. I'll text you when Em's on her way, and then if you'll let me know when she arrives, I'd appreciate it."

"You got it, Dad."

It's quiet for a few seconds before he whispers, "I'll never get tired of hearing you call me that." I can hear the emotion in his voice. Dad and I have always had a special bond. It's more than just being "the oldest" or his "first daughter." We grew up together, battled together, *learned* together.

"There's no other name I'd ever call you," I utter, my heart galloping in my chest and a massive lump forming in my throat.

"You used to call me Walk."

I smile at the memory, even though I don't really recall using that name. He started dating my mom when I was three, so while I have pieces of memories from my early childhood, I really only remember calling him Dad.

"Daddy Walk."

He clears his throat. "Okay, I gotta go. Dirt in my eye. Love you, Lou."

"Love you more, Daddy Walk."

He doesn't speak, but not because he doesn't have anything to say. He's emotional and is fighting it. I've only ever seen him cry twice. Once when Aunt Edna passed away, and the other when my sister crashed her bike and was found unconscious in the driveway. She had a pretty big concussion, a lot of superficial facial injuries that required stitches, and a broken arm. When she finally opened her eyes at the hospital, she asked him if her pink sparkled bike was okay, and I'll never forget the relief on Dad's face.

I sniffle and bat my eyes, clearing my own unshed tears. I need to get back to the bar and prepare for my shift. I push our conversation about Collin out of my head, because we're not there, and I don't know if we ever will be.

Does it feel good? Yes.

Does it feel different than previous relationships? Sure does.

Does that mean it'll progress to something more? Not necessarily.

That thought sits like acid in my gut.

Just as I prepare to pull out of the lot, my phone chimes with a text notification. Smiling, I check my device.

> Collin: I might know exactly who did that, and I'm positive he's looking forward to that thank you.

CHAPTER NINETEEN

Collin

THE MOMENT I WALK THROUGH THE DOOR, MY EYES SEEK HER out. She's behind the bar, pouring a draft beer, and laughing at something a customer says. Just seeing her brings out my own grin. "Hey, Collin!" Burt hollers.

Throwing my hand up in a wave, I hold her gaze as I head toward her and round the end of the bar. "Hi."

"Good afternoon," she replies.

I slip my bag on the shelf and nod to Guy as he exits the walk-in cooler with cases of beer to restock the bar. "Let me help," I offer, knowing he's probably ready to finish the restock and get the hell out of here.

When his tasks are done, he bags up the trash, while I place a new bag in the can behind the bar. "I'll take it on my way out." Guy clears out the tip jar and shoves the cash in his pocket before clocking out on the sheet in the office.

I know a new sales system, complete with employee timeclock, is the next purchase Lizzie wants to make for the bar, but it was put on hold, choosing to refinish the floors and take care of other updates first. The old register still works fine, so she hasn't been in too big of a rush to buy the new system.

"What time is your sister supposed to be here?" I ask after Guy takes off.

"Umm, between eight and eight thirty. Dad is going to text me when she is on her way. She's leaving straight from the game, not even bothering to change out of her uniform. The only reason Dad is okay with her not going home to shower is because he wants her on the road while it's still light."

"I get it," I reply, but before we can further the conversation, a new group of the post-work crowd stops by for a drink.

We're pretty busy for the next three hours, and it takes both of us to keep up with the crowd. Things have definitely picked up over the last few weeks, thanks to the changes she's made. And she's created a lot of positive buzz already with the announcement of the first live band next Saturday. Lizzie printed flyers and hung them around the bar and has been featuring a lot of that era of music on the jukebox tonight.

When the door opens once more, the younger version of Lizzie walks in with bright eyes and a wide smile. "I'm here!" she bellows, pulling everyone's attention.

"Oh Lord," Lizzie replies, shaking her head.

The two remaining regulars all turn to the bubbly blonde. "Little Lizard!" Gus hollers, offering a wide smile.

"Oh, I like that," Emberlyn states, coming up to the two older men and giving fist bumps.

I glance over at Lizzie and spot her typing on her phone. She mentioned last night, when I stopped by and escorted her to her apartment upstairs, her dad wanted her to let him know the second Emberlyn arrived. I helped her make a few final touches up there before I let her show her appreciation for the massage.

She was on her knees, and every time I close my eyes, I see her.

It's fucking glorious.

But now isn't the time to pull up those mental visuals.

"Hi, Collin," Emberlyn sings as she bounces up to the bar, bag slung over her shoulder.

"Hey, Em. Can I get you a drink?" I offer, drying off my hands from washing some of the glasses.

"No thanks." When she spots her sister, she runs around the bar, drops her bag, and throws her arms around her shoulders. "I've missed you so much!"

"Same, Em. Same," Lizzie whispers just loud enough I can hear over the noise.

"I can't wait to get to work on the stuff we were talking about earlier. I brought my laptop so I can log into all your social media accounts and start making videos."

Lizzie grins fondly. "Okay, but first up, run upstairs and shower."

Emberlyn makes a face.

"You're covered in dirt. Did you slide here?"

Her sister laughs. "No, but I did have two stolen bases, plus a slide home to score the final run of the game."

"Of course you did."

"Anyway, I guess I can run up and shower real quick and get into comfy clothes. But then I'll be back down here," Emberlyn states with a pointed look, as if daring her sister to tell her she has to stay in the apartment.

"Technically, you're not supposed to be here after nine, but I suppose I can make an exception, since you're family."

"And practically an employee. You can pay me with those brownies from the diner. Oh, and iced coffees. I saw this cute little coffee joint at the end of the block."

"My sister loves that place. It's her favorite," I interject into the conversation.

"Well, tell her to meet me in the morning for coffee. But not too early. It's Saturday, and I need my beauty sleep."

I nod, knowing Charli will be thrilled at the invite. Especially since she does nothing but sing Lizzie's praises.

"We can see what time Charli goes to work tomorrow. Maybe she can meet us for coffee," Lizzie says, her emerald eyes sparkling.

"Charli? Her name is Charli? I love it!"

"It's short for Charlotte," I tell her.

"Hey, I almost forgot. I have a surprise for you upstairs."

"A surprise?" Emberlyn asks, her matching green eyes sparkling.

"You'll know it when you see it. Go shower, and make sure the apartment door is locked when you're inside," Lizzie says before moving down the bar to fix a mixed drink.

Emberlyn squeals, grabs her bag, and takes off for the back hallway. She moves through the closed door to where the back entrance and stairs are located. About a minute later, Lizzie's phone chimes with a text. She checks the screen and smiles, holding the phone up so I can see it.

Emberlyn: OMG! I love it!! My very own room!!

Lizzie found a great daybed after a quick stop to a thrift store yesterday, after her massage, and got it for a steal. They even delivered it for her for a small fee. So, while she worked, I volunteered to go to the big box store over in Stockton, a short fifteen-minute drive. I picked up bedding she wanted and dinner, and then after she closed the bar, helped her wash everything and set it all up.

Of course, afterward, we got to the part where she thanked me for covering her massage, and I reciprocated because it's the polite, gentlemanly thing to do.

I try to push that image and the taste of her on my tongue out of my head. One, we're at work, and we've been trying to toe the line at keeping things divided between professional and personal. The other reason is simply because the last thing I need is to be spotted popping a woody behind the bar, and if there's one thing I've learned about Lizzie, she's completely boner-inducing. I can't help it. Just the sound of her voice, the slightest touch of her skin, the quickest glance her way has my body reacting in ways it hasn't since I was a teenager and learning what that damn thing was for.

We stay busy, me working one side of the bar and Lizzie the other.

Her side always seems to back up quicker, thanks to the guys. They line up at her end, getting as close to the gorgeous new woman in town. Not that I blame them, but I don't like the feeling that bubbles in my chest when I see them shooting their shot all night long.

"What's wrong?" the woman I can't stop thinking about asks as she comes over to grab the bottle of Jack Daniels from my hand.

"Nothing."

Her eyebrow arches in question, but she doesn't prod. She just goes about her business, mixing the drink and taking it to the guy who is practically drooling on the bar top. She laughs at something he says and takes his cash to the register. When she tries to hand him his change, he leans forward and says something only she can here. Lizzie smiles, but shakes her head no, triggering something that feels like happiness in my chest.

Did she just turn him down?

I return my focus to the customer in front of me, apologizing for the long delay in making her drink. She offers me a flirty smile, and I can feel Lizzie's eyes on me. I take the tip dropped on the bar and slip it inside the jar. Turning, I watch Lizzie grab a bottle of All American Crüe from the cooler, realizing it's low and prompting my need to grab a cold case from the cooler.

Just as I slip inside and retrieve the case, I feel a hand on my back. I don't need to worry about who's touching me. I'd know her touch anywhere. "Everything all right?" I ask when I turn around.

Her answer is to kiss me.

Hard.

Her tongue dives into my mouth, tangling with my own in a fierce kiss. It's all tongues and heat, and that erection I was worried about is very much alive and well right now. It's begging to get close to her, to feel her, and I'm weak. All I want to do is bend her over the stack of beer cases and remind her exactly how good we are together. To show her those assholes out in the bar are nothing in comparison to what I offer.

To what we have.

"Don't be jealous," she whispers, finally breaking the kiss.

"I'm not," I respond, the lie bitter on my tongue.

She smiles knowingly before adding, "You're the only one I want in my bed."

I shift the case to balance it on my right arm and adjust my dick in my jeans with my left. "How quickly can we make that happen again?"

She gives me a sad look. "Em is here until Sunday afternoon."

I sigh. "Then either you'll be in my bed that night or I'll be in yours."

A wicked smile spreads across her swollen lips. "Deal."

"What are you two doing in here? The natives are getting restless!"

Lizzie jumps back and spins around, facing her sister. I strategically hold the case of beer in my hands in front of my crotch, so she's not scarred for life. "Nothing! Grabbing beer," Lizzie insists with too much force.

Emberlyn just grins. "Right…" she replies with a smirk, drawing out that word.

I carefully hand off the case of beer, keeping it at crotch level, and then turn back around to make it look like I'm rearranging the cases and pulling a few from the taller stacks down so they're easier for Lizzie or Jani to grab if I'm not here.

"Take a few minutes. I'll cover the front until…you know," Lizzie practically sings, clearly understanding my need to cool off in the walk-in for a couple extra minutes. Then, they're both gone, leaving me alone with my thoughts and my hard dick.

Fortunately, I'm able to get myself under control quickly and return to the bar. Lizzie is slinging beers and mixing drinks, while Emberlyn is sitting at the end of the bar, her eyes wide with excitement as she watches, right next to the regulars. They'll protect her for sure, like she was one of their own.

As the night starts to wind down and the crowd thins, I move to where Lizzie's sister is sitting. She's on her laptop, typing away, and curiosity gets the best of me. "Whatcha doing?" I ask, wiping down the bar beside her.

"Well, I made myself an admin on the bar's social media pages and scheduled a bunch of posts and videos. Now, I'm saving video clips of the band coming next Saturday so we can use them throughout the week to promote." She meets my gaze. "They're really good. Not completely my style of music, but I grew up listening to it at my dad's place. What do you like to listen to?"

"I love classic country, but enjoy the cassette tape era too," I tell her.

She looks confused. "The what?"

I bark out a laugh. "Cassette tapes. They came before CDs."

She wrinkles her nose just like her sister does. "Oh, those weird little rectangles that you had to stick a pencil in to rewind them."

Chuckling, I nod. "Not always, but yeah. Those."

"Anyway," she says, her bubbly personality showing brightly in the dimly lit bar, "Lizzie also had me look for paint night ideas, and since the next one is the first part of June, I found this really cool water scene with the setting sun and prairie grass. It looks very summery and calm, perfect for her June event," she states, turning her laptop screen around and showing me the image.

"Nice," I confirm.

"And I've already started her a sign-up sheet. Notice the name at the top?" she asks, smiling widely when I see her name, followed by her mom's. "I'm going to text the aunts tomorrow morning and see if they want to come too, and if so, that'll be five of the twenty spots already reserved."

"I'll have to tell my sister to get up here soon and get her name on the list."

"Oh! The one who likes the little coffee spot down the block?"

"Yeah, Charli. Honestly, I'm surprised she didn't show up tonight. Hell, none of my siblings did. That's odd."

"Why so?" she asks, cocking her head to the side a bit.

I lean forward, elbows on the bar. "My siblings love to torture me, and they usually drop by when I'm working. Especially Cade, my twin brother."

Her eyes widen. "You have a twin?"

"Yep. Identical."

"Cool. Do you ever twin swap?"

I snort and shake my head. "Not anymore, but we may have done it a few times when we were younger."

"Oh my God, I bet that was epic."

"It was quite entertaining. Of course, when we'd get in trouble, my parents weren't very impressed."

She rolls her eyes. "Are they ever when their kid is in trouble? I have two older brothers, remember? Between those two and our cousins, there was always trouble."

"When I was younger, me, my brothers, and a group of our friends would ride our bikes to this swimming pool just outside of town. It was inside this campground, but they let anyone use it for a small fee. Anyway, when we'd get there, the woman who worked the counter would always grumble and say 'Here comes those Cooper Town boys.' It only fueled our need to cause a ruckus."

"I'm surprised you didn't get kicked out."

"Oh, we did. Often. But it was always for the day, and they'd make sure to call our parents, so we got a proper ass-chewin' when they got home from work."

She snorts and nods. "Yep, you and the boys sound a lot like my brothers and cousins. You'd probably all get along well."

I smile, wondering if I'll get the opportunity to know her brothers and cousins. I met both of her brothers when they helped Lizzie move stuff in, and even though I've heard a lot about the large family she has behind her, I have yet to meet the extended family. Well, besides the aunts and uncles.

"I'll let you get to it," I reply, tapping on the top of the bar and moving down to start washing the remaining dirty glasses.

By the time midnight rolls around, last call has been announced and we're pushing those few customers who remain out the door. Everyone appears to have a ride, something Lizzie has been adamant about from day one. If someone looks to be too drunk to drive, we take their keys and make them call a ride. I can't help but notice the final patron out the door is the douche who kept hitting on Lizzie all night. I don't know him, so he's clearly not from this town—or at least he's never frequented this bar much before.

"Thank you for the offer, but I'm not interested. I'm seeing someone."

The guy sighs. "All right, but at least keep my number in your phone. That other guy ever frees you up, call me." He practically shoves a bar napkin in her hand with his number written on it, and it takes every ounce of control I have not to walk over there and rip it out of her hand and toss it in the trash.

When the guy finally leaves and Lizzie locks the front entrance, Emberlyn says, "That was intense."

Her sister shrugs her shoulder, collecting a few cans and bottles from the tables and tossing them in the trash. "It wasn't, really. He was harmless."

"Maybe, but Collin over here looked like he wanted to run over there, piss on your leg, and throw you over his shoulder."

My eyes widen as I look between Lizzie and her sister. "I would not pee on her," I state, choosing to focus on humor.

"Maybe not physically, but metaphorically, you were marking your territory," Emberlyn practically sings. "It's okay. You two can pretend there isn't something going on between you two all you want, but I can see it. I stopped counting at sixteen. That's how many times I caught one of you watching the other when you thought no one was looking. Not to mention whatever was obviously happening in the cooler earlier that you both are pretending didn't happen. But I have eyes. And a brain. And you two are clearly doing the nasty and keeping it under wraps."

Lizzie's face turns redder than the fire engine I ride in every week for work. "Em!"

"What? I'm eighteen. I know all about sex."

Lizzie gasps and shakes her head. "All right, let us get the bar closed down and ready to go. You and I clearly have a conversation coming after."

Emberlyn rolls her eyes at her sister before throwing me a wink. "You can stay too. I'm across the hall. Just don't be too loud you wake me up, 'mkay?"

"Stop it," Lizzie chastises, her embarrassment evident.

"I think I'll let you two have your girls' night, but thanks for the offer. We'll see what tomorrow night brings," I reply with my own wink.

"Stop encouraging her!" Lizzie hollers at me, grabbing the broom and holding it out toward her sister. "Here. Maybe you won't run your mouth so much if your hands are busy."

Surprising me, Emberlyn jumps off her barstool and takes the broom. "You obviously don't know me as well as you think you do. I can talk *anytime.*"

And for the next twenty or so minutes, I learn that she is entirely correct.

Emberlyn talks the entire time.

But do you know what?

I love it.

And when I drive home to my quiet, lonely house, I miss them both instantly.

Sleep doesn't come nearly as easily as it normally does.

CHAPTER TWENTY

Lizzie

"OH MY GOD, THIS PLACE IS SO CUTE," EM ANNOUNCES THE moment we step inside the coffee shop.

"Isn't it? It's my fave," Charli agrees as she approaches. "You must be Emberlyn," she adds, pulling my sister in for a hug.

"I am. And you are definitely Collin's sister. You look a lot alike."

Charli snorts and links her arm through my sisters. "He wishes he was as good-looking as me."

Em laughs. "You can call me Em. All my friends do."

"And you can call me Charli. I only answer to Charlotte when it's my mom, and she's usually chastising me for something. Well, I suppose some of my old teachers still call me by my full name, but that's it."

Em giggles the sweetest sound that makes me smile. I love seeing my sister so happy and carefree. "Let's order some caffeine."

"A girl after my heart," Charli replies, escorting her to the front counter. I stand back, waiting my turn, and listen as the other two discuss their favorite iced coffee flavors.

"I think I'm gonna try the salted caramel iced coffee, with liquid sugar and cream, large, please," Em orders.

"Same," Charli states before turning to me.

"Might as well make it three." I pull out cash, thanks to healthy tips last night, but Charli waves me off.

"I got it," she says, pulling out her card.

"Well, then let me leave the tip," I announce, pulling some cash out and slipping it inside the jar.

When we have our drinks, we head over to one of the small, round bistro tables and have a seat. Em takes a sip, her eyes lighting up. "Oh my God, this is so good."

"It's one of my faves," Charli agrees, taking her own drink.

I barely have my lips around the straw when my sister asks, "So, did you know my sister and your brother are doing the nasty?"

If I had sucked any liquid up the straw, I would have spit it out all over the table. "Oh my God, Em!"

The other two giggle. "Actually, I was pretty certain they were when my brother called and paid for her massage."

"Aww," Em sings, covering her heart with her hand. "That's so sweet. Guys only do that kind of thing when they're either sleeping with someone or want to be."

I shake my head and take a drink of my iced coffee, wishing I weren't the main topic of their conversation and wondering how my little sister got so wise.

"What are you two doing today?" Charli asks.

"We're going shopping for a bit. I want to check out that thrift store Lizzie got my daybed from. She said they have lots of things I could use in my dorm this fall. Then, we're going to the diner for lunch so I can get some of those fudge brownies to take home with me, and then Lizzie has to work, so I'm hanging out at the bar."

"Oh! You're still going to be here later? I'll come up. I'll call my brothers and some friends."

"Yay!" Em sings, clapping her hands. "I want to meet Collin's twin brother and see if they really do look identical."

Charli snorts. "They really do, but I can tell them apart. Mostly it's the mischief Cade always seems to wear on his face that gives them away. Oh, and a small scar Collin has below his eye from when he was younger and fell out of a tree."

"I have scars by my left eye too! I cover them with makeup, but they're still there. I wrecked my bike when I was little. Broke my arm too."

"I broke my arm when I was little!" Charli announces, the two of them falling into an easy friendship almost instantly. My heart soars with happiness. "Mine was because Collin and Cade dared me to jump a skateboard off the concrete steps at the church."

"Ouch," Em groans, wrinkling her nose. "I bet that hurt."

"Don't all broken bones?"

"Yeah, probably," she replies with a giggle.

"Maybe we can all grab dinner beforehand." Charli looks at me, her eyes wide, as if realizing what she said. "I mean, if that's okay with you. I know you have to work, but I'd love to take Em with me to get food. Then, I'll deliver her safely to you at the bar."

"Oh, yes! Puh-lease, Lizzie?" my sister begs.

"I don't want to put you out," I reply to Charli, ignoring the way my sister gapes at me.

"You're not, believe me! I know Cade will want to go. I'll even call Cam."

"Cam?" my sister asks.

"My youngest brother," Charli says. "He and his friend, Quinn, are constant thorns in my side," she grumbles, making a face.

"Younger brother? Like how much younger?" My sister's eyes brighten.

"Still too old for you," I reply, giving her a pointed look over my plastic cup.

Her mouth drops open. "I'm eighteen."

"He's twenty-four," Charli says. "A touch too old for you."

"Six years isn't bad," my sister disagrees.

"I'll just call Dad and see what he thinks of you dating someone with an age gap," I tease.

Her eyes narrow. "Sure. And be sure you tell him you're doing the nasty with your employee."

My mouth drops open. "He'd be fine with it, because he dated Mom when she worked there. But you dating someone six years older? No way." I grin at her smugly, only because I know it'll piss her off.

Em rolls her eyes dramatically. To Charli she states, "I was just kidding about your brother. I just wanted to get a rise out of Lizzie."

I let out a huff as her words wash over me. I should have known she was just asking to piss me off. "You're terrible."

She takes a victorious sip of her drink before glancing at Charli. "So tell me about Cam's friend. The one that made you snarl when you mentioned him."

Charli's eyebrows shoot for the sky. "What? I didn't snarl."

"Oh, you definitely did. Spill the tea, new bestie." Em looks positively delighted to hear new gossip, especially involving Charli.

"No tea. Quinn is annoying at best."

"You like him!" Em announces, drawing the attention from the few other patrons inside the coffee shop.

"You're off your rocker! He's the most opinionated person alive, and he's always right. He does anything and everything he can to push my buttons. Quinn is the typical younger brother's annoying best friend, and he will never be anything more than that."

I can tell Em doesn't believe her, and to be honest, I'm not sure I do either. She's incredibly defensive and adamant of her annoyance of him, which is a big red flag. I can totally see where my sister would believe there's more there than just irritation at the man, but it's not my place to call her out more.

At least not now.

We sit and chat for the next thirty minutes, until Charli needs to head to the salon for her first appointment of the day. She says Saturdays are usually her busiest day, because more people have that day off.

When we all stand up and Em walks over to the trash can to dispose of her cup, Charli looks my way and quietly says, "If you're not okay with her going with us, that's fine and I'd completely understand. But the offer stands. We can take her to dinner and then bring her back safely afterward. We can even bring you something to eat."

I nod. "I'm okay with it, if she is." The truth is Em is eighteen, and I trust Collin's family. Despite only knowing them a short time, they're good people.

Before either of us can say anything about dinner, Em blurts out, "So what time is dinner? We're still going, right?"

I crack a smile as Charli replies, "We are. I'll text my brothers and find out what time works best for them. Do you like Mexican?"

"Love it!"

"Great, that's the plan. I'll text Lizzie with a time. I can swing by and pick you up."

"Sounds great!" Em replies, pulling her new friend into a hug. "See you soon!"

Charli gives me a quick hug before slipping out the door and heading for the salon. Em and I exit and get in my vehicle. The resale store isn't too far away, but I figure if we buy anything, it would be more convenient to have a vehicle there than to have to lug it all back to where we left it.

With a smile on my lips, we set out for the next part of our time together, and I wouldn't change a second of it.

"Hey."

I offer a small smile and step back, granting him access.

"Nope, come on."

I quickly scan his appearance, from his worn blue jeans to his fitted T-shirt and the work boots on his feet. "Where are we going?" I ask.

"For a ride." He flashes me one of his smiles, one that seems more comfortable and natural than it did before we started *hanging out*. "I know you're sad your sister just left, and I don't want you sulking in this apartment for the rest of the day or going downstairs to work early on your much-needed day off. So, let's go."

I just stare at him, hating the fact he's right. For the last thirty minutes, I've been super sad Em left, enjoying our time together and needing it more than I realized. And yes, after I switched the laundry, my plan was to go downstairs and catch up on a little paperwork in my office. I know Guy has the place under control, so I don't have to worry about him, but I figured there was something useful I could do to keep my mind occupied.

I huff and turn around, heading toward my bedroom.

"As much as I love seeing your ass in those cutoffs, I'm gonna need you in jeans, closed-toed shoes, and a T-shirt. Oh, and something to pull back your hair."

I pause and meet his gaze, raising a single eyebrow.

"Not for that, dirty girl." He winks and grins, setting my heart fluttering in my chest.

I move to my bedroom and change into the clothes he suggested before grabbing a hair tie and a pair of boots. "Are you going to tell me where we're going?" I ask, returning to the living room and taking a seat to put on my boots.

Collin is standing at the windows, looking out at the downtown area. "No."

I gape up at him, earning a small victorious grin.

"Come on, slow poke. We have stuff to do," he informs me, clapping his hands together and heading for the door.

I get up, grab my purse, and follow behind him. After making sure the door is secured, we move down the stairs and out the back door where I find his truck waiting. That's not what grabs my attention, however. It's what's in the bed. "Are we taking that?" I ask, pointing to the big orange four-wheeler in the bed.

"We are," he says, opening the passenger door for me. "But not from here, so let's go."

I jump inside the cab, and before I can fasten my seat belt, Collin leans in and steals a kiss. "Hi."

I press my lips to his once more before replying, "Hi."

He pulls back and smirks. "More of that later."

Once he closes my door, he moves around to get in on the driver's side and starts the truck. We make our way to the main drag, turning left in front of The Tall One and driving out of town. "Where are we going?" I ask, now that I know the mode of transportation.

"You remember my friend Wyatt, right?"

"The tall farmer?"

"Yeah, the big, ugly ogre. He has several acres we ride on, and since it's such a beautiful Sunday afternoon, I figured we'd go for a ride around his farm."

I'm already grinning eagerly as we make our way to the land his friend owns. The house is an older two-story place, with a big porch and large windows. There's a long driveway and a two-car detached garage with a breezeway between the structures. Not to mention two large, older barns that look like they've been well-maintained and a fenced-in pasture with cattle. "This place is great," I reply, taking it all in as we drive past the house and park by the second barn.

"It was his grandparents' place. His grandpa passed away a few years back, and they had to put his grandma in a place with memory care. Wyatt had been taking care of it, working with his dad, so they deeded it to him. His dad helps him with the cattle and farming the ground and lives about a mile up the road."

Just as we park, Wyatt walks out of the barn, dirt covering his jeans and shirt, with a wide grin on his face. "Well, well, well. Look who we have here. If it isn't my friend, Collin, and...a woman."

I turn toward Collin just in time to see him roll his eyes. "Shut up."

He holds up his dirty hands in surrender. "I'm just saying...it's been a while."

Moving to the bed of his truck, he lowers the tailgate and says, "I was here two days ago, asshole."

Wyatt just smiles, like the cat that ate the canary. "Not what I meant."

Collin doesn't respond, just preps the bed to remove the four-wheeler with ramps. "You don't mind if we take a spin around the farm, do you?" he asks, clearly already knowing the answer.

"No, no, of course not." He gives me his full attention. "Hey, Lizzie."

"Hi, Wyatt," I reply.

"You sure you want to hang out with this asshole? He's grumpy and ugly. You're more than welcome to come inside the barn with me."

Collin climbs up on the four-wheeler and gets ready to start the engine. "Sure, because that's what women want. To hang out in a dirty barn that smells like cow shit."

I can't help but crack a little smile at their banter. It's cut off by the roar of the engine, and I stand back and watch as Collin slowly reverses down the ramp. He drives forward and pulls up beside me. "Ready?"

I nod and pull my hair back. Then, I climb on the machine, pressing my front to his back and wrapping my arms around his waist. "Don't we need helmets?" I ask.

"We won't be going too fast. Plus, I know this property like the back of my hand. I can handle it," he tells me confidently, earning a nod from me.

I don't know why, but I trust him. More than I think I've ever trusted anyone else. "Let's do it."

"Have fun, kids, but remember, I have cameras. You get caught doing something spicy, I'm gonna post the video in the town-wide Facebook group."

Collin lifts his hand, flipping off his friend, who just walks away laughing. We jolt forward, my arms tightening around his body. The wind whips past me, making me grin, as the sun shines bright in the later-afternoon sky. We skirt around the field on grass and dirt paths that have been well-ridden. Everything else just falls away as I take in my surroundings. The green trees, the freshly planted fields, the pastured cattle watching us move by. It's calm, serene, and beautiful. I can see why someone would love to live in a country setting like this.

When we reach a path the veers into the trees, we slow and take the turn. It's cooler under the canopy of trees, and the breeze all but stops. I take it all in, closing my eyes a few times and just letting the air kiss my face.

After we ride for about an hour, he slows to a stop along a creek that runs through the back of the property. "Well?"

I can't help but smile. "Just what I needed."

"Good," he replies, slowly climbing off the machine and stretching his legs and back. "I hoped it might do your soul some good. I usually come out here and ride when I need to think or get away."

"I can see why," I respond, getting off the four-wheeler and taking in our surroundings. "It's beautiful here."

He nods. "Someday, I'll live in the country. I'd love to find a piece of timber like this and build a house in the middle. One you can't see from the road."

"Sounds perfect. And every time you come up the driveway, you're greeted by a dog, right?" I ask, closing my eyes and picturing it.

"What kind of dog?" he asks gently.

"I don't know, something big and fluffy, like a Lab or a shepherd."

"Both great breeds. We had a beagle when I was growing up. His favorite was Charli. He'd even let her do wild things like paint his nails. One night when Mom and Dad went out for dinner, he sat there while she put a dress on him. Cade and I were mortified."

A giggle spills from my lips. "What a good dog."

He nods. "His name was Buddy, and he was just that. Everyone's buddy."

"I love that. Maybe someday when I'm not in an apartment above the bar I'll get a dog."

"You should." He looks around, the faintest smile on his kissable lips. "Well, what do you say. Ready for a little more riding?"

"Of course," I reply, stretching my back a little before we climb back on.

He gets on first, but when I join him, I don't return to where I was sitting before. I shimmy myself right onto his lap, instantly feeling his cock growing hard between my legs. "This might make it hard to see."

I shrug, slipping my arms around his waist and pressing my chest to his. "Then we better be careful, huh?"

His hands move around to my ass. He squeezes the globes and rocks his hips, creating the most glorious friction. "Guess it's your turn to drive."

CHAPTER TWENTY-ONE

Collin

"YOU TALKING TO THE GIRL?"

I look up and find Gio and Frank standing in front of me, dopey smiles on their faces. "Excuse me?" I ask, slipping my phone back into my pocket.

"Oh, come on, man. You've been staring at that phone since we got on shift this morning. The only reason a man watches a device that long is either he's got porn on there, or he's talking to a woman. I'm going with the latter," Frank replies with a smirk.

"It could be porn," Gio chimes in, making a playful grab for the device.

"Get your hands away from my ass," I tell him, swiping at him to keep him from retrieving it.

"But…it's a fine ass, friend."

I roll my eyes, keeping my backside away from him. "What do you two assholes want?"

"When can we meet her?" Gio asks.

"Meet who?" Of course I play dumb.

"Oh hell," Frank groans. "If we gotta spell it out for you, you ain't doin' it right."

I shake my head and return my attention to finishing up the dishes I started before I got the first text from Lizzie. Frank and Emmitt cooked, and Gio and I were on cleanup and dish duty. "I'm doing it…just fine."

"Fine. Another word you never want to hear when *doin' it*." Gio's just goading me at this point.

I don't even acknowledge his comment, mostly because there's nothing *fine* about sex with Lizzie. It's pretty fucking outstanding, really. Better than I ever could have imagined for a man who spent a long time just trying to keep everything about sex.

"How's the bar?" Gio asks, leaning on the counter beside where I'm working.

"Good."

"I was thinking of grabbing a couple of buddies and coming down for the band this Saturday night."

"Really? That's cool. You sure you want to make the drive?" I ask, knowing it's an hour from Sycamore, where he lives.

"If you'll let us crash in your guest room again," he replies. About a year ago, he and two of his friends came to town during one of his break-ups with Clara. One took the couch, while the other two shared my guest bed. Not super comfortable for two large, grown male adults, but it sure as hell beats crashing on the floor.

"Anytime. You know that," I reply with a nod.

"I do, but I figured I should ask instead of just showing up. Hell, you probably won't even be there. Five bucks says you crash with Lizzie."

I don't reply with words, because if I have it my way, that's exactly what I'll do.

"Have you told her about…you know?"

I exhale, waiting for the past to wrap around me like a hot, smothering blanket, but that's not what happens. The heartache I usually feel isn't there. The pain isn't completely nonexistent, but it feels different. It's less consuming, less suffocating. I don't instantly drown in the misery of those memories from a time I can't forget.

"No, not yet. I almost did yesterday when we were on the four-wheeler, but I didn't want to put a damper a pretty amazing afternoon. It felt like talking about Whitney and what she did would end the good time I was having with Lizzie."

He slowly nods, understanding written all over his face. "I get that, but is there ever a good time to tell the woman you're seeing about your ex?"

I consider his question, knowing he's right. "No, probably not."

"Just get it over with. Cooper Town is awfully small. The fact they haven't run into each other is pretty rare."

"Yeah, Cade said the same thing."

He points at me. "And he's right."

"Yeah, I'll tell her."

"Soon," he encourages. Gio is one of the few guys I work with who I opened up to about what happened when I was in the military. He knows exactly how damaging that betrayal has been for me, how it's impacted my life to this day.

I open my mouth to smart off something, but the sound of the alarm cuts off anything I was about to say. Dropping the towel on the counter, we both take off, moving quickly to the apparatus room. Everyone runs in, grabbing their stuff from the gear wall and swiftly putting it all on.

Reports are coming in as we all board the trucks, ready to provide aid at a tire warehouse fire in the neighboring district. As we pull out of the station, sirens blaring, I push all thoughts of Lizzie, and the conversation we need to have, out of my head. Right now, I need to focus on what's ahead of me, so we all return back to the station safely at the end of the call.

It's the middle of the night when we pull back into the station. We're all dragging ass, dog tired, but unfortunately, the work isn't done. We need to restock supplies, inspect all gear and apparatuses, and conduct vehicle checks. An entire list of tasks needs to be completed before our asses hit the showers or our heads the pillows. The last thing you'd want is for us to not do what is needed and get a call because we were too tired to do it when we got back. Lives are at stake, and every second counts when a call comes in.

The captain calls out orders, and everyone gets to work. I'm in charge of making sure supplies are restocked, including much-needed medical items and water. When I've completed my list, I grab a bucket and hose and prepare to wash the rig. When we return to the firehouse, we always wash the trucks. They're covered in soot, smoke, and potential contaminants, which can be harmful to all of us.

Finally, after the trucks have been put back together, cleaned, and we're ready to roll out for the next call, we all head off to the living quarters. A few head straight for the kitchen, needing some nutrients, while most of the rest of us go straight to the showers. By the time I grab a clean pair of sweats and a T-shirt, there's a line, but I don't care. I'll wait as long as it takes.

As I stand in the hall with a handful of other firemen, I pull out my phone and check messages. I have six, but it's Lizzie's that I tap on first.

> Lizzie: I assume the radio silence means you got a call.
> Stay safe. Let me know when you're back.

Even though it's just after three, I decide to go ahead and fire off a reply so I don't worry her. Hopefully she's sleeping and the chime of her phone won't wake her.

> Me: Hope this doesn't wake you, but I wanted you
> to know I'm back at the station. Bad fire. Everyone's
> safe. Showering and crashing.

When I don't get a reply after a minute, I slip my phone back into my pocket, thankful she's still asleep. The line for the showers doesn't take long, thanks to six stalls inside the big communal bathroom, and before I know it, I'm able to finally grab my shower caddy and wash the scent of burnt rubber and charred wood off my skin.

After sliding into my bunk, exhaustion hits me hard. I remember to plug my phone in moments before I close my eyes. The last thing to go through my mind is the image of Lizzie, windblown and smiling from our four-wheeling ride on Sunday.

Damn, I can't wait to do that again.

Soon.

"Sleepy head, you have a visitor."

I crack my eyes open and find Gio's ugly mug smiling at me through the darkened room. "What time is it?"

"Almost eight," he replies. "Captain wants us all up and eating by nine. We got that first grade class coming in for a tour before lunch."

I groan, not because of the class tour, but simply because my body is still desperate for a little sleep. I'm used to this. For forty-eight hours, we push past the exhaustion and get the job done. We sleep when we're off duty, plain and simple.

But now I can prepare for the tour. This is one of my favorite parts of the job: the community engagement. Not the adults. Adults suck. But kids? They're fucking great. At that age, everyone wants to be a fireman or a doctor or a teacher. They want to save the world or make a difference, because that's who they see around them, always there and ready to help.

I slowly get up and stretch my arms. "Who is it?"

He shrugs. "No clue. I guess a woman was waiting at the door when Bozo came back in from grabbing donuts. Asked for you. Heard she's hot."

I sigh, trying to rack my brain over who it could be. I just don't see my sister, mom, or even Lizzie making the drive up to Sycamore to drop by and say hello, and anyone else I know in Sycamore is basically here already. "Let me get dressed. Give me five," I reply, grabbing some clothes and heading for the bathroom.

Since we have a tour coming, we'll be in department issued T-shirts and our work pants, so I quickly dress in what is required for the day. I take care of business, brushing my teeth and washing my face to help wake me up, before throwing on my boots and walking toward the front entrance. We don't really have a main entrance, per se, but we have the main glass door where visitors can enter when we're here.

When I round the corner, I take in the tall blonde standing near the wall, looking at the framed photographs of our commanding officers. Her long hair is hanging down her back, and her frame is a tad on the slender side. She's wearing flip-flops, cutoff shorts, and a tank top, and she's holding a big white box, similar to one you'd receive from a bakery.

And I have no idea who she is.

"Can I help you?" I ask, taking a few steps forward.

She spins to her left and plasters a huge smile on her face. Her dark eyes are bright, full of excitement, as she gazes up at me like I hung the moon and all the damn stars. "Oh my gosh, hi, Collin! It's so good to see you again!" she bellows, practically bouncing over to where I stand.

"I'm sorry," I start, slightly hesitant. "Do I know you?"

The happiness in her smile cracks before slowly fading completely. "It's Cherie!"

Cherie? Do I know a Cherie?

And then it hits me.

The note left at my sister's work.

"Cherie. Yes, of course."

That makes her smile again. "I brought you this." She carefully thrusts the box toward me. "They're my famous chocolate brownies. You can share them with the others, if you want."

"Umm, thanks. Appreciate it." I have no idea what to say. This is awkward as fuck. "So, uh, Cherie. You dropped off a note at my sister's work. Can I ask how you found her?"

She waves her hand, as if dismissing my concern. "Social media."

"I don't have social media," I state, that same annoyance I had a couple weeks ago when she dropped off that note returning.

"No, but she does. Camden and Cade too. They all have photos of you. That's how I found her."

"Okay," I reply, taking a deep breath. "But why?"

"Well, because I wanted to spend time with you. After you helped rescue my cat from a tree, I just kept thinking about you. I saw you come and go a few times here and after a while, I knew I had to make my move." Her face sobers. "But you didn't show up to the bistro where I thought we'd meet up."

"Oh."

"But I forgive you," she beams, grinning from ear to ear. "I thought we could go get breakfast when you get off shift tomorrow morning."

The fact she knows when I would be leaving work is a little unsettling. "Uh, I don't think that's a good idea."

Again, her face falls, and I swear I see tears in her eyes. "Why?"

My mind reels as I scramble for a reason that lets her down easily and doesn't send her in to a tizzy, because, frankly, I don't know this woman or how she's going to react. Then, it hits me. Honesty. "I'm seeing someone."

"You are?" She looks completely despondent as my words sink in.

"I am. It happened right around the time of your note. I probably should have met up with you and told you then, but to be honest, I didn't know you."

She gives me a sad smile. "Safety first, right?"

I nod. "It's been drilled into me," I reply.

"I get it." After a beat, she adds, "So, this woman? It's serious?"

"Yes." The answer is out before I even think about it. The truth is, yes, it's serious, even if we haven't officially had that conversation yet. I love hanging out with her, working with her, talking to her, but my favorite part is falling asleep with her in my arms. And since we jumped into our casual relationship, I've spent more nights outside of work with her than without her. Not to mention the line we firmly drew in the sand, keeping personal and professional separate, has been slowly blurring.

I just like her in my life.

It feels more enriched this way.

"I'm sorry, I don't mean to hurt you."

She sniffles, clearly upset by the news. "It's okay. I mean, it sucks, but

I get it. I just waited too long to make my move. Maybe if I had reached out to you sooner, things would be different, right?"

Her dark eyes are laced with hope, and even though it's a little white lie, I go ahead and give her what she's looking for. "Perhaps."

She smiles and relaxes, rocking from heel to toe. "Okay, well, maybe now isn't our time, but that doesn't mean it's not going to happen at all. Promise me, if you and the woman you're dating break up, you'll call me."

I nod, refusing to say the words.

"Great! In the meantime, keep the brownies, because they're the best brownies in the world." Leaning forward, she asks, "Do you know what the secret ingredient is?"

"No?"

"Love, silly," she replies with a giggle. "Anyway, when you're ready, let me know. I'll bake you more brownies. Naked." She throws in a wink.

I clear my throat, wishing this conversation were over. "I need to get back to work."

She nods, the sadness returning to her eyes. "So long, Collin. Maybe our paths will cross again one day."

Before I can reply, she goes up on her tiptoes and presses her lips to mine. "Goodbye."

And then she's gone, leaving me standing here, holding a box of brownies and wondering what in the hell just happened.

Spinning around, I find Gio there with a grin on his face. "That looked…"

I exhale deeply. "That was nuts."

"She kissed you," he states, walking forward and taking the box from my hands. "Gimme." He practically dives into the box and steals the first one he can get his big paws on.

"Who was that?" he asks between bites.

"Remember the woman who dropped off the note at my sister's work?"

His eyes widen almost comically. "Shut up, really? That was her?"

I nod. "That was her."

He shovels half the brownie into his mouth. "What was her name again?"

"Cherie. Don't eat those."

"Why not?" he asks, reaching into the box for a second one. "They're good."

"They're probably laced with something," I mutter, closing the box and setting it aside.

"Like what? A woman trying to woo a man isn't going to lace his brownies with Ex-Lax. There's nothing sexy about shitting through a screen." He takes another bite. "Viagra, maybe."

I pause and look at the brownie my friend is consuming. "You think she'd do that?"

He shrugs. "We'll see in a bit if I get an erection that lasts longer than four hours."

I huff in exasperation. "Stop eating them."

"Can't. They really are good." Another bite.

"Fine, I don't want you crying to me if you get some weird side effect from them," I state, watching as he takes the box and starts heading back to where the guys are gathered for breakfast.

Shaking my head, I take a moment to wrap my head around what in the hell just happened. I can't believe she just dropped by here—with baked goods, no less—and thought I'd go out with her. A woman I only met once, more than six months ago, after we rescued her cat from a tree.

Talk about the weirdest firefighter story I've heard yet…

Pulling out my phone, I realize Lizzie will be getting up soon. More than anything, I want to talk to her as she starts her day. With a hint of a smile, I start typing.

Me: You won't believe what just happened…

CHAPTER TWENTY-TWO

Lizzie

T HE PLACE IS PACKED, AND I'VE NEVER FELT A DEEPER SENSE OF pride than I do right now.

I did this.

All my hard work over the last few months—hell, years—has paid off.

"If we're not careful, the fire marshal is gonna show up," Collin hollers over the music as he pours two draft beers.

"Yeah, but I'm not sure there's anything I can do about it now," I state, worrying my lip between my teeth.

Collin gives me a soft smile, one that barely touches his lips. But I see it in his eyes, so that's how I know it's there. "If he shows up, let me talk to him. I've known Troy for years. Volunteered on the department for a few years after I got out of the Air Force."

I nod, though I'm certain he's going to want to deal with me as the property owner. "We'll cross that bridge when we get there," I say over the noise.

Cade walks behind us, carrying two cases of beer to restock, singing along with the band. I crack a smile, mostly because he's been doing that since the moment the band started playing, and also because he's so different than his twin, who has barely tapped his foot along with the beat once or twice.

Thank God for Cade. Earlier this week, I went to Collin and asked what he thought about hiring one of his siblings to work tonight for cash. I realized we could potentially need help with restocking coolers, picking up empties around the tables, and making sure the trash is taken out when it starts to get full. Jani has her son this evening and really didn't want to work, and Guy worked the afternoon for me. Knowing his brother as well as he does, Collin knew Cade would be more than willing to work, and when asked, he agreed readily.

Now, he's saving our asses, since both Collin and I have been so damn busy refilling drinks we never would have had time to do what is needed. I haven't even had time to pee, let alone take a drink of water.

Collin uses what's left in a bottle of rum and glances at the shelf. "Hey, Cade, can you grab two bottles of Bacardi and anything else we may be low on?" He tosses his twin the lanyard of keys, which has everything for the bar, including one for the dry storage room where the liquor is kept.

"On it," Cade hollers between lines of a Billy Ray Cyrus song. Gathering up the empty boxes he just tore down, he turns to me and says, "When I get back, I'll watch the bar. You take a quick break."

"I'm good," I reply, even though I really have to pee.

He snorts. "You look like your eyeballs are floating."

I turn and make a face. "How in the world would you know that?"

He just gives me that knowing, cocky grin. "You've been extra squirmy, and Charli gets like that when we're four-wheeling and she has to pee."

I chuckle and shake my head. "Fine. Two minutes."

He glances at the liquor counter behind the bar and makes a mental list of a few things we're low on before digging for the right key and taking off for the storage room.

"Take longer than two minutes, Lizzie," Collin says gently, his body practically pressed behind mine. To the naked eye, it would look like two coworkers moving around each other to work, but to me, it's much more. I can feel the heat of his body, feel the pulse of his energy. His warm breath tickles my neck, and all I want to do is stop, cock my head to the side just a bit, and feel the brush of his lips against me.

That won't happen, of course—at least not down here. We've managed to maintain a very professional working relationship while at the bar, and tonight is no exception. His touches have been brief and warranted but have packed a punch to my libido, nonetheless.

"You should go first," I reply, grabbing two beers from the cooler.

"Nope, ladies first. Always." He turns and gives me a look that indicates he's not necessarily referring to the use of the restroom. He's big on making sure I get off first, or at the very least with him, before he takes his own release. "Stop that." His breath is hot against my ear, his hand brushes against my side.

"Stop what?" I ask, holding his gaze.

His lips curl up in a smirk. "You know what. I can practically read your thoughts, and they're dirty."

I feel my cheeks blush hot, but Cade returns with the bottles of liquor, breaking the mounting sexual tension behind the bar.

"All right, take a break. I've got this," he states, clapping his hands together and smiling widely. To his brother, he asks, "You ready to make some money? Magic Cade is here."

"Oh God," I groan, sharking my head. "The shirt and pants stay on!"

He barks out a laugh. "I make no promises, Lizzie Lou. I give my fans what they want."

I point to Collin. "Keep him off the bar."

Collin grins. "I'll do my best."

I move quickly toward the hallway, noticing instantly the lines for the bathroom. No way am I waiting out here, so I carefully slip between the people and make my way through the first back door that's closed and head for the stairs. Pulling my keys out of my pocket as I go, I have the door unlocked the moment I hit the landing.

I bolt toward the bathroom and take care of business, grateful to finally have an empty bladder. As I'm washing my hands, I hear what sounds like my door opening and closing, even over the hum of the band through the floor.

Did I lock the door behind me?

I know I was in a hurry to use the bathroom, what if someone followed me up here?

I look around the bathroom for a weapon, really only finding my hair dryer. I grab it regardless and prepare to use it against whoever is in my apartment. Ignoring the pounding in my chest, I place my hand on the doorknob and gently crack it open. Just as I start to pull the door open, steeling my spine to defend myself and my home, I spot a familiar face leaning against the wall across from me.

"What the hell?" I ask, opening the door completely.

He glances at my hand and cracks a smile. "What were you gonna do with that?"

"Whack you with it! Jesus, Collin, you scared the shit out of me. I heard the door and freaked out," I reply, dropping the hair dryer on the ground.

Trying to be stern, he steps forward and pulls me into his arms. "You should make sure you lock your door, especially on a night like this."

I huff, threading my arms around his waist. "I know, stupid mistake, but all I could think about was peeing."

He presses his warm lips to my own, his tongue delving inside my mouth. "Mmm, best break I've ever taken."

"Uhh, yeah, speaking of that. Not that I'm not relieved it was you in my apartment and not someone else, but what are you doing up here? Did you really just leave your brother, the man who'd give anything to perform a Magic Mike routine on the top of my bar, downstairs to man everything?"

He snorts. "He has help. Charli and Cam stepped in so I could go to the bathroom too. I'm sure it's fine."

I'm not convinced, and I'm sure my face shows exactly that. "You left your brothers behind my bar? Thank God for Charli."

He chuckles a low, gravelly sound that is like a jolt of electricity to my lady bits. "That's funny, if you think Charli would be any more responsible behind the bar than Cam or Cade. She's just as much of a menace. She'll be the one to give away free drinks."

My eyes narrow. "Again…and yet, you left them all down there."

Finally, he smiles widely. "It's okay, I promise. They vowed to be on their best behavior, but I'm not sure they're the best at mixing drinks, so we should probably get back down there as soon as possible."

Exhaling, I brush my lips across his once more, wishing we had more time. "I'd rather stay right here and kiss you."

"Same, Lizzie, same." He places a chaste kiss to my lips and slips around me. "Give me a minute to use the bathroom and then we can get back down there."

While he goes in to use the facilities, I grab two bottles of water from the fridge and twist the first cap open, taking a hearty drink. When Collin joins me, I hand him the other bottle. "Thanks."

"Of course." With one more pull from the bottle, I replace the cap and walk toward the door. "Ready?"

"Yep," he states, following behind me to the door. He makes sure the lock is engaged before we carefully descend the steps. "What do you think of the band?" he asks, having to raise his voice over the noise.

"I love them! I think they're doing a great job."

"Agreed. The patrons seem pretty pleased with them."

We round the counter and walk through the doorway separating the bar from the back. My eyes instantly go to the bar, where I see Cade, Camden, and Charli grabbing drinks. Charli seems to be the one using the register, which I'm grateful for. Not that it's too difficult, but I'm sure she's not certain on the prices of everything, so hopefully their assistance didn't create too much of a mess for me to figure out later.

Just as we approach the end of the bar, someone waves at Collin. He changes our trajectory, taking my hand so I'm forced to follow him. "Hey, you made it!"

"Of course I did. This place looks great!" the man says, offering me a friendly smile.

"That's all thanks to this woman. Gio, meet Lizzie, the owner of The Tipsy Lizard. Lizzie, this is Gio, a coworker for the Sycamore Fire Department and a good friend."

I take his extended hand. "It's nice to meet you. Collin mentioned you may come."

"Well, I had to meet the woman who's finally put a smile on my friend's face," he states with a wink. I feel my cheeks flush as he grins knowingly at me. "I see the feeling is mutual."

I glance at Collin, who doesn't seem to have any of the worry or stress lines around his mouth and eyes like he used to. He looks relaxed, confident, and dare I say it, happy. "Well, he's a great guy. I'm enjoying spending time with him."

"Anyway, I know you're busy, but I wanted to say hey. Hopefully we'll be able to get to know each other soon."

"You still crashing at my place?" Collin asks his friend.

"Yep, if the offer stands. Drake and Emilio are over in the corner. I was just heading up to get us our first round of drinks."

"Well, what can I get you? First round's on me," I reply, grateful to meet one of Collin's close work friends.

"That's not necessary, but we'll take three Night Crüe bottles, please."

Nodding, I slip behind the bar and grab the drinks. I twist off the tops and place them on the corner, where Collin and Gio are standing. "Thanks for these," he says, handing a twenty to his friend. "Tip jar." With a wink, he takes the drinks and heads toward his friends, easily getting lost in the mass of people.

"I emptied the tip jar in your office," Charli states, coming to stand beside me. "It was overflowing, and I didn't want to start having money spilling out on the floor. Cade gave me the keys, so I slipped into your office and dumped it all in your top drawer."

I offer a warm smile. "Thank you. I appreciate your help."

She waves off my thanks. "Happy to do it."

Just then, the song changes to a classic Mötley Crüe song, one that instantly brings a smile to my face. It's one of my dad's favorites, and I remember listening to it a lot when I was younger. Hell, I've heard it a ton even when I was older. On Friday and Saturday nights, he would play a Crüe hit at the stroke of eleven. I've even heard he used to get up on the bar and dance, something I've not witnessed.

Suddenly, Cade hollers, "That's my jam!"

Before I know what's happening, he jumps up on the bar and the crowd roars to life. All I can do is stand here—laughing along—as he dances on the top of my bar, careful not to spill anyone's drink. I pull out my phone and hit record, needing to document this moment to send to my dad later. Of course, dozens of phones are out and pointing at the bar, recording Cade's moment of freedom. After getting about twenty seconds of his antics, I stop recording and just watch him dance.

"I'm sorry," Collin says in my ear over the band and cheers.

I sigh, feeling his hand snake around my waist and leaning into his touch just a bit. "It's fine. In fact, it's sort of poetic, isn't it? One of the big things that made my dad's place famous on the weekends. Now, your brother is continuing the tradition here, at my place."

"I'm not sure it needs to be a tradition, but as long as you're okay with it, I won't go rip him off the bar and pummel him for making a mess."

"I'm fine with it," I tell him, leaning my head back and resting it on his shoulder. I don't even realize I'm doing it until I feel eyes turn our way. Suddenly, I recognize how close Collin and I are, the fact we're touching in a less than professional way.

But do I care?

I realize immediately I don't.

I like this man. I'm enjoying spending my time with him, dating him, so if people see that, who cares? As long as we're fine with the status of our relationship, it shouldn't matter what anyone else thinks.

Cade pulls out some killer air guitar moves, making the crowd cheer and sing along. When the song finally reaches the end, he throws his arms up in the air and hollers, "Don't forget to tip the band and your bartenders!" He reaches down and grabs the large jar we use for tips and holds it out. To my shock, money is shoved inside.

"Look."

I turn to where he's pointing and notice people making their way up to where the band is set up, and even though I can't see their actions through the masses, I assume they're throwing money in their tip jar too.

"Thank you all for coming out tonight. I think this is one of the biggest crowds we've ever had," the lead singer states, earning cheers. "And a huge thanks to Lizzie for having us here. I saw on her social media page she's having a paint night coming up and has a few other fun events on her calendar, so be sure to check those out and give a new business owner your support. We're gonna take a quick break and be back in fifteen."

Collin drops his hand and moves over to the jukebox. He cranks up some Reba, and the entire place starts to sing and dance. All I can do is stand there and take it all in again. Well, just not for too long though, because the moment the band stops playing, the bar picks up.

I jump to it, filling drinks with Collin. Cade and Camden both make sure coolers are filled before heading out to collect empties and throw them away. I feel incredibly blessed and supported, something I thought would take more time to build. I just moved here and purchased this old bar less than two months ago, and here I am, surrounded by a close group of friends who are willing to do whatever it takes to help me succeed.

That's love.

My throat tightens as my eyes automatically move to Collin. He's pouring a draft beer, listening to what someone is saying. There's a hint of a smile on his lips as he delivers the glass to the patron. He leans forward to hear what the guy is saying before his eyes slam into mine. He replies to the man, but keeps his gaze locked on me. It feels intimate, like maybe he's talking about me.

The night is better than I ever could have expected, and at the end of it, I'm both relieved and exhausted. Plus, the fire marshal didn't come, so we'll chalk that up to a win. The band is working on tearing down their setup. Cade is working on doing the final stock of the cooler and alcohol bottles, while Collin is out in the bar, collecting trash left on all the tables.

I'm washing the dirty glasses and cleaning the bar top, the jukebox playing softly in the background.

"We're gonna head out," Gio says to Collin, walking over to where he is at a table.

Collin pulls out his key and hands it over. "I went ahead and changed the sheets on both my bed and the guest room so there should be plenty of space for you guys."

Gio grins. "You're not going home then?"

Collin's eyes automatically look my way. "I'll stop by in the morning to change before work." They are both on duty tomorrow morning at eight, and I know Collin likes to give himself extra travel time. It takes an hour to get from Cooper Town to Sycamore, so that means he's going to have to get up extra early in the morning to be on his way. Would it be easier for him to just go home and crash in his own bed? Probably. Do I still want him to stay with me here? Absolutely.

"Nice to meet you, Lizzie," Gio hollers, throwing me a wave, along with his two friends who I got to meet at one point during the night.

"Nice to meet you, Gio. You guys be safe heading back."

"We will," he replies, giving one of those bro hugs to Collin before they make their way to the front door. Collin lets them out and says something about seeing him in the morning, bright and early.

We work quickly and quietly to get the bar somewhat put back together before we leave. Since it doesn't open until noon, I'll have plenty of time to do the deep clean in the morning, including sweeping and mopping the nasty floors. After tonight's crowd, they definitely need it.

"Here," I say, handing Cade an envelope of cash when we're all done and the band has left.

He waves it off. "I don't want your money."

I practically shove the stack of bills into his chest, finding a hint of satisfaction when the force of my shove causes him to move. "Take it. You earned this. We couldn't have done it without you."

Reluctantly, he finally takes the envelope and slips it into his back pocket. "You're welcome. I actually enjoyed it. And since my dance earned you all some extra tips, I think we should discuss adding it to the future lineup."

"Not gonna happen," I counter, fighting a grin.

"Spoilsport. That little bit got me a dozen new phone numbers," he replies, waggling his eyebrows.

"Well, you're just gonna have to earn those pages in your black book the old-fashioned way. Stay off my bar," I state, noting the lack of bite behind my bark.

"Yeah, yeah." To his brother he asks, "You good?"

"Yep." It's obvious he meant with his night plans.

"All right, then I'm out of here." He heads toward the back door, bellowing as he goes, "Suit up, kids! I don't want any grumpy baby Collins joining us in nine months."

The door slams shut, echoing through the bar. "He's adopted."

I bark out a laugh at Collin's comment and gather up the register. "Your tips, kind sir."

He slips his envelope into his back pocket without checking it. Taking my hand, he escorts me to the office to lock up the deposit and register, flipping off lights as we go. When we reach the back, he makes sure all doors are secured before turning toward the steps. "Ready for bed?"

Smiling, my heart crashes against my chest.

With him?

"Always."

CHAPTER TWENTY-THREE

Collin

THE MOMENT THE DOOR IS CLOSED, I SPIN HER AROUND AND PRESS my lips to hers. My fingers glide against the side of her face and her hair, which is pulled up in a high ponytail. "I've been needing to do that for a while now."

She grins against my mouth. "You just did that a few hours ago," she reminds me, referring to when we came up here to use the bathroom.

"Too long ago," I inform her, rocking my hips against her, letting her feel my erection. I feel like I've had one for hours, watching her work. She moves so easily around her bar, laughing and smiling with customers without flirting. It was a huge fucking turn-on tonight; despite the fact I wasn't able to react to her the way I wanted to.

Every time one of those assholes came up and hit on her, I wanted to turn into a caveman. Throw her over my shoulder and stake my claim right then and there, but that's not toeing the professional line we both agreed to.

"I enjoyed meeting Gio and his friends," she murmurs, gripping the side of my shirt.

"I don't want to talk about him," I say, sliding my knee between her legs and reveling in the feel of her grinding against my thigh.

"What do you want to talk about? Cade dancing on the bar?"

She's teasing, I know it, but I still growl at her question. "Fuck no, Lizzie. I want to talk about getting you out of these clothes."

"I should shower. It was hot and sweaty all evening," she says. "Plus, spilled beer."

"Hmmm," I murmur against her neck, sliding my nose against the long column. "I have an idea."

"Does it involve the shower?"

Smirking, I give a quick nod before bending down and scooping her up and over my shoulder in a matter of seconds. The sound of Lizzie squealing makes my heart soar higher than ever before. I carry her to her ugly bathroom and slowly lower her onto the floor.

"Undress," I instruct, watching her eyes widen and dilate. She enjoys this side of me too, loves it when I get all bossy.

Quickly, I turn around and spin the knobs. Knowing it'll take a handful of seconds before the water temperature warms, I return my attention to her, cracking a smile when she's trying to strip in record time. When her foot gets tangled in the leg of her pants, I reach forward and assist. "What's the rush, sweetheart?" I ask, sliding my palm along her calf as I help her detangle.

"You naked in the shower is the rush, Collin," she mutters, a wicked glimmer reflecting back at me in those hypnotic green orbs.

When her leg is free, I toss the jeans onto the floor and reach for her panties. "These should go too," I murmur softly, taking my time to remove the thin material. She's better than any gift I could open on Christmas, all warm, wet, and mine.

Mine.

It's been too damn long since I even considered the concept of a woman being mine again, but this feels right. Hell, it feels more than right, and surprisingly, that doesn't scare me as much as I expected. In fact, I want more.

No, I *need* more.

And I'm not just talking about this, getting naked in the shower with her.

I need more of us, together.

My heart is trying to beat out of my chest, and if it weren't for having to remove my hands from her body, I'd rub the spot where it aches. But I keep my hands where they are, sliding around to her backside and kneading her ass in my palms. Lizzie moves forward, pressing her entire front to mine, and I'm completely torn between wanting to strip us both naked immediately and savoring our time together by dragging it out as long as I can.

But the fact remains, I have to work in only a handful of hours, and even though Lizzie will be able to sleep in a bit longer, she has a long day at the bar as well. So, as much as I want to keep her here, drawing out the pleasure and release, it's irresponsible of me to do so.

So, I'll just have to have my wicked way with her fast and hard in the shower.

I make quick work at removing her panties and bra, and while she steps out of her socks, I strip away all my clothes, leaving them in a pile on the floor. The room fills with steam, and even though my cock is seeping precum and I want nothing more than to bury it deep inside her, I move to adjust the water temperature to a comfortably hot level.

"Come." I extend my hand, and she gently places hers against my palm.

We slip behind the curtain, the hot water hitting my side and stinging. "Too hot?"

"No way, this is perfect," she replies, dipping beneath the spray.

She pulls me toward her, snaking her arms around my neck. I claim her lips in a bruising kiss, our tongues tangling as my hands move over her wet skin. "Are you ready for me, Lizzie?"

"I've been wet all night."

I groan, picturing her behind the bar, wet and achy. "Well, we should do something about that now, shouldn't we?"

She nods insistently.

"Turn around," I instruct, taking in her naked, wet, red skin. Moving behind her, I lift her right leg, propping it on the edge of the tub. My fingers glide through her pussy. "Are you wet for me?"

"So wet," she murmurs, rocking her hips and pushing them back to grant me better access.

"Hands on the wall."

She does as instructed immediately.

"I can't wait, Lizzie. I need in your pussy so fucking bad," I whisper in her ear, thrusting two fingers inside her.

She moans and pushes her sweet ass into my groin. "Yes. Please. Hurry."

I reach down and line myself up with her entrance from behind. Just as I start to thrust forward, it hits me. "Shit. I don't have a condom."

"I'm on birth control," she replies, gazing at me over her shoulder. "And I'm clean."

My heart hammers so hard, it's as if the band is still playing downstairs and echoing through the apartment. "I've never…" My brain seems to short circuit at the thought.

She holds my stare as she says, "Me either. And I trust you."

"I'm clean. I'd never risk you, Lizzie. Ever."

The sweetest smile spreads across her lips. "I know."

"Are you sure? I can get out and grab a rubber from my wallet."

Her answer is to push just enough to take the head of my cock inside her.

I close my eyes and let a curse fly, instantly surrounded in fire. Grasping for any ounce of control I possess, I place my hands on her hips and slowly push forward.

Pure.

Fucking.

Heaven.

When I'm fully seated inside her, I know I'll be hanging on by a thread the moment I start to move. Fortunately, I can already feel the muscles of her pussy tighten, so I know it's not going to take much to get her there.

"Don't move your hands," I instruct, gently pushing her forward a little so her sweet ass is pointed back at me.

And then I move.

I start to pump, long, deliberate motions. With each rock of my hips, she reciprocates, rolling her body and taking me as deep as she can. Reaching up, I wrap one hand gently around her ponytail and give it just the slightest tug. The result? I feel her pussy squeeze as she cries out.

She's so fucking close, which is good because my body is teetering on the edge of release, barely hanging on myself. The feel of her bare is overwhelmingly amazing, and I'm barely holding on.

"I need you to come, Lizzie. Let me feel it. Let me feel you," I coax, dropping my hand from her hair and reaching around between her legs. All it takes is a few swipes of my fingers across her swollen clit and she detonates.

The grip on my dick is so fierce, I have no choice but to follow. I come hard, pumping my hips and emptying myself until I'm spent and breathless. I lean forward, spooning her body against mine.

Lizzie starts to sag, and as much as I'd love to stay right here, wrapped around her like a glove, I know we need to get washed up and to bed. Backing up, I dislodge my cock and step back into the water spray. "Come on, Lizzie."

She turns around, a mixture of euphoria and exhaustion in her stunning eyes, and joins me under the direct spray. Neither of us says a word as I grab her bodywash and squirt a glob in my hand. I didn't think to take a washcloth from the cabinet, but this'll do just fine for tonight. All we really want to do is clean the alcohol and sweat off our bodies.

Lizzie does the same, placing her hands on my chest and washing. Our eyes are locked, and I realize this is the most intimate moment I've ever shared with a woman, sex excluded. This is pure, our vulnerability and flaws on full display, and I'm not just talking about our bodies. It's as if we see each other, all the parts you try to hide from the world.

But I see her.

And the fact that not only does she see me, but I want her to, is pretty telling.

I'm in love with her.

When we've both scrubbed work off our bodies, I turn us so she's fully beneath the spray. As the water cascades down her body, I lean in and press my lips to hers. This kiss is tender and full of meaning. I'm just not ready to say it yet, but maybe she'll feel it.

"Come on, Lizzie. Let's get to bed."

Shutting off the water, I reach out and grab a big fluffy towel off the bar and wrap it around her. "I didn't think to grab another. Let me get you one," she says before carefully stepping out of the tub and pulling a second towel from the cabinet.

"Thanks," I tell her, rubbing the soft material over my body before wrapping it around my waist.

She pauses at the sink to brush her teeth, while I go out and check the door and turn off the kitchen light. When I return, she's finishing up, so I slip into the bathroom and do the same, using the extra brush I started keeping at her place. Finally, it's time to hit the hay, and my body is ready.

When I get to her bedroom, I find Lizzie lying in bed, the sheet and thin blanket covering her naked body. I drop my towel onto the floor with hers and climb beneath the covers. Instantly, she moves, shifting her small body to curl against mine. I can't get over how perfectly she fits there.

With me.

She exhales, her fingers wrapping around my arms as she rests her cheek against my chest. "Night, Collin," she murmurs softly.

"I'm not going to wake you up in the morning, okay?" I ask, referring to when I leave for work.

"Be safe tomorrow."

"I will," I tell her, kissing her forehead and just holding her close.

Her skin is soft and warm, maybe even a bit tacky still from the shower. But it still feels good.

She sighs and wiggles, shimmying even closer. I'm hot, but there's no way in hell I'm moving right now. "I like you here. With me."

The corner of my lip ticks with a hint of a smile. "I like being here with you too."

My throat is thick, my emotions running high. All I can think about is...what if? What if we really make a go of this? What if I finally let go of the past that's had a death grip on me for the last decade? What if I grab on to this woman and never let go? What if I finally get everything I never even realized I wanted?

Her soft snore fills the room, and as exhausted as I am, I don't find sleep right away. I lie here, listening to her sleep and thinking about the future. A future I want with her.

Why?

Because I've fallen completely in love with her.

And those lines we've tried to walk, keeping our relationship professional when needed and private when not?

Well, I'm so far past those lines, I can't even see them anymore.

And that's okay.

We don't need lines or rules. I want to date this woman, and if that means I need to quit so things don't get confusing at work, then so be it. I'll quit tomorrow. Because being with her is more important than a job. So, if she wants me to choose, I choose her.

It's that simple.

She once asked me to give her thirty days. It was her request when she bought the business.

Well, what if I want more? Not just thirty days or sixty. Not a year or five. I want it all. All her time, all her love. I want forever.

That's my simple request.

As I finally start to drift off to sleep, I whisper, "I love you."

It's the first time I've said it in more than ten years.

But it feels right.

She's the one.

I feel it deep in my soul.

She's forever.

When the alarm on my phone sounds, I almost shut it off. I'm too comfortable, too tired, but that's not fair to my teammates at the station. So, I reach over and tap my screen, silencing the noise. Lizzie wiggles in my arms, snuggling closer. Her warm, naked skin is too tempting, but I can't stay.

Not this morning, anyway.

Pressing my lips to her forehead, I slowly coax her to her back and extract my arm from beneath her body. Fortunately, she doesn't wake. Instead, she rolls over onto her side and buries her face in the pillow. With a little mumble, she drifts back to sleep.

I move to the bathroom and grab my clothes. Even though I should dress in the living room and take off so I'm quieter, I return to her bedroom. With my eyes locked on her sleeping form, I dress in last night's clothes. Finally, when I have nothing left to do but put my shoes on, I move to where she lies and lightly brush my lips across hers. "Goodbye, Lizzie."

"Bye," she mumbles, turning onto her stomach.

I stand here for a minute, watching her sleep and repeating those three words just said. I've never heard anything sweeter, and I know what I have to do.

Taking a step back, and then another, I keep moving until I'm exiting her bedroom. I put on my boots and make sure I have my wallet before leaving her apartment, checking to make sure it's locked, and heading down the stairs. I want nothing more than to just go back up and be with her, but that can't happen. Not today.

I have a job to do.

My feelings for Lizzie will have to wait.

For now.

CHAPTER TWENTY-FOUR

Lizzie

WHAT A WEEK!
Ever since last Saturday night's band, we've been busier. The after-work crowd is growing, and the regulars have noticed. They've been making daily comments about the uptick in traffic, telling me it's because Cade danced on the bar.

Lord, I hope not, because I don't want to seem like I'm recreating or copying my dad's business.

Collin had worked Sunday through Tuesday, and while I got to see him a bit Tuesday night, I've barely seen him since. He was supposed to work Thursday but ended up sick. He was going to power through, but his stomach wasn't having it. So, I covered his shift, which did not make him happy because I worked that afternoon too. But I don't mind. It's my business, and my responsibility to step in and fill the gaps when needed. Was I exhausted at the end of the day? Sure, but nothing too terrible. If anything, it didn't give me an opportunity to help Collin when he was under the weather. I did leave a care package on is front porch on Friday morning, and we've texted a lot throughout the week, but I haven't been able to see him, throw my arms around his neck, and kiss him the way I wanted to. He was adamant about me not coming over until he was better. The last thing he wants is for me to get sick, especially when I have a business to run.

Things have been…good.

So good, really, despite not physically seeing him much this week.

Our conversations are deeper, more meaningful, and it feels like we've taken a giant step over that little line we drew in the sand all those weeks ago. I still recall him telling me he loved me when he thought I was sleeping last weekend. And I was sleeping, but not deep enough that I couldn't hear him. Or remember. Neither of us have brought it up, nor has he said it again, so that makes me wonder if he really did mean to say it. I mean, I was asleep. I very easily could have dreamed his words, but I truly don't believe I did. It was so clear, so real.

Tonight is paint night, and Jani is working behind the bar, but I'll be there to help her. My focus will be on making sure the attendees are taken care of and having fun and the food is restocked. Keeping busy will definitely help me not think about Collin or the fact he left for work this morning, finally feeling better, and I won't be able to see him again until Monday. Almost a week after the last time I laid eyes on him.

So, yeah. It's been a long week.

I have the food set up on the table and made sure to make plenty again for the regulars. This time, I didn't have to do any desserts, because Aunt Lyndee insisted on sending them. She was supposed to come tonight, but she and Aunt Madelyn both had something come up. And BJ is working tonight, so it's just Mom and Em coming over.

The good news is, earlier in the week, I posted about the three cancellations and someone came in within a few minutes of the social media post and filled the spots. So, once again, I'll have a full class this evening, and I couldn't be prouder.

Mom and Em arrive first, carrying in boxes of sweet treats. "You better take these before I eat them all," my sister announces as soon as she steps inside the bar.

"Hey! Little Lizard!" The regulars have taken to my sister as quickly and easily as they did me, and I can't help but smile at their reaction to seeing her.

"Friends!" Em replies, walking over to where they sit and offering high fives as she passes. "I brought amazing, yummy desserts from my aunt Lyndee's bakery. Come over and get some before the good stuff is gone."

Because they were instructed by the mini-me, all four of them get up off their stools and follow her to the table. First they help her unload, then snatch a few treats from the boxes.

"She's been talking about coming back here all week," Mom says, stopping beside me.

"Funny, so have they," I reply, nodding to the regulars as my sister jokes around and catches up with them back at the bar.

"I'm glad you have a good group of customers to keep an eye on you."

I stick out my tongue, earning an eye roll from my mom. "Don't give me that look. You're a capable adult, but we still worry. That's what parents do."

"I know," I state, taking the few boxes she's carrying and heading over to the table. With her help, I start arranging desserts with the rest of the food.

Anita arrives and gets everything set up, including the sample painting she did earlier in the week so everyone can see what it will look like— or what it's supposed to look like. Mom and Em take a table for four, and before long they're joined by Charli and her friend, Sommer. Before long I have the rest of the attendees checked in, with the exception of the three additions I added earlier in the week.

"I'm gonna use the restroom before we start," Charli states.

"I'll grab fresh drinks," Sommer chimes in, asking my mom and sister if they want anything from the bar. Even though Mom could probably drink, she and Em are both enjoying one of the nonalcoholic options I created for tonight's girls' night paint night.

"Sorry we're late."

I spin around and find the woman who signed up for the remaining spots tonight. "It's fine, Keira. We haven't started yet," I tell her, offering a friendly smile to all three.

"This is Emily and Whitney," she says, introducing her friends.

I nod to both, noticing instantly how…intently they're staring at me. Clearing my throat, I add, "Well, grab a drink if you want one. There's some food over on the table you can help yourself to throughout the evening."

They all nod before turning their attention to the bar. They're smiling and carrying on as they go, so I assume I must have just imagined what felt like a touch of hostility.

Anita asks for everyone's attention and starts to talk about the steps they're gonna take to paint their picture. I head toward the food to see if anything needs refreshed, and as I'm adding a few more pastries to the platter, I sense someone step up beside me.

"What the hell?"

I glance to my left and find Charli standing there, staring at the group with her mouth gaping open. I can practically feel the anger radiating off her. "What?"

"What is that bitch doing here?" she practically growls.

I spin around, my eyes darting around the room, trying to figure out who in the hell she's talking about. "Who?"

"Whitney."

I scan the crowd once more, landing on the three newcomers who just arrived at the last table. As if sensing our eyes, the woman I just met as Whitney looks our way and smiles. No, that's not accurate. She smirks.

"I can't believe she'd have the balls to come here, after everything she did."

"What'd she do?" I find myself asking, wondering if these women used to be friends once upon a time. I know what it's like to have a falling out with an old friend. I had one in high school with a girl who was a pathological liar. Junior year, I couldn't take it anymore and ended our friendship. I no longer knew what was real and what wasn't.

When I turn to face Charli, she's standing there with a horrified look on her face. "You don't know?"

Trying to scan what I know from my short time here, I come up empty where a woman named Whitney is concerned. Finally, I shake my head.

She huffs out a deep breath. "Of course you don't," she grumbles, almost to herself.

"Maybe we can talk about it after the class?" I suggest, mostly because it's already started and Anita is showing everyone how to paint the background.

She turns and gives me a pointed look. "You need to talk to Collin."

My eyebrows shoot toward my hairline. "Collin? What's wrong?" I ask, even though something that feels like dread starts to churn in my stomach.

"It's not my story to tell," Charli finally says, clearly having a hard time finding the right words. I can tell she's upset, maybe even a bit angry at that Whitney woman.

I steal another look toward the woman who has suddenly upset the apple cart, even though I don't even know why she had the power to. She has long, gorgeous dark hair she keeps flipping back over her shoulder, as if she's made that very move a million times in her life and just does it naturally. Her clothes are expensive, in a cowgirl sort of way. She's wearing fitted blue jeans and boots, and her top is western and shows a ton of cleavage, as if she's perhaps had the girls done and wants them on display.

And all I keep wondering is why Collin would have anything to do with this situation, but the nagging feeling I have in the back of my mind tells me the answer.

They were together.

He's mentioned a difficult past, a break-up that almost killed him, and now I can't help but feel like it all revolves around this woman.

Sadly, I can't even ask him about her. He started his shift today, and they got called out on a big fire earlier this afternoon. At least that's what he texted moments before it went radio silent. I know their job doesn't end when the trucks pull back into the station, so there's no telling when I'll be able to speak to him again. Not to mention this feels like a face-to-face conversation, not something you ask via text.

"Why don't you go join the table and catch up?"

She narrows her eyes at Whitney, as if shooting invisible daggers all the way across the room. "I hate her."

I reach up and place my hand on her arm, grabbing her attention. "Thank you."

She looks at me confused. "For what?"

"For being…you. For being a friend."

She pulls me into a huge hug. "I've got you, girl. And I'll be the one kicking my brother's ass all the way to the state line and back if he ever fucks this up with you."

I bark out a laugh. "Something tells me you will."

"Oh, I will. And he knows it."

I nod to where my sister is waving Charli over, so she doesn't fall too far behind on her painting. "Go. Have fun. Don't get blood on my freshly refinished floor."

She laughs hard and grins somewhat evilly. "I make no promises."

I watch her walk away, taking the long way to her seat and making a trip past Whitney and her friends. As expected, she says something to her I can't hear, causing Whitney to gasp and glare back at the woman strolling past. She replies, but there's no way I can hear it over the noise. Charli just laughs, a maniacal sound that filters all the way back to where I stand. She looks completely satisfied, as if whatever she said to Whitney had the exact result she was looking for.

Remind me to never get on Charli's bad side.

Choosing to not speculate any further over what Whitney means to Collin, I return to the food table and straighten what's been picked over and refill what I can. Jani is easily able to handle the bar, so there's no need for me to go back there and just get in her way. Instead, I keep myself busy with the food, inviting the regulars to grab another plate and checking on my mom and sister whenever I can.

They're doing great, both of their paintings resembling the one Anita is doing at the front of the room, and they're having so much fun. I make a mental note to try to take one of the classes with them this summer before

Em heads off for school. As long as the bar is covered, I should be able to paint and keep up with the food, since that doesn't require as much attention once the painting starts.

As the night starts to wind down and everyone is adding the final touches to their pieces, I return to the food table to make sure what's left is out and ready for the ladies. I stir the meatballs and put the last tray of pastries out on the table, waiting for tonight's attendees to get one last plate of snacks.

"He's still in love with me, you know."

My hands pause and my heart hammers in my chest. I school my features and slowly turn to face the woman beside me. "Whitney, hi. Enjoying your evening?" I ask, pasting a smile on my face.

Ignoring my question, she places her hands on her hips and narrows her eyes. "You can try all you want, but it'll never go past a few months. He's been in love with me forever. It's why he rarely dates and won't commit."

My smile falters but only for a moment. "Thank you for coming tonight. I hope your friends and you had a good time." With that, I move around her and head behind the bar.

My brain is swimming with her words on constant repeat.

He's still in love with me.

It's why he rarely dates and won't commit.

I move behind the bar, needing to keep myself busy. I note what needs to be restocked and make a quick trip to the cooler to grab what I can. "What did she say to you?"

No need to turn around to confirm who joined me in the small, cold space. "It doesn't matter," I state, digging up every ounce of gumption I can grab and pasting on a fake smile.

"Bullshit it doesn't!" Her words are loud, echoing throughout the cold storage, but she doesn't notice. "That woman is...terrible. Everywhere she goes is a trail of hurt. Don't believe her, whatever she said. She's scum."

I crack a little, real smile. "She seems very full of herself."

Charli huffs. "She's the worst. Like, she's walking gonorrhea with a side of crabs."

A giggle flies from my lips. "That's…eww."

"Well, it's true. She's a nasty bitch, and I don't say that lightly or easily." She sobers, the anger slowly ebbing from her face. "It's not my story to tell, Lizzie. Just talk to Collin. Make him tell you."

I swallow over the sudden lump of emotion lodged in my throat. "I don't want to push him."

Before I even get that statement out, she's already shaking her head. "No, he needs pushing. You were completely unprepared for whatever the hell that was out there, and that's not right. He's an idiot."

That makes me smile. I want to reply, *"He may be an idiot, but he's my idiot."*

But is that accurate? If what Whitney said was true, there's a lot of baggage to unpack with their history, and maybe that's why he's never committed to someone long term.

"Don't do that. Don't buy into whatever she told you. I'm serious. You need to talk to Collin."

I nod, knowing she's right. I need all the facts before I let my imagination fill in all the missing pieces to the story. "You're right."

She grins back at me. "I'm always right, you'll realize that." With a wink she adds, "Now, let's get out of here. I'm freezing my tits off."

A bark of laughter flies from my mouth as I scoop up the cases and exit the cooler. Charli closes the door behind me and follows me as I return to the bar. I glance around, not spotting Whitney or her friends anywhere.

"They left," Mom says.

I nod, not having to explain anything. No surprise she picked up on my tension and the uneasiness I felt. Hell, she probably caught the exchange by the food table. Just like when we were younger, my mom misses nothing.

She doesn't say anything, but the look she gives me lets me know this conversation isn't over. She's going to want details, but she's not going to request them now. "Come on, Em, let's help get all this food packed up."

"There are some large baggies in the storage room if you want to bag up what's left in little goodie bags. I'll send them home with everyone," I state, turning back to help tidy up the painting area.

Thirty minutes later, we have everything put back together, and Mom and Em are preparing to leave. "Take what you want back with you," I tell them as Mom pulls me into a big hug.

"We will, honey. I put two bags in the cooler for you and Jani and handed the rest of them to your regulars who are still sitting at the bar."

The fact she's doing exactly what I'd do and taking care of the regulars makes me smile. "Thank you, Mom."

"Of course," she replies, stepping back and letting Em slip in for a hug.

"Text me when you get home," I tell them, making Mom smile at the irony.

"I will, sweetie."

"And tell Dad you're on your way. He'll worry," I add, causing her to laugh.

"He's already texting me asking."

"Be safe. Love you."

"Love you more," she replies.

Grabbing their paintings and their snack bags, which I'm certain Em will dive into on their hour-long drive back to Stewart Grove, they head for the exit, waving as they go. A wave of sadness washes over me like a spring rain. I love it when my family is here, but it seems I miss them even more when they leave.

Robotically, I make it through the rest of the evening, and when it's time to close down, Jani and I are more than ready. Collin is on my mind once more, but now those thoughts are filled with questions and uncertainty. I'm aware the only way to get the answers to the questions bouncing around in my head is to ask Collin. Unfortunately, I probably won't get those answers until sometime Monday.

When the building is locked up and the lights are off, I head upstairs, ready for bed. I move through my nightly routine, including taking a quick shower. Finally, I climb into bed and feel my energy just drain from my body.

Of course, my bed is cold, and it makes me miss the one man I wish were here with me. Grabbing my phone off my nightstand, I look at our most recent text exchange, the one from earlier today. He hasn't sent anything in more than ten hours. I'm sure he's just busy, or perhaps the fire call they received is still an issue. Either way, a bubble of worry churns in my stomach.

I flip from side to side, trying to find a comfortable position to no avail. Finally, I tap my phone screen once more and bring up his name. I might not be able to talk to him, but I sure as hell can let him know I'm thinking of him. I can't stop thinking about him. He's always on my mind, sending my heart fluttering.

> Me: Thinking about you and hoping work is going well. Stay safe. Good night.

Setting my phone back on my nightstand, I curl onto my side and hug my pillow. I don't know how long it takes me to find sleep, but it's longer than normal.

And my dreams?

They're full of Collin...

And Whitney.

CHAPTER TWENTY-FIVE

Collin

I'M STARTLED AWAKE BY THE NOTIFICATION CHIME ON MY PHONE. With heavy arms, I reach for the device, hoping to silence it before it wakes up the rest of the crew. Everyone is still sleeping, thanks to a massive office building fire in downtown Sycamore. We got called out yesterday afternoon around three and didn't pull the trucks back into the station until twelve hours later.

By that point, we were zombies and when the work was complete and we finally hit the hay, I crashed. I never even glanced at my phone, even though Lizzie wasn't far from the front of my mind.

I tap on the screen and input my password, noting a couple of new messages from my sister. Running my hand over my face, I click on her name and read.

> Charli: You're the biggest idiot ever.
>
> Charli: Seriously, Collin. What the hell?! You've got to be the dumbest man alive, and considering the company our brothers keep, that's saying something.

Charli: You better be sleeping, because it's taking everything I have not to drive there and kick your ass.

I run my hand over my face once more, trying to figure out what in the world I did to piss in her Cheerios this early on a Sunday morning. When I come up with nothing, I fire off a reply.

Me: What'd I do? Been a long night. We're all still sleeping.

I catch the time at the top of the screen, noting it's just after eight. Won't be long and we'll have to get up and start chores for the day, including making breakfast. Those thoughts are cut off by my sister's reply.

Charli: Whitney showed up at paint night last night.

Blood starts to swoosh in my ears as I read her words. My heart starts to pound as dread fills my entire being.

Me: Shit.

Charli: Yep. And in true Whitney fashion, she ran her mouth to Lizzie. I don't know what about—she wouldn't tell me. But gauging by the look on Lizzie's face, I'm sure it wasn't the ho-bag speaking your praises.

Charli: Fix this. Now. She's the best thing that's happened to you and if you mess this up because of the walking STD, I'm gonna kick you square in the balls. Twice.

I lean forward and rest my elbows on my knees. My eyes close, and I picture Lizzie's face. She's smiling at me, just like the afternoon we rode my four-wheeler. Or she's cradled in my arms while we fall asleep, like last weekend. The night I whispered I loved her, wishing I was strong enough to tell her when she was fully awake.

Charli: You there?

> Me: Yeah. I'm working until tomorrow morning. I'll get ahold of her.
>
> Charli: And fix this!!
>
> Me: Yes, Charli. I'll fix this.

God, I hope I can.

My sister's right. There's no telling what Whitney told Lizzie, but I'm sure it's not flattering toward me. She blamed me for everything, from being gone too much while I was serving in the Air Force to being the reason she stepped out of our relationship. According to her, I wrecked everything we were supposedly working toward together.

Yet, I wasn't the one sleeping with my friends—or, my former friends. Plural.

But the guilt trip she put on me was pretty intense. Fuck, I blamed myself for quite a while after it all went down. If only I had married her during my time in the military, then I could have taken her with me. Of course, she probably would have cheated at some point then too, so marrying her wouldn't have fixed anything.

If anything, it saved half my pension and the division of marital assets.

My phone chimes with Charli's reply, but I don't read it. Instead, I pull up Lizzie's name, noticing a message she sent just before one this morning.

> Lizzie: Thinking about you and hoping work is going well. Stay safe. Good night.

My fingers hover over the screen. How do I reply? Everything I want to say—*need* to say—really should be done face-to-face. Sending a text and wanting to talk about my ex is shitty as hell, and I refuse to do that. Instead, I let my heart do the talking.

> Me: Good morning, beautiful. Yesterday and this morning were pretty intense. Bad fire. I've been thinking about you nonstop. There are some things I need to tell you, I know, and when I get back home, we'll talk. Until then, know you consume me. I miss you.

I bite my tongue to keep from typing the three little words I want to say. Not because there's drama happening, thanks to the appearance of my ex, but simply because I need to tell her. I should have said it before I left for work last weekend, yet I kept those words to myself. Well, I said them, but only when she was asleep.

I'm a fucking mess.

But this is something I can rectify. I can fix this, I know it.

I just need to get to Lizzie so I can fill in the details of my past, the ones I should have told her before now. Even if we started off as casual, that's not how it feels now. The moment we started to teeter into more exclusive and a bit more formal, I should have told her. That's on me.

We need to talk. Soon.

Until then, I'll keep communicating, despite doing a shitty job thus far.

Come Monday morning, I'm beat. The drive back to Cooper Town is filled with listening to my mom talk through my speakers, but wishing it were Lizzie. Not that I'm not grateful my mom calls to keep me company on the trip back to town so I don't fall asleep behind the wheel, but I've barely spoken to the one woman I want more than anything to have a conversation with.

Between her work schedule and mine, our only communications Sunday were sporadic texts between fire calls and patrons. My morning started with a big car accident on the interstate not thirty minutes after I talked to my sister, and it was practically nonstop until it was time to clock out this morning. I don't know if it was a full moon or what, but there was definitely something wonky going on out there.

Now, I'm pulling into town and want nothing more than to drive straight to her apartment and talk to her. Kiss her. Crash in her bed with her in my arms. In that exact order.

But I'm running on barely any sleep, and that's not fair to her. So, instead of driving to where I want to be, I go home. To my cold, lifeless house. But at least there's hot water and a comfortable bed to crash in for a while.

After signing off with Mom, I make my way into my place, dropping my bag on the floor by the washing machine to deal with later. My plan is to catch a few hours of much-needed sleep, shower, and head over to the bar to see her. I'm assuming Guy is working today, so she'll probably be on later. I'll give her the first half of the day, but then I'm coming for her.

> Me: I'm home. Gonna crash for a bit then I'll come find you. I know we need to talk. I miss you and can't wait to see you.

I hit send before dropping my phone onto the charger in my bedroom. Then, I crawl into bed and let sleep pull me under.

I wake at three and practically jump out of bed. I had hoped to be up by one, but apparently my body had other plans. I knew I needed sleep, but I was hoping I'd catch up later tonight, after talking to Lizzie. Of course, I could have set an alarm, so the fact I actually slept as long as I did is on me.

After running through the shower, brushing my teeth again, and re-dressing in a pair of comfortable jeans and T-shirt, I slip on athletic shoes, grab my keys and wallet, and head for the door. My anxiety level is high, with both a mixture of wanting to see her so fucking bad and knowing this conversation is going to be one of the hardest I've ever had. Even harder than the time I came home and broke up with Whitney.

I jump in my truck and head straight to the bar. Parking in the back lot, I climb from the cab and jog around the building to the front. It's almost four, not quite time for the shift to change, but that's okay. It'll give me about an hour with Lizzie to talk.

Pulling open the door, I'm greeted with the familiar round of hellos from the regulars, all who are sitting at the bar, watching an old episode of *Gunsmoke*. Most of them aren't even drinking. They're just enjoying the atmosphere and the comradery of friends, something I've noticed happening more and more. They just like being together, talking about life and whatnot, and it makes me smile. These men are an integral part of what makes The Tipsy Lizard so damn special.

"Hey, Collin," Guy says as I approach. "Thought you were off today?"

"I am. Was gonna run up and talk to Lizzie," I reply casually, even though I feel anything but.

"Lizzie, huh?" Jarrod asks, a smirk on his face.

"You sweet on our little Lizzie?" Tom asks, a knowing grin stretching across his mouth.

"You two would make such a great pair," Larry chimes in.

"She's not here," Burt announces.

"She's not?"

Guy jumps in. "Nope, she took the day off. I'm not sure where she went, but she left a little more than an hour ago. Jani's coming in at five."

My heart sinks, and I'm certain my disappointment is written all over my face.

"If it's any consolation, she didn't appear upset or anything. Just said she was taking the afternoon off. Something about needing some wind therapy and wanting to go where the trees talk and she could think in peace."

My brain is spinning, my heart's trying to leap out of my chest.

Where would she go for wind therapy?

I mentally run through all the places she likes to go, but nothing fits the bill. As far as I know she doesn't frequent a park or a hiking trail, and she's never gone on a run with me.

Then it hits me.

Could it be that easy?

"I gotta go," I tell them, tapping the bar top as I practically bolt toward the door.

"Go get her, tiger!"

"Get your girl!"

"About time he figured it out."

I make it to my truck in record time, jumping in and taking off like a bat out of hell. I drive straight out of town, traveling the familiar roads that lead to the farm. I pull onto the lane and head for the barn, bypassing the house completely. As if waiting for my arrival, Wyatt is there, smiling like the cat that ate the canary.

"Been waiting on you."

"Where is she?" I ask, making my way to my oldest, truest friend.

He just grins. "You mean the pretty girl who stole your four-wheeler?"

I crack my own smile at the thought. "Yeah. Her."

"Well, let's see here," he starts, leaning against the barn as if he has all the time in the world. "I think I recall seeing her take off that'a way." He points to the path we took when I brought her out here a couple weeks back.

I don't even reply, just head straight to his four-wheeler that's sitting beside the barn. "I'll be back."

"Sure, go ahead and take it. I'm not using it," he responds, his smile evident in his voice. I jump on the machine and fire it up, taking off as if my ass were on fire. "Watch the cameras!" he hollers over the engine noise.

I'm comfortable on ATVs, his included, so it takes me no time to work my way around the farm, following the same route I took Lizzie on. I keep my eyes peeled for my machine. When I turn into the trees and the temperature drops without direct sunlight, I finally spot her. She's sitting on my four-wheeler, her legs hanging off the back with her head resting between the handlebars. It doesn't look entirely comfortable, but I'm not going to judge. She still looks completely mesmerizing lying there.

I head in her direction and smile when she lifts her head to look my way. There's no missing the way her kissable lips turn up as she watches me approach. I park next to my ATV and turn off the engine. Lizzie sits up completely and turns to face me, and I do the same.

"Hi," she states.

"Hi. Everything okay?" I ask, worried about her tremendously.

She gives me a small grin and nods. "Yeah, it is. I hope it's okay I took your four-wheeler for a ride," she says a bit sheepishly.

"I don't care about that," I tell her. "You can take it whenever you want."

When she looks up at me and our eyes lock once more, I feel this instant shift in my chest, like all the pieces finally click into place. It's not painful or dramatic. It's…right.

She's the piece I didn't even know I was missing.

"I owe you an apology."

Her eyebrows shoot up, but she doesn't say a word, so I continue.

"I heard you met Whitney," I start, letting out a deep breath. "Whitney and I dated while I was in the Air Force. She was a year younger than me in school, right between Cade and me and Charli. From the beginning, I had been a little reluctant to start a relationship with someone who lived back here, while I was in Washington. She insisted she didn't care about the distance, telling me we had all the time in the world."

I close my eyes for a brief moment, but it's not Whitney's face I see. It's Lizzie's.

"After the first six months of long-distance dating, she brought up the idea of her moving to Washington, but the only way to do that was for me to get married housing. She didn't want to just get her own place there in town. She wanted to live with me, and that meant I would have to marry her. I wasn't ready for that, and I told her. She insisted that's not what she wanted either, yet her insistence that I was the one keeping us apart said otherwise. She played with my mind, telling me one thing and then either doing another or making me feel a different way. It was a constant game, but I thought I loved her, so I kept playing.

"It wasn't until we'd hit the year mark of our relationship that her demands for a ring started to hit pretty frequently. She blamed me for our separation and started telling everyone back home I wouldn't commit to her, even though I was fully committed. I tried to talk to her, to remind her she agreed in the beginning that it was only temporary and, as soon as I was released from the Air Force, I'd move back home with her. She constantly told me to hurry up, as if I could somehow make my enlistment go faster. I was in for four years, and had one left to go.

"One night, I got a call from Wyatt. He was upset. Told me he didn't want to tell me what he was about to say, but as my friend, he had to. He informed me Whitney was cheating on me. Not with one guy, but with two. Two I considered friends back in Cooper Town. Worse, the rumor was going around that she was pregnant, and I knew the baby couldn't be mine. I hadn't been home for a leave in more than six months."

The pain slices through my chest, but I know I need to finish. Lizzie doesn't say a word, just watches me and listens, but I don't miss the different emotions that sweep across her face. Outrage, anger, shock, and sadness. It's all there.

"When I called her, she denied it. Told me it was all just rumors, and at first, I believed her. I knew how small towns work. Wouldn't have been the first time my name was thrown in the middle of a rumor scandal. But as the weeks went on and the messages I got from people back here started to increase, I realized I was being played.

"I talked to my CO and he granted me a short leave. I had forty-eight hours to fly home and figure out what the hell was going on. The moment I showed up on her doorstep and my friend, Chris, answered the door, I had my answer. He was shocked to see me but didn't fight back when I threw the punch. I knew doing so could get me kicked out of the military, but I did it anyway. I was so fucking hurt, so mad at him and her."

I shake my head for a moment and finish the story. "She came to the door, clearly pregnant. Told me I was a waste of space and a loser, that I could never give her what Chris had. For over a year, she strung me along like a puppy dog, toying with my emotions and using the distance as a weapon."

She clears her throat and asks, "What happened to Chris?"

The corner of my mouth curls up. "You mean when he learned the baby wasn't actually his because she was also sleeping with Jackson? He left her. Works construction with Cade, but I don't think they talk. I know we don't."

"Good," she states venomously. "A friend doesn't fuck another friend's girl."

I give her a full-on smile this time. "I agree."

"And Jackson?"

I snort. "Stupid asshole married her, just like she wanted. But when he caught her cheating about a year after the baby was born, he left her ass."

"Good," she repeats.

Exhaling, I say, "So that's it. That's the past I was embarrassed to share. It hurt pretty badly, and I carried her betrayal with me for years. Hell, I was still carting it along like daily luggage until…"

After a beat, she encourages, "Until…"

Getting up off the machine, I move to where she sits and wrap my hands around her waist, drawing her toward me. "Until you came along and showed me what my future might actually look like." Deep breath. "You, Lizzie. You're the future I want. You're the only one I want, and I'm sorry I didn't tell you about Whitney—"

She cuts me off by placing her fingers against my lips. "No more talking. Only kissing."

CHAPTER TWENTY-SIX

Lizzie

I'M PISSED.

But not at Collin.

I'm angry on his behalf, at the woman who trampled all over his giving heart and made him feel less than he is.

"I'm sorry she did that to you. Now I know why Charli referred to her as walking gonorrhea with crabs."

He snorts a laugh, but the moment my legs wrap around his hips, lining up his instant erection with the apex of my thighs, his smile fades. "I wasn't kidding when I said everything just seemed to get better when I met you. I spent so much time keeping people at arm's length because I didn't want to be hurt like that again, but with you, you just…broke through."

"I'm persistent like that," I tell him, wearing a smirk.

He slides his hands up my neck, framing my face. "I love your persistence."

Clearing my throat, I hold his gaze and whisper, "I won't ever hurt you like that, Collin. Ever. I'm not saying I won't disappoint you or upset you from time to time, because that happens in all relationships, but

I'd never intentionally do anything close to what she did to you. In just a short amount of time, I've learned you are the most loyal, most giving person I've ever met. You have a caring and nurturing heart, and I think you're amazing."

He cracks a small smile as a blush creeps up his neck. "You make me sound like a wimp."

"No way," I reply, shaking my head. "You are most definitely all man." I go ahead and waggle my eyebrows suggestively to punctuate my point.

"I'm sorry I didn't tell you before she had the chance to ambush you. That never should have happened," he says.

"I forgive you," I reply instantly. "Now, that's enough about her. I have something else I want to talk about."

"Anything," he says.

"It's a simple request, honestly."

The corner of his mouth ticks with a smile. "Yeah? Name it."

"I think I already did, and you still haven't kissed me yet."

His fingers flex on the side of my face as he slowly bends down. "Yes, ma'am."

And then his mouth is pressed to mine in the most glorious kiss. It's the perfect mixture of sweet and heat, his tongue coaxing my mouth open and delving inside to taste. I get completely lost in the kiss, my hands moving to his back to hold him close. It's not the most convenient position, with me sitting and him standing between my legs, but it's never felt more right.

"I have something else I want to say," he whispers, placing a gentle kiss on the corner of my mouth.

"Okay," I reply, feeling a little breathy and lightheaded from his kisses.

He takes a breath and holds my gaze as he whispers, "I love you. I didn't plan on it happening, but somewhere between the bar and our late-night talks, I fell completely head over heels in love with you."

My heart literally did some sort of pirouette in my chest at his declaration. I've been told those words before, but it never felt like this, like he's the air I breathe. "I love you too."

He seems surprised for a moment. "Yeah?"

"Yes, you big idiot," I reply with a chuckle, repeating what Charli likes to call him. "I can't believe you didn't pick up on that."

"I *am* an idiot, according to my sister, and I've learned to never assume where love is concerned."

I pull him closer, pressing my cheek to his chest. "Well, you will never have to assume or wonder about my love. I'll make sure to always show you."

He flashes me a Cheshire cat grin. "Yeah? Show me? How you gonna show me?"

I feel him grow harder against me. "I have a list. A pretty long, detailed one."

"Let's go," he states, taking my hand and carefully pulling me off the four-wheeler.

"What? Where are we going?"

"To my truck."

"But...your ATV," I reply with a chuckle.

"I'll come get it later. Or Wyatt can."

Before I know it, we're both on Wyatt's four-wheeler and heading back to the farm at a clipped pace. The wind blows through my hair, and I have a smile on my face as I wrap my arms tightly around Collin's chest. With my cheek resting against his back, I close my eyes and just...feel.

This is what real love feels like.

I know it.

Everything about this man has felt different from the first day I met him, and I can't wait to spend my days getting to know him better. To share my life with him and grow, both individually and together. I don't know what our future holds, but I'm anxious to find out.

A few months ago, I was dreaming of the life I wanted, and now I'm living that dream. I moved an hour away, purchased an old bar, and am transforming it into something I can be proud of. It's not complete, but I'm okay with a work in progress. Why? Because it's mine.

Then there's Collin. I wasn't planning on him, but sometimes that's exactly how God works. When you least expect it, that's when someone amazing walks into the bar.

Life isn't easy, but it's worth living to the fullest.

And that's what I want to do.

Will that lead me to a future with Collin? Maybe a house in the country, a few kids, and a dog chasing them around the backyard? It's too soon to plan all that, but maybe someday, down the road, I hope so.

I've always had a pretty good head on my shoulders. I'd figure out what I want and how to make it happen, and for the first time, I see a man by my side—the one I love—riding the storms of life with me. Someone who sees my dreams as equal to his and wants to help me reach them. Likewise, I'll do whatever I can to support him in any way I can.

So now, the big question.

What do I want out of life?

It's simple, really.

I want it all.

That's my request.

EPILOGUE

Collin

"YOU NERVOUS?" SHE ASKS, GIVING ME A LITTLE SMILE FROM THE passenger seat of my truck.

"Nope," I state confidently, though that's not entirely true. I'm definitely a little anxious, and the closer we get to Stewart Grove the sweatier I feel.

"Liar," she mutters, bringing our joined hands to her mouth and kissing my knuckle. "Don't be nervous. You've met them all before."

I glance over at her, those sexy blond curls framing her gorgeous face. "I have met them before, yes, but this will be the first time I meet them as the man you love," I state, repeating the words her father told her over the phone a handful of weeks ago.

Lizzie smiles. "It's going to be fine," she says, and it feels like she's telling herself that just as much as she's telling me.

I give her hand a squeeze and then bring her knuckles to my own lips, placing a tender kiss across each finger. "It's absolutely going to be fine."

She turns her attention to the landscape as we head toward her hometown. As I drive, I steal glances at her, loving how relaxed and happy she looks. It's not that I'm nervous, per se, but believe it or not, I actually want her dad to like me. Why, when I've never really cared what others thought of me? Because he's one of the most important people in her life. They're incredibly close, and I'd never want to jeopardize their relationship in any way.

This isn't the first time I've been to Stewart Grove, but it's the first time I've been here like this, attending a summer cookout with the woman I love, preparing to spend the whole afternoon and evening with her family. Not just her parents and siblings either, but her extended family will all be there. The uncles and aunts I know, thanks to meeting them at the bar over the course of the last few months, but all the cousins are new to me. And I've been told there are a lot of them.

"Make a right up here," she says casually from the passenger seat.

I know we're getting close, having passed the welcome sign. I also know her parents live on the edge of town, on a street where the houses aren't too close and the yards are big. She's talked a lot about growing up in this house and having the space to play and grow.

"I'll show you the small place I used to rent tomorrow when I give you a tour," she adds, taking in the familiar neighborhood. There's a faint smile on her lips, the contentment of coming home, and I pray she never loses that look. She's happy to be here, I can tell, but that doesn't diminish the love she feels for her new town, her new life. This will always be the past that got her to where she is today, and I know she'll never forget that.

"Left," she murmurs as we approach a big T intersection.

The moment I turn, I know we've arrived. Not just because she's told me all about this place, but simply because of the massive line of cars on the side of the street, and there's only one driveway packed with cars.

I park at the end of the line and shut off the engine. I ignore how quickly it starts to get warm in the cab, my eyes watching the house as if it holds world secrets or something, but when I feel her gaze on me, I give her my complete attention.

"We got this," she says, flashing a little grin.

"Of course we do. We can handle anything." I sound way more confident than I feel in the moment.

"We can. Even if Dad who is going to give you a very hard time because you're dating his oldest daughter," Lizzie says.

"And I'm ready for it. Wanna know why?"

"Why?"

"Because I know he's giving me the biggest inquisition I ever experienced because he loves you and wants only the very best for his oldest daughter. We've got this."

She smiles from ear to ear, her green eyes sparkling under the sunshine. "You're right, we do."

Leaning forward, she presses her lips to mine in a chaste kiss. "Ready?"

"Let's do this."

ANOTHER EPILOGUE

Lizzie

H E TAKES MY HAND AS WE WALK TOWARD THE HOUSE, AND IT feels like my heart is going to leap from my chest and take off running in the other direction. I'm incredibly nervous, but only because of the meaning of this moment.

"Let's go around back," I say, taking the sidewalk around to the back-yard where I know everyone is gathered.

Even though we're right on time, it appears everyone is already here. The moment we step around the house into the yard, the noise level ele-vates, and we're spotted. "Lizzie!"

Immediately, we're surrounded by my family, all wanting hugs and to officially meet the man at my side.

"Everyone, this is Collin. Collin, this is everyone!" I glance over at him, noticing the slightly overwhelmed look on his face. "I'm not going to go through all the names right now, because you'll never remember them."

He nods, his eyes a bit wide.

"Come on, let's go say hello to my parents." Taking his hand, I move him out of the middle of the pile and head toward where Mom and Dad stand.

They're on the patio alone, as if everyone understands the magnitude of this moment and is giving us space. "Hi," I say lamely as I approach.

Mom smiles at us both, stepping forward and giving me a hug. "Breathe, sweetheart," she whispers, kissing my cheek before stepping back.

I turn my attention to my dad. He's staring at Collin, his expression unreadable. I've witnessed this look on his face many times over the years, and I know he'll give nothing away until he's ready. "Hi, Dad," I state, stepping in to give him a hug.

When he looks at me, his face instantly relaxes, and a little smile spreads across his mouth. "Hi, Lou."

He kisses my forehead, just like he used to do when I was little, before I step back and turn to look at Collin. "Mom, Dad, this is Collin. Collin, these are my parents, Mallory and Walker Meyer."

Collin reacts first, stepping forward and offering his hand to my mom. She smiles but doesn't take it. "Nice to see you again, Collin." Stepping closer, she adds, "Around here, we hug family."

My heartbeat slows almost immediately as I watch Collin give my mom a polite hug. "Thank you for having me."

"Of course," she replies, moving back to stand next to my dad.

Collin turns his attention to the man who has always been there. Who wiped away my tears and held me when I was scared. He made me laugh and always told me how much he loved me more times than I could possibly count. He always likes to tell the story of how much I changed his life, but the reality of it is, he changed mine. He gave me something I never had.

A real dad.

I find myself holding my breath as I watch Collin extend his hand to shake. My dad stares at him, then down at the offered hand. Just as I'm about to chastise my dad for being rude, he steps forward and takes Collin's hand, giving it a firm shake. "Welcome, Collin. It's nice to officially meet you."

My heart flies right out of my chest and I feel tears gathering in my eyes. I knew this was going to be a big moment, but seeing my dad take Collin's hand feels better than I ever imagined. I didn't expect my dad to give him a hard time, per se, but I expected a little more discomfort.

Dad holds Collin's eyes and adds, "Take care of my baby girl." His words are thick, and I swear I can see his eyes shining a little brighter than they were just moments ago.

"Always, sir. You have my word."

Dad nods before releasing his hand.

"I'm going to go get the rest of the food ready," Mom announces, placing a supportive kiss on my dad's cheek before heading into the house.

I'm about to excuse myself to go help, when I see a wall of uncles walk up behind my dad. "Do you need help burying a body?"

I almost roll my eyes, but I can tell by the look on my uncle Tank's face, he's dead serious.

Dad's lips tick in the slightest grin. "No, we're good. Guys, meet Collin, the man my Lou loves."

Hearing my dad say those words, introducing Collin to my uncles that way, causes a few of those tears I've been keeping at bay to spill.

"Fuck, you made her cry!" Uncle Jasper announces, a look of panic and anger on his handsome face.

Dad just smiles. "I didn't mean to, Lou." He moves straight for me to pull me into a hug, but he's too late. Collin is there, his arms sweeping around me and his thumb swiping across the apple of my cheek.

My dad notices immediately, a flash of hurt mixed with respect on his face. But he pushes it away instantly, replacing that pain with a gentle smile.

"I'm good," I insist to Collin and everyone standing around us. "These are happy tears."

"They better always be happy tears," Uncle Tank grumbles, already saying more words in a short amount of time than normal. But he's always acted a little different with me. We've been tight my entire life, and I don't see that changing anytime soon. He crosses his arms over his chest and stares down Collin, who doesn't so much as flinch.

"Food's ready!" Mom hollers from the doorway, and everyone starts to scramble for the house.

No one around me moves, and suddenly, there's tension once more. It's as if everyone is waiting for what comes next, whatever that may be.

But it's Dad that makes the move.

He takes a step forward, a soft smile on his face as he claps Collin on the shoulder. "Come on, Collin. Let's eat."

THE END

BONUS SCENE

Collin

July

TODAY WAS THE PERFECT DAY.

Period.

We spent the entire day kicking up dust and tearing up the trails. The best part was, for the first time ever, I had someone riding with me. Not just anyone.

Lizzie.

We met up with her entire family for a cookout recently and made our relationship official. Even though I had already met most of the people in attendance, it was our first meeting in the capacity of boyfriend and girlfriend, and to be honest, it wasn't as bad as I thought it would be. Sure, I got interrogated by her uncles, but that was to be expected. What I wasn't expecting was how welcoming her dad was. I fully anticipated him being...harder. But it was a pretty damn good day, much like this one.

My siblings, friends, and I booked a four-wheeling trip to our favorite place to ride in Indiana. We arrived when the park opened at eight, found our camping spots, and unloaded the machines. We spent the morning running the trails before returning to the campground for lunch and to get everything set up.

Lizzie has been right beside me—or specifically, when we're riding, behind me—the entire day. Hearing her laughter as we went racing down hills and splashing through ravines has been the highlight of the trip. Well, that and feeling her arms wrapped around my waist. The problem with that is my little soldier south of the belt noticed too and has been hard way more than appropriate.

By the time the afternoon riding session was done, we were all starved and covered in grime. It's a mixture of sweat and dirt making a nice paste of nastiness all over our bodies. Since I favor tent camping over using a camper, we were stuck using the shower house to clean up, right along with the rest of the crew we're here with.

Now, we're enjoying a few beers and some s'mores, sitting around the campfire and talking shit.

"I'm telling you, she was into me," Camden insists, making everyone around us laugh.

"She was into your sandwich. The woman was drooling, and it wasn't over your mediocre looks," Cade teases

Even though some of us have heard this story, it's still good to listen to everyone laugh and pick on Cam a little. Lizzie is curled up in the chair beside me, her fingers threaded through mine. Her giggle makes me smile, something I rarely did before she came into my life.

"Are we bringing up old shit now? Because I have stories. How about the woman who tried to sleep with Collin so she could say she slept with twins?" Camden spits out. The moment the question leaves his mouth, I hear Lizzie gasp beside me.

"What?" she asks, her green eyes twinkling with shock through the reflection of the flames.

"What the hell? I was just sitting here, being quiet," I argue, earning laughter from everyone around us. They've all heard the story, probably a few times over, but that doesn't mean I want it shared with Lizzie.

"All's fair in love and old stories, man," Camden states with a smirk.

"So, Lizzie, there was this woman about five years ago, and she did the horizontal mambo with that one over there," he says, pointing to my twin.

"I don't recall being horizontal," Cade chirps with a grin. "There was a wall and her legs wrapped around me while I—"

"Do not finish that sentence," Charli hollers, plugging her eyes and singing loudly.

Cade just smiles and throws her a wink.

"Anyway, after she was…vertical with Cade, she went searching for his twin brother," Camden announces smugly.

Lizzie turns my way, grinning from ear to ear. "Did you…"

"No," I reply, shifting uncomfortably. Not because talking about previous sexual partners with Lizzie causes unease, but simply because of what that woman said to me.

"Tell her the rest of it," Cade barks out.

"I'll tell it!" Wyatt announces, standing up across the bonfire from where Lizzie and I sit. "She showed up—"

"Naked!" everyone hollers, interrupting Wyatt.

"That's right, *naked*, and insists she must determine once and for all which Miller twin is better in bed."

Lizzie's eyes dart toward me. "She did that?"

"Some women are nasty," Charli mutters, turning to Cade. "Just like some men. Dirty, dirty peens and vagges."

"Is that a word?" Lizzie asks my sister.

"Of course it is," she insists, taking a drink of her beer. "And I stand by my statement where some people are concerned."

"Come on," I say softly, while everyone around us carries on and tells more stories. "Let's go to bed."

With her hand still tucked inside mine, she stands up and tosses her can in the trash. "Good night, everyone," she says, following me toward our tent.

"Remember, we can hear you. Those canvas walls are thin!" someone hollers, probably Quinn.

I unzip the entrance of the tent and wait for her to enter first. It's a little stuffy inside, even with the windows all open, but that's what you get when you tent camp in July. Usually, it doesn't bother me, but I worry Lizzie will have a bad experience because of it.

I close the zipper and turn on the small battery-operated light I keep inside. A few bugs managed to slip through the screened windows, so as soon as we're ready for bed, I'll shut the light off. Flipping my slides off my feet, I turn my attention to watching Lizzie. She slips off her sandals and removes her shorts. My eyes are glued to the globes of her ass, which are on full display, thanks to the tiny pair of panties she's wearing.

"Camping panties?" I whisper. Even though we're a bit away from the fire where we all congregate, I don't want anyone to hear us talking about her thong.

She flashes a quick grin. "Of course. I knew it was going to be hot, so I figured the less coverage the better."

My dick is fully on board with her reasoning. "Makes sense," I reply with a wink.

As soon as we're both down to sleeping attire, I flip out the light. Usually, when I would camp alone, I'd bring a bedroll and be fine, but with Lizzie along for the experience, I wanted us as close and comfortable as possible. So, I purchased an extremely expensive air mattress, promising not to lose one breath of oxygen throughout the night. The worst thing about them is when you go to bed fully aired and wake up in the morning in a crater of a deflated mattress.

"This is nice," she murmurs, getting comfortable in bed.

I slip my shirt and shorts off, leaving just my boxers. As much as I'd love to sleep naked next to the woman I love, I don't trust any of the assholes out by the fire. Not when you can't lock a door or close the windows without risking suffocation.

Climbing onto the bed, I slip beneath the sheet I brought, knowing it was going to be hot. I've got a thinner blanket too, just in case it gets a touch cool through the night, but for now, all we need is a sheet. "Come here," she whispers, moving toward me.

The moment my arms wrap around her, I ignore the heat radiating from our bodies and focus on the feel of her against mine. She's my favorite person in the whole world, and the fact I'm getting to hold her tonight—and most nights—makes me the luckiest bastard to walk this earth.

I still can't believe how different it feels this time around. Sure, I'm older and wiser, but it's not just that. It's the woman. Lizzie Meyer is the one for me, and even though it's only been a few months, I can tell. Everything is brighter and better, as if the sun is shining a little more than ever before. I know that sounds weird, and perhaps a little feminine, but it's the truth.

"You seem to be thinking awfully hard over there," Lizzie murmurs, her warm breath tickling my arm. "Whatcha thinking about?"

"You," I answer honestly. "How everything is just…better with you."

She slides even closer, forcing me to turn on my side so we're facing each other. "I agree."

"I'm glad you're here," I state, brushing my lips across hers. "I wasn't sure if this would be your thing or not."

"Are you kidding? I love riding with you at Wyatt's farm. Today was so fun, and I really hope we do it again soon. I've never been to a place this big."

"I'm glad you enjoyed it, because even though I would give it up for you, I'm glad I don't have to," I confess with a chuckle.

She runs her hands across my cheek. "Never. I'd never ask you to skip something you love, especially since it's a release for you. With the stresses of your job, you need to have something that's for you."

"I have you now," I whisper, inching even closer to the heat between her legs.

"You have me no matter what, but you still have this. And, if I get to come with you, then great, but if you wanted to do this on your own, I'd understand."

"Did you not hear me when I said everything is better with you?" I ask, lifting her leg over mine and rocking my hips forward. The friction is sweet and so desperately wanted.

Suddenly, she moves. Even though the darkness surrounds us in the tent, I can see her sit up and strip away the tank top she's wearing. Before I can advise her against it, merely because we're not far from a group of assholes I know would sneak a peek if given the opportunity, she's beneath the sheet and in my arms once more.

"There, that's better." She wiggles against me. "Now, what were you saying?"

"Was I saying something?" I ask, my mind already focused solely on the beautiful woman pressed against me.

"Something about everything being better with me," she whispers, her lips dancing across my jaw.

I grunt, my hips automatically flexing forward. "Yeah, I guess I was saying something about that fact. Like camping. *So* much better with you here."

She giggles. "Even in the hot, sticky tent, I'm a huge fan of camping," she informs me, reaching between us and wrapping her hand around my cock.

A groan of pure pleasure slides past my lips. "Camping for the win," I state before flexing forward once more.

"We can hear you!" someone hollers from the bonfire area.

Reaching over, I turn on the music app on my phone, not even caring what song plays.

"Now, where were we?"

THE END

BOOKS ALSO BY LACEY BLACK

Rivers Edge series
Trust Me, Rivers Edge book 1 (Maddox and Avery) –
FREE at all retailers
Fight Me, Rivers Edge book 2 (Jake and Erin)
Expect Me, Rivers Edge book 3 (Travis and Josselyn)
Promise Me: A Novella, Rivers Edge book 3.5 (Jase and Holly)
Protect Me, Rivers Edge book 4 (Nate and Lia)
Boss Me, Rivers Edge book 5 (Will and Carmen)
Trust Us: A Rivers Edge Christmas Novella (Maddox and Avery)
~ *This novella was originally part of the Christmas Miracles Anthology*
With Me, A Rivers Edge Christmas Novella (Brooklyn and Becker)

Bound Together series
Submerged, Bound Together book 1 (Blake and Carly)
Profited, Bound Together book 2 (Reid and Dani)
Entwined, Bound Together book 3 (Luke and Sidney)

Summer Sisters series
My Kinda Kisses, Summer Sisters book 1 (Jaime and Ryan)
My Kinda Night, Summer Sisters book 2 (Payton and Dean)
My Kinda Song, Summer Sisters book 3 (Abby and Levi)
My Kinda Mess, Summer Sisters book 4 (Lexi and Linkin)
My Kinda Player, Summer Sisters book 5 (AJ and Sawyer)
My Kinda Player, Summer Sisters book 6 (Meghan and Nick)
My Kinda Wedding, A Summer Sisters Novella book 7
(Meghan and Nick)

Rockland Falls series
Love and Pancakes, Rockland Falls book 1
Love and Lingerie, Rockland Falls book 2
Love and Landscape, Rockland Falls book 3
Love and Neckties, Rockland Falls book 4

Standalone
Music Notes, a sexy contemporary romance standalone
A Place To Call Home, a Memorial Day novella
Exes and Ho Ho Ho's,
a sexy contemporary romance standalone novella
Pants on Fire
Double Dog Dare You
Grip
Bachelor Swap, A Bachelor Tower Series Novel
Perfect Kiss, Mason Creek Series book 9
Waiting For Love, The Love Vixen Series book 11
Quarterback Keeper, a surprise baby novella
Kissing A Stranger, book 4 in the multi-author
The Kissing Games series

Burgers and Brew Crüe Series
Kickstart My Heart, book 1
Don't Go Away Mad, book 2
Same Ol' Situation, book 3
Wild Side, book 4
What's It Gonna Take, book 5
Home Sweet Home, book 6
Too Young to Fall in Love, book 7
Without You, book 8
Time For Change, book 9
You're All I Need, book 10

Pine Village Series
Pretty Remarkable, a free prequel short story
Pretty Incredible, book 1
Pretty Dependable, book 2
Pretty Drunk, book 3
Pretty Relentless, book 4
Pretty Wild, book 5

Cooper Town Boys Series
A Simple Request, book 1
A Simple Hello, book 2
A Simple Mistake, book 3
A Simple Regret, book 4

Co-Written with *NYT Bestselling* Author, Kaylee Ryan
It's Not Over, Fair Lakes book 1
Just Getting Started, Fair Lakes book 2
Can't Get Enough, Fair Lakes book 3
Fair Lakes Box Set
Boy Trouble
Home To You, a second chance novella
Beneath the Fallen Stars, Never Too Far book 1
Beneath the Desert Sun, Never Too Far book 2
Tell Me A Story
Royal
Crying Shame
Watch and Learn

ABOUT THE AUTHOR

USA Today Bestselling Author Lacey Black is a Midwestern girl with a passion for reading, writing, and shopping. She carries her e-reader with her everywhere she goes so she never misses an opportunity to read a few pages. Always looking for a happily ever after, Lacey is passionate about contemporary romance novels and enjoys it further when you mix in a little suspense. She resides in a small town in Illinois with her husband and two children.

Website: www.laceyblackbooks.com

Email: laceyblackwrites@gmail.com

Newsletter: www.laceyblackbooks.com/newsletter

www.ingramcontent.com/pod-product-compliance
Lightning Source LLC
Chambersburg PA
CBHW071426260626
47170CB00008B/2614